Best Ghost Short Stories 1850-1899
A Phantasmal™ Ghost Anthology

ANDREWBARGER.COM

The Best Ghost Short Stories
1850-1899
A Phantasmal™ Ghost Anthology

First Edition
ISBN: 978-1-933747-59-0

Bottletree Books LLC
United States of America

BottletreeBooks.com

Fonts: Bookman Old Style, Chiller

Andrew's Fiction

Divine Dantes: Squirt Guns in Hades (Infernal Trilogy #1)
Divine Dantes: Paella in Purgatory (Infernal Trilogy #2)
Divine Dantes: Cruising in Paradise (Infernal Trilogy #3)
Mailboxes – Mansions – Memphistopheles
Coffee with Poe: A Novel of Edgar Allan Poe's Life

Andrew's Anthologies

Phantasmal: Best Ghost Short Stories 1800-1849
Best Horror Short Stories 1850-1899: A 6a66le Horror Anthology
BlooDeath: Best Vampire Short Stories 1800-1849
6a66le: Best Horror Short Stories 1800-1849
Mesaerion: Best Science Fiction Short Stories 1800-1849
Middle Unearthed: Best Fantasy Short Stories 1800-1849
Shifters: Best Werewolf Short Stories 1800-1849
Leo Tolstoy's 5 Greatest Novellas Annotated
Leo Tolstoy's 20 Greatest Short Stories Annotated
Edgar Allan Poe Annotated Entire Stories and Poems
Orion: An Epic English Poem

I am deeply and horribly convinced, that there does exist beyond this a spiritual world—a system whose workings are generally in mercy hidden from us—a system which may be, and which is sometimes, partially and terribly revealed.

"The Familiar" 1872
JOSEPH SHERIDAN LE FANU

There be spirits that are created for vengeance, which in their fury lay on sore strokes; in the time of destruction they pour out their force, and appease the wrath of him that made them.

Ecclesiasticus 39:28
KING JAMES VERSION

CONTENTS

Victorians
Victors of the Ghost Story

On rare occasions there arises a country, in a particular time period, which is so dominate in one particular area that its denizens forever change it, whether it be in art, sports, engineering, culinary delights, etc.

As I write this the day after the 120th Boston Marathon, one instance that comes to mind is the decades-long supremacy of the Kenyans in distance running. Another is Swiss watchmaking or German engineering or early philosophy of the Greeks. The Italian Renaissance painters must be remembered as well as the chocolatiers of Belgium, which have wreaked havoc on my waistline. Thank you very much, Belgians.

And then there are the British whose power in spinning a fantastic ghost story was unparalleled in the last half of the nineteenth century. Apart from Robert Chambers and Francis Marion Crawford, the best ghost short stories in the English language during this period were penned by Victorians.

Technically, the Victorian age was a decade or so longer than the fifty year period under review. It is defined as the period in British history when Queen Victoria ruled—June 1837 to January 1901. Makes perfect sense. This timeframe ushered in the modern ghost short story and the world has the Brits to thank for many a sleepless night. In this little dark corner of the art world that hovers around midnight, it is little surprise after reading a legion of ghost short stories from 1850-1899 that one cannot spell Victorian without the word *victor*.

And who were the Victorian kingpins of the paranormal? Perched squarely in the literary scene of the Victorian age was Charles Dickens. Ole Boz. Regardless of the knocks on some of his kitschy character names, he is one of the most widely known English authors of all time.

Dickens was an excellent ghost short story writer. Nothing less would be expected from the author of *A Christmas Carol*, first published in December of 1843. In it Scrooge is visited by four ghosts: Jacob Marley (his former law partner) and the ghosts of Christmas past, present and future. You know the story well. *A Christmas Carol* offers up the first instance of time travel in English literature where the protagonist travels to *both* the future and the past.

The ghosts streaming from the pen of Dickens were highly communicative with the living. They were no longer stagnate beings of the spirit world who moved silently among the darkling corners of haunted houses, but rather interacted with the sorry lot of the living in ways never before seen in literature.

Dickens's earlier tale, "The Goblins Who Stole a Sexton" (1836) is a precursor to *A Christmas Carol* and involves a gravedigger who is going about his morbid trade on Christmas Eve when horror strikes among the gravestones. It is the first short story to contain time acceleration, where a family's life flashes before the protagonist's eyes.

For us lovers of a good supernatural story, let's all tip our top hats to Charles Dickens.

He was so fixated with ghost stories that he wrote nearly twenty of them among his short stories and novels. His "No. 1 Branch Line, The Signal Man" of 1866 sits firmly in this collection. As if his many ghost stories weren't enough for the genre, Dickens fostered the literary careers of many talented supernatural authors by publishing them in his weekly magazine—*All the Year Round*, including Joseph Le Fanu, Wilkie Collins, Edward Bulwer-Lytton and Elizabeth Gaskell.

The latter was but one of a number of British female writers in the ghost story genre who shined during this period. Mary Braddon, Rhoda Broughton, Catherine Crowe, Amelia Edwards, Mary Anne Evans (aka George Eliot), Florence Marryat (daughter of horror story writer Captain Frederick Marryat), Mary Louise Molesworth, Rosa Mulholland, Edith Nesbit, and many others stood out as fine ghost story writers of the Victorian age.

This is when female ghost story writers emerged from the shadowy recesses of the proverbial closet. They became less timid and that always makes for the creation of better art. They no longer had to write under pseudonyms or use the initials of their first and middle names to make it appear they were men.

In the Victorian age, with a strong queen at the helm, the women of Britain felt empowered to write in the supernatural genre if they wished. It was no longer viewed as a waste of time for a woman to pen a ghost story when morals could have been taught to the reading public in other genres. The perception of readers in relation to female supernatural writers changed in the Victorian age.

What's more, during the nineteenth century the perception of colors altered, too. The color yellow morphed from the cheerful glow of flowering snapdragons and daffodils on the English countryside to one that forewarned of evil in Britain and the United States. It became a color to describe the sickly, instead of the happy. Yellow fever entered the vernacular and those outside of the African continent became fearful of the viral disease spread by female mosquitos. This was especially true given the active slave trade in parts of America.

The color yellow soon became treated as a precursor to death thanks to writers in the supernatural community. By 1892, American Charlotte Perkins Gilman published her classic horror story "The Yellow Wallpaper." In it the sickly colored wallpaper has a terrible effect on the occupant of the room. Three years later, fellow American Robert Chambers published his collection of short stories *The King in Yellow* that begged the overriding question "Have you found the yellow sign?" It contains the haunting ghost story "The Yellow Sign" (1895) included in this anthology and his treatment of the color in *The King in Yellow* has evolved into what is now referred to as the yellow mythos in supernatural literature.

In addition to Robert Chambers another American managed to whip up a ghost story worthy of this collection. It was titled "The Upper Berth" (1894) by Francis Marion Crawford and is the only one set on a ship. Both stories by Chambers and Crawford were highly regarded by H. P. Lovecraft. They are two of the most haunting in this collection.

And speaking of Americans writing supernatural fiction during this period, Ambrose Bierce and Henry James have to be mentioned. There will be calls from the literary community that at least one of their ghost stories should be included. There is no question that some of their ghost stories were quite good.

Ambrose Bierce penned nearly thirty supernatural stories though not all were ghost stories. "The Damned Thing" (1893) is often cited as one of his best. It is a horror story and an enhanced knock-off of the much earlier "What Was It?" (1859) by Fitz James O'Brien. Given the setting and focused storyline, "The Secret of Macarger's Gulch" (1891) is Bierce's finest short work. Again, it is not a ghost story.

Henry James, on the other hand, was a proponent of the subtle ghost story. Enter the timid ghosts. As if filled by English sensibilities, they were rarely overt in their actions. They never jump out from behind the curtain and say "Boo!" Their presence was felt all the same yet in a more nuanced way than traditional ghost stories. James wrote cigar smoking, single malt scotch sipping tales. His "The Romance of Certain Old Clothes" (1868), "Sir Edmund Orme" (1892) and "The Friends of the Friends" (1896) are each well worth a read.

In this collection you will fail to find a humorous ghost story though a number where written in this period; nor is there one where a living individual is mistaken for a ghost. Give me the scary ghost, the evil ghost, the one bent on destruction or give me none at all. M. R. James pre-echoed these sentiments of mine a century earlier. "Another requisite, in my opinion, is that the ghost should be malevolent or odious: amiable and helpful apparitions are all very well in fairy tales or in local legends, but I have no use for them in a fictitious ghost story."[1]

---

[1] *More Ghost Stories of an Antiquary*, M. R. James, Preface, 1911

You will learn much more about these ghost stories from the introduction given for each. They have been chosen for their ability to frighten and leave an indelible impression on the reader. I only wish I could experience them again for the first time.

Ghost stories! You can almost feel them whispering on the back of your neck. Fantastic, scary, wide-eyed around the campfire, check under the bed, make you sleep with the lights on, ghost stories. The Victorians had no shortage of them. They were naturals at the craft and the undisputed victors in the genre.

Andrew Barger
April 18, 2016

Francis Marion Crawford
(1854-1909)

This collection begins with a ghost story H. P. Lovecraft deemed "one of the most tremendous horror-stories in all literature."[1] So who was Francis Marion Crawford and how did he come about penning the fantastic ghost story, "The Upper Berth" that Lovecraft went on to call his "weird masterpiece?"[2]

Born in Italy, his father was Thomas Crawford, an American sculptor. Crawford studied in both the United States and Europe and was an American citizen. As a young man he began submitting stories to various magazines for publication and then started writing novels. His first—*Mr. Isaacs: A Tale of Modern India*—was published in 1882. It had supernatural elements interwoven throughout.

Crawford wrote across many genres including such far-reaching areas from the supernatural as the romance genre. His stories set in Italy became popular in America. F. Scott Fitzgerald's *Tender is the Night*[3] mentions Crawford, though offhandedly: "Until one o'clock Baby Warren lay in bed, reading one of Marion Crawford's curiously inanimate Roman stories . . .."

---

[1] *Supernatural Horror in Literature*, H. P. Lovecraft, 1927, pg. 29

[2] Ibid.

[3] *Tender is the Night*, F. Scott Fitzgerald, Chap. XXIII, 1934, pg. 193

It is his supernatural tales were he excelled and for which he is most remembered today. His 1903 novella "Man Overboard!" is his longest work of supernatural fiction, though Crawford penned a number of short stories in the genre. These include "The Dead Smile" (1899) a horror story, "For the Blood is the Life" (1905) a vampire tale, "The Screaming Skull" (1908) that draws a number of parallels to H. G. Wells's "Pollock and the Porroh Man" (1895) and "The Doll's Ghost" (1911) a unique take on the ghost story theme.

In 1881 he penned the short novel *The Witch of Prague* and five years later "The Upper Berth." It first appeared in a periodical called *The Broken Shaft*. The ghost story was met with interest and subsequently published in other magazines of the day.

"The Upper Berth" was printed at a time when transatlantic cruising was becoming popular. Ships were getting larger and faster, which decreased the time of the voyage between England and the United States. Crawford made this voyage on a number of occasions and was known as being versed in sea navigation.

It was in 1885, the year before "The Upper Berth" was published by Crawford, that the Etruria Cunard steamship broke the transatlantic voyage time by making the Queenstown to Sandy Hook passage in 6 days, 5 hours and 31 minutes.[4]

---

[4] *Trans-Atlantic Passenger Ships, Past and Present*, Eugene W. Smith, 1947, pg. 11

The Upper Berth
1886

CHAPTER I

SOMBODY ASKED FOR the cigars. We had talked long, and the conversation was beginning to languish; the tobacco smoke had got into the heavy curtains, the wine had got into those brains which were liable to become heavy, and it was already perfectly evident that, unless somebody did something to rouse our oppressed spirits, the meeting would soon come to its natural conclusion, and we, the guests, would speedily go home to bed, and most certainly to sleep. No one had said anything very remarkable; it may be that no one had anything very remarkable to say. Jones had given us every particular of his last hunting adventure in Yorkshire.

Mr. Tompkins, of Boston, had explained at elaborate length those working principles, by the due and careful maintenance of which the Atchison, Topeka, and Santa Fe Railroad not only extended its territory, increased its departmental influence, and transported live stock without starving them to death before the day of actual delivery, but, also, had for years succeeded in deceiving those passengers who bought its tickets into the fallacious belief that the corporation aforesaid was really able to transport human life without destroying it.

Signor Tombola had endeavored to persuade us, by arguments which we took no trouble to oppose, that the unity of his country in no way resembled the average modern torpedo, carefully planned, constructed with all the skill of the greatest European arsenals, but, when constructed, destined to be directed by feeble hands into a region where it must undoubtedly explode, unseen, unfeared, and unheard, into the illimitable wastes of political chaos.

It is unnecessary to go into further details. The conversation had assumed proportions which would have bored Prometheus on his rock,[1] which would have driven Tantalus to distraction,[2] and which would have impelled Ixion to seek relaxation[3] in the simple

---

[1] In Greek mythology Prometheus was chained to a rock by Zeus

[2] He was sentenced to everlasting punishment in Greek mythology, standing in a body of fresh water that would recede just enough so he could not drink from it and above him a tree of ripe fruit just out of his reach

[3] In Greek mythology Ixion was sentenced to ride on a wheel of fire for eternity

but instructive dialogues of Herr Ollendorff,[4] rather than submit to the greater evil of listening to our talk. We had sat at table for hours; we were bored, we were tired, and nobody showed signs of moving.

Somebody called for cigars. We all instinctively looked towards the speaker. Brisbane was a man of five-and-thirty years of age, and remarkable for those gifts which chiefly attract the attention of men. He was a strong man. The external proportions of his figure presented nothing extraordinary to the common eye, though his size was about the average. He was a little over six feet in height, and moderately broad in the shoulder; he did not appear to be stout, but, on the other hand, he was certainly not thin; his small head, was supported by a strong and sinewy neck; his broad, muscular hands appeared to possess a peculiar skill in breaking walnuts without the assistance of the ordinary cracker, and seeing him in profile, one could not help remarking the extraordinary breadth of his sleeves, and the unusual thickness of his chest. He was one of those men who are commonly spoken of among men as deceptive; that is to say, that though he looked exceedingly strong he was in reality very much stronger than he looked. Of his features I need say little. His head is small, his hair is thin, his eyes are blue, his nose is large, he has a small moustache and a square jaw. Everybody knows Brisbane, and when he asked for a cigar everybody looked at him.

"It is a very singular thing," said Brisbane.

Everybody stopped talking. Brisbane's voice was not loud, but possessed a peculiar quality of penetrating general conversation, and cutting it like a knife. Everybody listened. Brisbane, perceiving that he had attracted their general attention, lit his cigar with great equanimity.

"It is very singular," he continued, "that thing about ghosts. People are always asking whether anybody has seen a ghost. I have."

"Bosh! What, you? You don't mean to say so, Brisbane? Well, for a man of his intelligence!"

A chorus of exclamations greeted Brisbane's remarkable statement. Everybody called for cigars, and Stubbs, the butler, suddenly appeared from the depths of nowhere with a fresh bottle of dry champagne. The situation was saved; Brisbane was going to tell a story.

I am an old sailor, said Brisbane, and as I have to cross the Atlantic pretty often, I have my favorites. Most men have their favorites. I have seen a man wait in a Broadway bar for three quarters of an hour for a particular car which he liked. I believe the

---

[4] In 1840 Herr G. Ollendorff published *A New Method of Learning to Read, Write and Speak the German Language in Six Months*, which explains in the Preface that it is "founded on the principle, that each question contains nearly the answer which one ought or which one wishes to make to it. The slight difference between the question and the answer is always explained before the question."

bar-keeper made at least one third of his living by that man's preference. I have a habit of waiting for certain ships when I am obliged to cross that duck-pond.[5] It may be a prejudice, but I was never cheated out of a good passage but once in my life.

I remember it very well; it was a warm morning in June, and the Custom House officials, who were hanging about waiting for a steamer already on her way up from the Quarantine,[6] presented a peculiarly hazy and thoughtful appearance. I had not much luggage—I never have. I mingled with a crowd of passengers, porters, and officious individuals in blue coats and brass buttons, who seemed to spring up like mushrooms from the deck of a moored steamer to obtrude their unnecessary services upon the independent passenger. I have often noticed with a certain interest the spontaneous evolution of these fellows. They are not there when you arrive; five minutes after the pilot has called "Go ahead!" they, or at least their blue coats and brass buttons, have disappeared from deck and gangway as completely as though they had been consigned to that locker which tradition unanimously ascribes to Davy Jones.[7]

But, at the moment of starting, they are there, clean shaved, blue coated, and ravenous for fees. I hastened on board. The *Kamtschatka* was one of my favorite ships. I say was, because she emphatically no longer is. I cannot conceive of any inducement which could entice me to make another voyage in her.

Yes, I know what you are going to say. She is uncommonly clean in the run aft, she has enough bluffing off in the bows to keep her dry, and the lower berths are most of them double. She has a lot of advantages, but I won't cross in her again. Excuse the digression. I got on board. I hailed a steward, whose red nose and redder whiskers were equally familiar to me.

"One hundred and five, lower berth," said I, in the businesslike tone peculiar to men who think no more of crossing the Atlantic than taking a whiskey cocktail at downtown Delmonico's.[8]

The steward took my portmanteau, greatcoat, and rug. I shall never forget the expression of his face. Not that he turned pale. It is maintained by the most eminent divines that even miracles cannot change the course of nature. I have no hesitation in saying that he did not turn pale; but, from his expression, I judged that he was either about to shed tears, to sneeze, or to drop my portmanteau. As the latter contained two bottles of particularly fine old sherry presented to me for my voyage by my old friend Snigginson van

---

[5] Atlantic Ocean

[6] Harbor area where ships arriving from Central American, South American and African countries were held for yellow fever inspection of passengers and crew members

[7] An idiom for the bottom of the ocean and the sailors who are put there by the evil spirit of the ocean—Davy Jones

[8] Famous New York steakhouse that opened in 1837 and is in operation to this day at 56 Beaver Street near Wall Street

Pickyns, I felt extremely nervous. But the steward did none of these things.

"Well, I'm d—d!" said he in a low voice, and led the way.

I supposed my Hermes,[9] as he led me to the lower regions, had had a little grog, but I said nothing and followed him. 105 was on the port side, well aft. There was nothing remarkable about the stateroom. The lower berth, like most of those upon the *Kamtschatka,* was double.

There was plenty of room; there was the usual washing apparatus, calculated to convey an idea of luxury to the mind of a North American Indian; there were the usual inefficient racks of brown wood, in which it is more easy to hang a large sized umbrella than the common toothbrush of commerce. Upon the uninviting mattresses were carefully folded together those blankets which a great modern humorist has aptly compared to cold buckwheat cakes.[10] The question of towels was left entirely to the imagination.

The glass decanters were filled with a transparent liquid faintly tinged with brown, but from which an odor less faint, but not more pleasing, ascended to the nostrils, like a far-off seasick reminiscence of oily machinery. Sad-colored curtains half closed the upper berth. The hazy June daylight shed a faint illumination upon the desolate little scene. Ugh! how I hate that stateroom!

The steward deposited my traps and looked at me as though he wanted to get away—probably in search of more passengers and more fees. It is always a good plan to start in favor with those functionaries, and I accordingly gave him certain coins there and then.

"I'll try and make yer comfortable all I can," he remarked, as he put the coins in his pocket.

Nevertheless, there was a doubtful intonation in his voice which surprised me. Possibly his scab of fees had gone up, and he was not satisfied; but on the whole I was inclined to think that, as he himself would have expressed it, he was "the better for a glass." I was wrong, however, and did the man injustice.

CHAPTER II

Nothing especially worthy of mention occurred during that day. We left the pier punctually, and it was very pleasant to be fairly under way, for the weather was warm and sultry, and the motion of the steamer produced a refreshing breeze. Everybody knows what the first day at sea is like. People pace the decks and stare at each other, and occasionally meet acquaintances whom they did not know to be on board.

---

[9] Greek god of transition and for which stewards are sometimes called
[10] Author Bret Harte (1836-1902) described the blankets as such in his short story "A Sleeping-Car Experience" (1878)

There is the usual uncertainty as to whether the food will be good, bad, or indifferent, until the first two meals have put the matter beyond a doubt; there is the usual uncertainty about the weather, until the ship is fairly off Fire Island. The tables are crowded at first, and then suddenly thinned. Pale-faced people spring from their seats and precipitate themselves towards the door, and each old sailor breathes more freely as his seasick neighbor rushes from his side, leaving him plenty of elbow-room and an unlimited command over the mustard.

One passage across the Atlantic is very much like another, and we who cross very often do not make the voyage for the sake of novelty. Whales and icebergs are indeed always objects of interest, but, after all, one whale is very much like another whale, and one rarely sees an iceberg at close quarters. To the majority of us the most delightful moment of the day on board an ocean steamer is when we have taken our last turn on deck, have smoked our last cigar, and having succeeded in tiring ourselves, feel at liberty to turn in with a clear conscience.

On that first night of the voyage I felt particularly lazy, and went to bed in 105 rather earlier than I usually do. As I turned in, I was amazed to see that I was to have a companion. A portmanteau, very like my own, lay in the opposite corner, and in the upper berth had been deposited a neatly folded rug, with a stick and umbrella. I had hoped to be alone, and I was disappointed; but I wondered who my roommate was to be, and I determined to have a look at him.

Before I had been long in bed he entered. He was, as far as I could see, a very tall man, very thin, very pale, with sandy hair and whiskers and colorless grey eyes. He had about him, I thought, an air of rather dubious fashion; the sort of man you might see in Wall Street, without being able precisely to say what he was doing there—the sort of man who frequents the Café Anglais,[11] who always seems to be alone and who drinks champagne; you might meet him on a racecourse, but he would never appear to be doing anything there either.

A little over-dressed—a little odd. There are three or four of his kind on every ocean steamer. I made up my mind that I did not care to make his acquaintance, and I went to sleep saying to myself that I would study his habits in order to avoid him. If he rose early, I would rise late; if he went to bed late I would go to bed early. I did not care to know him. If you once know people of that kind, they are always turning up. Poor fellow! I need not have taken the trouble to come to so many decisions about him, for I never saw him again after that first night in 105.

I was sleeping soundly when I was suddenly waked by a loud noise. To judge from the sound, my roommate must have sprung with a single leap from the upper berth to the floor. I heard him fumbling with the latch and bolt of the door, which opened almost

---

11 From 1802-1913 the Café Anglais was a small hotel and famous restaurant in Paris

immediately, and then I heard his footsteps as he ran at full speed down the passage, leaving the door open behind him. The ship was rolling a little, and I expected to hear him stumble or fall, but he ran as though he were running for his life. The door swung on its hinges with the motion of the vessel, and the sound annoyed me. I got up and shut it, and groped my way back to my berth in the darkness. I went to sleep again; but I have no idea how long I slept.

When I awoke it was still quite dark, but I felt a disagreeable sensation of cold, and it seemed to me that the air was damp. You know the peculiar smell of a cabin which has been wet with seawater. I covered myself up as well as I could and dozed off again, framing complaints to be made the next day, and selecting the most powerful epithets in the language. I could hear my roommate turn over in the upper berth. He had probably returned while I was asleep. Once I thought I heard him groan, and I argued that he was sea-sick. That is particularly unpleasant when one is below. Nevertheless I dozed off and slept till early daylight.

The ship was rolling heavily, much more than on the previous evening, and the grey light which came in through the porthole changed in tint with every movement according as the angle of the vessel's side turned the glass seawards or skywards. It was very cold—unaccountably so for the month of June.

I turned my head and looked at the porthole, and saw to my surprise that it was wide open and hooked back. I believe I swore audibly. Then I got up and shut it. As I turned back I glanced at the upper berth. The curtains were drawn close together; my companion had probably felt cold as well as I. It struck me that I had slept enough. The stateroom was uncomfortable, though, strange to say, I could not smell the dampness which had annoyed me in the night. My roommate was still asleep—excellent opportunity for avoiding him, so I dressed at once and went on deck.

The day was warm and cloudy, with an oily smell on the water. It was seven o'clock as I came out—much later than I had imagined. I came across the doctor, who was taking his first sniff of the morning air. He was a young man from the West of Ireland—a tremendous fellow, with black hair and blue eyes, already inclined to be stout; he had a happy-go-lucky, healthy look about him which was rather attractive.

"Fine morning," I remarked, by way of introduction.

"Well," said he, eyeing me with an air of ready interest, "it's a fine morning and it's not a fine morning. I don't think it's much of a morning."

"Well, no—it is not so very fine," said I.

"It's just what I call fuggly weather," replied the doctor.

"It was very cold last night, I thought," I remarked. "However, when I looked about, I found that the porthole was wide open. I had not noticed it when I went to bed. And the stateroom was damp, too."

"Damp!" said he. "Whereabouts are you?"

"One hundred and five—"

To my surprise the doctor started visibly, and stared at me.

"What is the matter ?" I asked.

"Oh—nothing," he answered; "only everybody has complained of that stateroom for the last three trips."

"I shall complain, too," I said. "It has certainly not been properly aired. It is a shame!"

"I don't believe it can be helped," answered the doctor. "I believe there is something—well, it is not my business to frighten passengers."

"You need not be afraid of frightening me," I replied. "I can stand any amount of damp. If I should get a bad cold, I will come to you."

I offered the doctor a cigar, which he took and examined very critically.

"It is not so much the damp," he remarked. "However, I dare say you will get on very well. Have you a roommate?"

"Yes; a deuce of a fellow, who bolts out in the middle of the night, and leaves the door open."

Again the doctor glanced curiously at me. Then he lit the cigar and looked grave.

"Did he come back?" he asked presently.

"Yes. I was asleep, but I waked up, and heard him moving. Then I felt cold and went to sleep again. This morning I found the porthole open."

"Look here," said the doctor quietly, "I don't care much for this ship. I don't care a rap for her reputation. I tell you what I will do. I have a good-sized place up here. I will share it with you, though I don't know you from Adam."

I was very much surprised at the proposition. I could not imagine why he should take such a sudden interest in my welfare. However, his manner, as he spoke of the ship, was peculiar.

"You are very good, doctor," I said. "But, really, I believe even now the cabin could be aired, or cleaned out, or something. Why do you not care for the ship?"

"We are not superstitious in our profession, sir," replied the doctor, "but the sea makes people so. I don't want to prejudice you, and I don't want to frighten you, but if you will take my advice you will move in here. I would as soon see you overboard," he added earnestly, "as know that you or any other man was to sleep in 105."

"Good gracious! Why?" I asked.

"Just because on the three last trips the people who have slept there actually have gone overboard," he answered gravely.

The intelligence was startling and exceedingly unpleasant, I confess. I looked hard at the doctor to see whether he was making game of me, but he looked perfectly serious. I thanked him warmly for his offer, but told him I intended to be the exception to the rule by which everyone who slept in that particular stateroom went overboard.

He did not say much, but looked as grave as ever, and hinted that, before we got across, I should probably reconsider his proposal. In the course of time we went to breakfast, at which only an inconsiderable number of passengers assembled. I noticed that one or two of the officers who breakfasted with us looked grave. After breakfast I went into my stateroom in order to get a book. The curtains of the upper berth were still closely drawn. Not a sound was to be heard. My room-mate was probably still asleep.

As I came out I met the steward whose business it was to look after me. He whispered that the captain wanted to see me, and then scuttled away down the passage as if very anxious to avoid any questions. I went toward the captain's cabin, and found him waiting for me.

"Sir," said he, "I want to ask a favor of you."

I answered that I would do anything to oblige him.

"Your roommate has disappeared," he said. "He is known to have turned in early last night. Did you notice anything extraordinary in his manner?"

The question, coming as it did in exact confirmation of the fears the doctor had expressed half an hour earlier, staggered me.

"You don't mean to say he has gone overboard?" I asked.

"I fear he has," answered the captain.

"This is the most extraordinary thing—" I began.

"Why?" he asked.

"He is the fourth, then?" I explained. In answer to another question from the captain, I explained, without mentioning the doctor, that I had heard the story concerning 105. He seemed very much annoyed at hearing that I knew of it. I told him what had occurred in the night.

"What you say," he replied, "coincides almost exactly with what was told me by the roommates of two of the other three. They bolt out of bed and run down the passage. Two of them were seen to go overboard by the watch; we stopped and lowered boats, but they were not found. Nobody, however, saw or heard the man who was lost last night—if he is really lost. The steward, who is a superstitious fellow, perhaps, and expected something to go wrong, went to look for him this morning, and found his berth empty, but his clothes lying about, just as he had left them. The steward was the only man on board who knew him by sight, and he has been searching everywhere for him. He has disappeared! Now, sir, I want to beg you not to mention the circumstance to any of the passengers; I don't want the ship to get a bad name, and nothing hangs about an ocean-goer like stories of suicides. You shall have your choice of any one of the officers' cabins you like, including my own, for the rest of the passage. Is that a fair bargain?"

"Very," said I; "and I am much obliged to you. But since I am alone, and have the stateroom to myself, I would rather not move. If the steward will take out that unfortunate man's things, I would as lief stay where I am. I will not say anything about the matter, and I think I can promise you that I will not follow my roommate."

The captain tried to dissuade me from my intention, but I preferred having a stateroom alone to being the chum of any officer on board. I do not know whether I acted foolishly, but if I had taken his advice I should have had nothing more to tell. There would have remained the disagreeable coincidence of several suicides occurring among men who had slept in the same cabin, but that would have been all.

That was not the end of the matter, however, by any means. I obstinately made up my mind that I would not be disturbed by such tales, and I even went so far as to argue the question with the captain. There was something wrong about the stateroom, I said. It was rather damp. The porthole had been left open last night. My roommate might have been ill when he came on board, and he might have become delirious after he went to bed. He might even now be hiding somewhere on board, and might be found later. The place ought to be aired and the fastening of the port looked to. If the captain would give me leave, I would see that what I thought necessary were done immediately.

"Of course you have a right to stay where you are if you please," he replied, rather petulantly; "but I wish you would turn out and let me lock the place up, and be done with it."

I did not see it in the same light, and left the captain, after promising to be silent concerning the disappearance of my companion. The latter had had no acquaintances on board, and was not missed in the course of the day. Towards evening I met the doctor again, and he asked me whether I had changed my mind. I told him I had not.

"Then you will before long," he said, very gravely.

CHAPTER III

We played whist in the evening, and I went to bed late. I will confess now that I felt a disagreeable sensation when I entered my stateroom. I could not help thinking of the tall man I had seen on the previous night, who was now dead, drowned, tossing about in the long swell, two or three hundred miles astern.

His face rose very distinctly before me as I undressed, and I even went so far as to draw back the curtains of the upper berth, as though to persuade myself that he was actually gone. I also bolted the door of the stateroom. Suddenly I became aware that the porthole was open, and fastened back. This was more than I could stand. I hastily threw on my dressing-gown and went in search of Robert, the steward of my passage. I was very angry, I remember, and when I found him I dragged him roughly to the door of 105, and pushed him towards the open porthole.

"What the deuce do you mean, you scoundrel, by leaving that port open every night? Don't you know it is against the regulations? Don't you know that if the ship heeled and the water began to come in, ten men could not shut it? I will report you to the captain, you blackguard, for endangering the ship!"

I was exceedingly wroth. The man trembled and turned pale, and then began to shut the round glass plate with the heavy brass fittings.

"Why don't you answer me?" I said roughly.

"If you please, sir," faltered Robert, "there's nobody on board as can keep this 'ere port shut at night. You can try it yourself, sir. I ain't a-going to stop hany longer on board o' this vessel, sir; I ain't, indeed. But if I was you, sir, I'd just clear out and go and sleep with the surgeon, or something, I would. Look 'ere, sir, is that fastened what you may call securely, or not, sir? Try it, sir, see if it will move a hinch."

I tried the port, and found it perfectly tight.

"Well, sir," continued Robert, triumphantly, "I wager my reputation as a A1 steward that in 'arf an hour it will be open again; fastened back, too, sir, that's the horful thing—fastened back!"

I examined the great screw and the looped nut that ran on it.

"If I find it open in the night, Robert, I will give you a sovereign. It is not possible. You may go."

"Soverin' did you say, sir? Very good, sir. Thank ye, sir. Goodnight, sir. Pleasant reepose, sir, and all manner of hinchantin' dreams, sir."

Robert scuttled away, delighted at being released. Of course, I thought he was trying to account for his negligence by a silly story, intended to frighten me, and I disbelieved him. The consequence was that he got his sovereign, and I spent a very peculiarly unpleasant night.

I went to bed, and five minutes after I had rolled myself up in my blankets the inexorable Robert extinguished the light that burned steadily behind the ground-glass pane near the door. I lay quite still in the dark trying to go to sleep, but I soon found that impossible. It had been some satisfaction to be angry with the steward, and the diversion had banished that unpleasant sensation I had at first experienced when I thought of the drowned man who had been my chum; but I was no longer sleepy, and I lay awake for some time, occasionally glancing at the porthole, which I could just see from where I lay, and which, in the darkness, looked like a faintly luminous soup-plate suspended in blackness.

I believe I must have lain there for an hour, and, as I remember, I was just dozing into sleep when I was roused by a draught of cold air, and by distinctly feeling the spray of the sea blown upon my face. I started to my feet, and not having allowed in the dark for the motion of the ship, I was instantly thrown violently across the stateroom upon the couch which was placed beneath the porthole. I recovered myself immediately, however, and climbed upon my knees. The porthole was again wide open and fastened back!

Now these things are facts. I was wide awake when I got up, and I should certainly have been waked by the fall had I still been dozing. Moreover, I bruised my elbows and knees badly, and the bruises were there on the following morning to testify to the fact, if I myself had doubted it.

The porthole was wide open and fastened back—a thing so unaccountable that I remember very well feeling astonishment rather than fear when I discovered it. I at once closed the plate again, and screwed down the loop nut with all my strength. It was very dark in the stateroom. I reflected that the port had certainly been opened within an hour after Robert had at first shut it in my presence, and I determined to watch it, and see whether it would open again.

Those brass fittings are very heavy and by no means easy to move; I could not believe that the clump had been turned by the shaking of the screw. I stood peering out through the thick glass at the alternate white and grey streaks of the sea that foamed beneath the ship's side. I must have remained there a quarter of an hour.

Suddenly, as I stood, I distinctly heard something moving behind me in one of the berths, and a moment afterwards, just as I turned instinctively to look—though I could, of course, see nothing in the darkness—I heard a very faint groan. I sprang across the stateroom, and tore the curtains of the upper berth aside, thrusting in my hands to discover if there were any one there. There was some one.

I remember that the sensation as I put my hands forward was as though I were plunging them into the air of a damp cellar, and from behind the curtains came a gust of wind that smelled horribly of stagnant seawater. I laid hold of something that had the shape of a man's arm, but was smooth, and wet, and icy cold. But suddenly, as I pulled, the creature sprang violently forward against me, a clammy, oozy mass, as it seemed to me, heavy and wet, yet endowed with a sort of supernatural strength.

I reeled across the stateroom, and in an instant the door opened and the thing rushed out. I had not had time to be frightened, and quickly recovering myself, I sprang through the door and gave chase at the top of my speed, but I was too late. Ten yards before me I could see—I am sure I saw it—a dark shadow moving in the dimly lighted passage, quickly as the shadow of a fast horse thrown before a dogcart by the lamp on a dark night. But in a moment it had disappeared, and I found myself holding on to the polished rail that ran along the bulkhead where the passage turned towards the companion. My hair stood on end, and the cold perspiration rolled down my face. I am not ashamed of it in the least: I was very badly frightened.

Still I doubted my senses, and pulled myself together. It was absurd, I thought. The Welsh rare-bit[12] I had eaten had disagreed with me. I had been in a nightmare. I made my way back to my stateroom, and entered it with an effort. The whole place smelled of stagnant seawater, as it had when I had waked on the previous evening. It required my utmost strength to go in, and grope among my things for a box of wax lights. As I lighted a railway reading lantern which I always carry in case I want to read after the lamps are out, I perceived that the porthole was again open, and a sort of creeping horror began to take possession of me which I never felt before, nor wish to feel again. But I got a light and proceeded to examine the upper berth, expecting to find it drenched with seawater.

But I was disappointed. The bed had been slept in, and the smell of the sea was strong; but the bedding was as dry as a bone. I fancied that Robert had not had the courage to make the bed after the accident of the previous night—it had all been a hideous dream. I drew the curtains back as far as I could and examined the place very carefully. It was perfectly dry. But the porthole was open again. With a sort of dull bewilderment of horror I closed it and screwed it down, and thrusting my heavy stick through the brass loop, wrenched it with all my might, till the thick metal began to bend under the pressure. Then I hooked my reading lantern into the red velvet at the head of the couch, and sat down to recover my senses if I could. I sat there all night, unable to think of rest— hardly able to think at all. But the porthole remained closed, and I did not believe it would now open again without the application of a considerable force.

The morning dawned at last, and I dressed myself slowly, thinking over all that had happened in the night. It was a beautiful day and I went on deck, glad to get out into the early, pure sunshine, and to smell the breeze from the blue water, so different from the noisome, stagnant odor of my stateroom. Instinctively I turned aft, towards the surgeon's cabin. There he stood, with a pipe in his mouth, taking his morning airing precisely as on the preceding day.

"Good-morning," said he quietly, but looking at me with evident curiosity.

"Doctor, you were quite right," said I. "There is something wrong about that place."

"I thought you would change your mind," he answered, rather triumphantly. "You have had a bad night, eh? Shall I make you a pick-me-up? I have a capital recipe."

"No, thanks," I cried. "But I would like to tell you what happened."

---

[12] A vegetarian spread placed on sliced bread or toast and that derives its name as a joke on Welsh rabbit because the Welsh could not afford meat dishes

I then tried to explain as clearly as possible precisely what had occurred, not omitting to state that I had been scared as I had never been scared in my whole life before. I dwelt particularly on the phenomenon of the porthole, which was a fact to which I could testify, even if the rest had been an illusion. I had closed it twice in the night, and the second time I had actually bent the brass in wrenching it with my stick. I believe I insisted a good deal on this point.

"You seem to think I am likely to doubt the story," said the doctor, smiling at the detailed account of the state of the porthole. "I do not doubt it in the least. I renew my invitation to you. Bring your traps here, and take half my cabin."

"Come and take half of mine for one night," I said. "Help me to get at the bottom of this thing."

"You will get to the bottom of something else if you try," answered the doctor.

"What?" I asked.

"The bottom of the sea. I am going to leave this ship. It is not canny."

"Then you will not help me to find out—"

"Not I," said the doctor, quickly. "It is my business to keep my wits about me—not to go fiddling about with ghosts and things."

"Do you really believe it is a ghost?" I enquired, rather contemptuously. But as I spoke I remembered very well the horrible sensation of the supernatural which had got possession of me during the night.

The doctor turned sharply on me. "Have you any reasonable explanation of these things to offer?" he asked.

"No; you have not. Well, you say you will find an explanation. I say that you won't, sir, simply because there is not any."

"But, my dear sir," I retorted, "do you, a man of science, mean to tell me that such things cannot be explained?"

"I do," he answered stoutly. "And, if they could, I would not be concerned in the explanation."

I did not care to spend another night alone in the stateroom, and yet I was obstinately determined to get at the root of the disturbances. I do not believe there are many men who would have slept there alone, after passing two such nights. But I made up my mind to try it, if I could not get any one to share a watch with me. The doctor was evidently not inclined for such an experiment. He said he was a surgeon, and that in case any accident occurred on board he must be always in readiness.

He could not afford to have his nerves unsettled. Perhaps he was quite right, but I am inclined to think that his precaution was prompted by his inclination. On enquiry, he informed me that there was no one on board who would be likely to join me in my investigations, and after a little more conversation I left him. A little later I met the captain, and told him my story. I said that, if no one would spend the night with me, I would ask leave to have the light burning all night, and would try it alone.

"Look here," said he, "I will tell you what I will do. I will share your watch myself, and we will see what happens. It is my belief that we can find out between us. There may be some fellow skulking on board, who steals a passage by frightening the passengers. It is just possible that there may be something queer in the carpentering of that berth."

I suggested taking the ship's carpenter below and examining the place; but I was overjoyed at the captain's offer to spend the night with me. He accordingly sent for the workman and ordered him to do anything I required. We went below at once. I had all the bedding cleared out of the upper berth, and we examined the place thoroughly to see if there was a board loose anywhere, or a panel which could be opened or pushed aside.

We tried the planks everywhere, tapped the flooring, unscrewed the fittings of the lower berth and took it to pieces—in short, there was not a square inch of the stateroom which was not searched and tested. Everything was in perfect order, and we put everything back in its place. As we were finishing our work, Robert came to the door and looked in.

"Well, sir—find anything, sir?" he asked, with a ghastly grin.

"You were right about the porthole, Robert," I said, and I gave him the promised sovereign. The carpenter did his work silently and skillfully, following my directions. When he had done he spoke.

"I'm a plain man, sir," he said. "But it's my belief you had better just turn out your things, and let me run half a dozen four-inch screws through the door of this cabin. There's no good never came o' this cabin yet, sir, and that's all about it. There's been four lives lost out o' here to my own remembrance, and that in four trips. Better give it up, sir—better give it up!"

"I will try it for one night more," I said.

"Better give it up, sir—better give it up! It's a precious bad job," repeated the workman, putting his tools in his bag and leaving the cabin.

But my spirits had risen considerably at the prospect of having the captain's company, and I made up my mind not to be prevented from going to the end of the strange business. I abstained from Welsh rare-bits and grog[13] that evening, and did not even join in the customary game of whist.[14] I wanted to be quite sure of my nerves, and my vanity made me anxious to make a good figure in the captain's eyes.

CHAPTER IV

The captain was one of those splendidly tough and cheerful specimens of seafaring humanity whose combined courage, hardihood, and calmness in difficulty leads them naturally into

---

13 Cheap beer

14 Card game where points are scored on tricks won against other players

high positions of trust. He was not the man to be led away by an idle tale, and the mere fact that he was willing to join me in the investigation was proof that he thought there was something seriously wrong, which could not be accounted for on ordinary theories, nor laughed down as a common superstition. To some extent, too, his reputation was at stake, as well as the reputation of the ship. It is no light thing to lose passengers overboard, and he knew it.

About ten o'clock that evening, as I was smoking a last cigar, he came up to me, and drew me aside from the beat of the other passengers who were patrolling the deck in the warm darkness.

"This is a serious matter, Mr. Brisbane," he said. "We must make up our minds either way—to be disappointed or to have a pretty rough time of it. You see I cannot afford to laugh at the affair, and I will ask you to sign your name to a statement of whatever occurs. If nothing happens tonight, we will try it again tomorrow and next day. Are you ready?"

So we went below, and entered the stateroom. As we went in I could see Robert the steward, who stood a little further down the passage, watching us, with his usual grin, as though certain that something dreadful was about to happen. The captain closed the door behind us and bolted it.

"Supposing we put your portmanteau before the door," he suggested. "One of us can sit on it. Nothing can get out then. Is the port screwed down?"

I found it as I had left it in the morning. Indeed, without using a lever, as I had done, no one could have opened it. I drew back the curtains of the upper berth so that I could see well into it. By the captain's advice I lighted my reading lantern, and placed it so that it shone upon the white sheets above. He insisted upon sitting on the portmanteau, declaring that he wished to be able to swear that he had sat before the door.

Then he requested me to search the stateroom thoroughly, an operation very soon accomplished, as it consisted merely in looking beneath the lower berth and under the couch below the porthole. The spaces were quite empty.

"It is impossible for any human being to get in," I said, "or for any human being to open the port."

"Very good," said the captain, calmly. "If we see anything now, it must be either imagination or something supernatural."

I sat down on the edge of the lower berth.

"The first time it happened," said the captain, crossing his legs and leaning back against the door, "was in March. The passenger who slept here, in the upper berth, turned out to have been a lunatic—at all events, he was known to have been a little touched, and he had taken his passage without the knowledge of his friends. He rushed out in the middle of the night, and threw himself overboard, before the officer who had the watch could stop him. We stopped and lowered a boat; it was a quiet night, just before that heavy weather came on; but we could not find him. Of course his suicide was afterwards accounted for on the ground of his insanity."

"I suppose that often happens?" I remarked, rather absently.

"Not often—no," said the captain; "never before in my experience, though I have heard of it happening on board of other ships. Well, as I was saying, that occurred in March. On the very next trip—What are you looking at?" he asked, stopping suddenly in his narration.

I believe I gave no answer. My eyes were riveted upon the porthole. It seemed to me that the brass loop-nut was beginning to turn very slowly upon the screw—so slowly, however, that I was not sure it moved at all. I watched it intently, fixing its position in my mind, and trying to ascertain whether it changed. Seeing where I was looking, the captain looked too.

"It moves!" he exclaimed, in a tone of conviction. "No, it does not," he added, after a minute.

"If it were the jarring of the screw," said I, "it would have opened during the day; but I found it this evening jammed tight as I left it this morning."

I rose and tried the nut. It was certainly loosened, for by an effort I could move it with my hands.

"The queer thing," said the captain, "is that the second man who was lost is supposed to have got through that very port. We had a terrible time over it. It was in the middle of the night, and the weather was very heavy; there was an alarm that one of the ports was open and the sea running in. I came below and found everything flooded, the water pouring in every time she rolled, and the whole port swinging from the top bolts—not the porthole in the middle. Well, we managed to shut it, but the water did some damage. Ever since that the place smells of seawater from time to time. We supposed the passenger had thrown himself out, though the Lord only knows how he did it. The steward kept telling me that he cannot keep anything shut here. Upon my word—I can smell it now, cannot you?" he enquired, sniffing the air suspiciously.

"Yes—distinctly," I said, and I shuddered as that same odor of stagnant seawater grew stronger in the cabin. "Now, to smell like this, the place must be damp," I continued, "and yet when I examined it with the carpenter this morning everything was perfectly dry. It is most extraordinary—hallo!"

My reading lantern, which had been placed in the upper berth, was suddenly extinguished. There was still a good deal of light from the pane of ground glass near the door, behind which loomed the regulation lamp. The ship rolled heavily, and the curtain of the upper berth swung far out into the stateroom and back again. I rose quickly from my seat on the edge of the bed, and the captain at the same moment started to his feet with a loud cry of surprise.

I had turned with the intention of taking down the lantern to examine it, when I heard his exclamation, and immediately afterwards his call for help. I sprang towards him. He was wrestling with all his might with the brass loop of the port. It seemed to turn against his hands in spite of all his efforts. I caught up my cane, a heavy oak stick I always used to carry, and thrust it through the ring and bore on it with all my strength. But the strong wood snapped suddenly, and I fell upon the couch. When I rose again the port was wide open, and the captain was standing with his back against the door, pale to the lips.

"There is something in that berth!" he cried, in a strange voice, his eyes almost starting from his head. "Hold the door, while I look—it shall not escape us, whatever it is!"

But instead of taking his place, I sprang upon the lower bed, and seized something which lay in the upper berth.

It was something ghostly, horrible beyond words, and it moved in my grip. It was like the body of a man long drowned, and yet it moved, and had the strength of ten men living; but I gripped it with all my might—the slippery, oozy, horrible thing—the dead white eyes seemed to stare at me out of the dusk; the putrid odor of rank seawater was about it, and its shiny hair hung in foul wet curls over its dead face.

I wrestled with the dead thing; it thrust itself upon me and forced me back and nearly broke my arms; it wound its corpse's arms about my neck, the living death, and overpowered me, so that I, at last, cried aloud and fell, and left my hold.

As I fell the thing sprang across me, and seemed to throw itself upon the captain. When I last saw him on his feet his face was white and his lips set. It seemed to me that he struck a violent blow at the dead being, and then he, too, fell forward upon his face, with an inarticulate cry of horror.

The thing paused an instant, seeming to hover over his prostrate body, and I could have screamed again for very fright, but I had no voice left. The thing vanished suddenly, and it seemed to my disturbed senses that it made its exit through the open port, though how that was possible, considering the smallness of the aperture, is more than anyone can tell. I lay a long time upon the floor, and the captain lay beside me. At last I partially recovered my senses and moved, and instantly I knew that my arm was broken— the small bone of the left forearm near the wrist.

I got upon my feet somehow, and with my remaining hand I tried to raise the captain. He groaned and moved, and at last came to himself. He was not hurt, but he seemed badly stunned.

Well, do you want to hear any more? There is nothing more. That is the end of my story. The carpenter carried out his scheme of running half a dozen four inch screws through the door of 105; and if you ever take a passage in the *Kamtschatka*, you may ask for a berth in that stateroom. You will be told that it is engaged—yes— engaged by that dead thing.

I finished the trip in the surgeon's cabin. He doctored my broken arm, and advised me not to "fiddle about with ghosts and things" any more.

The captain was very silent, and never sailed again in that ship, though it is still running. And I will not sail in her either. It was a very disagreeable experience, and I was very badly frightened, which is a thing I do not like.

That is all. That is how I saw a ghost—if it was a ghost. It was dead anyhow.

Ralph Adams Cram
(1863-1942)

Ralph Adams Cram was a denizen of the Ivy League. He was a Yale-trained architect who designed the Princeton University Chapel in 1928 that is still viewed today as one of its finest structures. Ralph Adams Cram's forte was cathedrals and he designed numerous churches in the northeast including such notable Gothic edifices as the Cathedral of Saint John the Divine in New York City, which is still being used nearly a hundred years later.

The author of this gut-wrenching ghost story penned many non-fiction books espousing his views of modern gothic architecture. Yet it was his collection of fictional ghost stories in 1895, *Black Spirits and White*, which placed him in lofty literary company. His most famous horror story, "The Dead Valley" (1895), was lauded by H. P. Lovecraft.

Most importantly for spectral literature, he also published a seminal ghost story called "In Kropfsberg Keep" that was contained in the 1895 collection. It is a masterpiece of Gothic writing, unmatched in atmosphere and structural sense of dread for the last half of the nineteenth century.

The setting is Germany in an eldritch inn that makes full use of Cram's expertise in describing Gothic structures. Consider this passage:

> The Keep rose absolutely isolated among the ruins, yet on passing through the wall Rupert found himself in a long, uneven corridor, the floor of which was warped and sagging, while the walls were covered on one side with big

faded portraits of an inferior quality, like those in the corridor that connects the Pitti and Uffizzi in Florence.

By publishing "In Kropfsberg Keep," Ralph Adams Cram gave the world great writing and a ghost story with a continuing sense of dread. The surprise ending should be savored to its fullest.

His protagonists are "ghost hunters," which is one of the first uses of the now popular term in a ghost short story. It's time to begin the chase.

In Kropfsberg Keep
1895

TO THE TRAVELER from Innsbruck to Munich, up the lovely valley of the Silver Inn, many castles appear, one after another, each on its beetling cliff or gentle hill,—appear and disappear, melting into the dark fir trees that grow so thickly on every side,—Laneck, Lichtwer, Ratholtz, Tratzberg, Matzen, Kropfsberg, gathering close around the entrance to the dark and wonderful Zillerthal.

But to us—Tom Rendel and myself—there are two castles only: not the gorgeous and princely Ambras, nor the noble old Tratzberg, with its crowded treasures of solemn and splendid mediævalism; but little Matzen,[1] where eager hospitality forms the new life of a never-dead chivalry, and Kropfsberg,[2] ruined, tottering, blasted by fire and smitten with grievous years,—a dead thing, and haunted,—full of strange legends, and eloquent of mystery and tragedy.

We were visiting the von C—s at Matzen, and gaining our first wondering knowledge of the courtly, cordial castle life in the Tyrol,—of the gentle and delicate hospitality of noble Austrians.

Brixleg had ceased to be but a mark on a map, and had become a place of rest and delight, a home for homeless wanderers on the face of Europe, while Schloss Matzen was a synonym for all that was gracious and kindly and beautiful in life. The days moved on in a golden round of riding and driving and shooting: down to Landl and Thiersee for chamois, across the river to the magic Achensec, up the Zillerthal, across the Schmerner Joch, even to the railway station at Steinach.

And in the evenings after the late dinners in the upper hall where the sleepy hounds leaned against our chairs looking at us with suppliant eyes, in the evenings when the fire was dying away in the hooded fireplace in the library, stories. Stories, and legends, and fairy tales, while the stiff old portraits changed countenance constantly under the flickering firelight, and the sound of the drifting Inn came softly across the meadows far below.

---

[1] Schloss Matzen castle is a historic Austrian castle

[2] Fictitious castle, the closest in name being Kransberg Castle in Kransberg, Germany

If ever I tell the Story of Schloss Matzen, then will be the time to paint the too inadequate picture of this fair oasis in the desert of travel and tourists and hotels; but just now it is Kropfsberg the Silent that is of greater importance, for it was only in Matzen that the story was told by Fræulein E—, the gold-haired niece of Frau von C—s, one hot evening in July, when we were sitting in the great west window of the drawing-room after a long ride up the Stallenthal.

All the windows were open to catch the faint wind, and we had sat for a long time watching the Otzethaler Alps turn rose-color over distant Innsbruck, then deepen to violet as the sun went down and the white mists rose slowly until Lichtwer and Laneck and Kropfsberg rose like craggy islands in a silver sea.

And this is the story as Fræulein E— told it to us,—the Story of Kropfsberg Keep.[3]

A great many years ago, soon after my grandfather died, and Matzen came to us, when I was a little girl, and so young that I remember nothing of the affair except as something dreadful that frightened me very much, two young men who had studied painting with my grandfather came down to Brixleg from Munich, partly to paint, and partly to amuse themselves,—"ghost-hunting" as they said, for they were very sensible young men and prided themselves on it, laughing at all kinds of "superstition," and particularly at that form which believed in ghosts and feared them.

They had never seen a real ghost, you know, and they belonged to a certain set of people who believed nothing they had not seen themselves,—which always seemed to me very conceited.

Well, they knew that we had lots of beautiful castles here in the "lower valley," and they assumed, and rightly, that every castle has at least one ghost story connected with it, so they chose this as their hunting ground, only the game they sought was ghosts, not chamois.[4] Their plan was to visit every place that was supposed to be haunted, and to meet every reputed ghost, and prove that it really was no ghost at all.

There was a little inn down in the village then, kept by an old man named Peter Rosskopf, and the two young men made this their headquarters. The very first night they began to draw from the old innkeeper all that he knew of legends and ghost stories connected with Brixleg and its castles, and as he was a most garrulous old gentleman he filled them with the wildest delight by his stories of the ghosts of the castles about the mouth of the Zillerthal.

Of course the old man believed every word he said, and you can imagine his horror and amazement when, after telling his guests the particularly blood-curdling story of Kropfsberg and its haunted keep, the elder of the two boys, whose surname I have forgotten, but whose Christian name was Rupert, calmly said,

---

[3] In this instance the "keep" is large, central tower of the castle
[4] Mountain goat

"Your story is most satisfactory: we will sleep in Kropfsberg Keep tomorrow night, and you must provide us with all that we may need to make ourselves comfortable."

The old man nearly fell into the fire. "What for a blockhead are you?" he cried, with big eyes.

"The keep is haunted by Count Albert's ghost, I tell you!"

"That is why we are going there tomorrow night; we wish to make the acquaintance of Count Albert."

"But there was a man stayed there once, and in the morning he was dead."

"Very silly of him; there are two of us, and we carry revolvers."

"But it's a ghost, I tell you," almost screamed the innkeeper; "are ghosts afraid of firearms?"

"Whether they are or not, we are not afraid of them."

Here the younger boy broke in,—he was named Otto von Kleist. I remember the name, for I had a music teacher once by that name. He abused the poor old man shamefully; told him that they were going to spend the night in Kropfsberg in spite of Count Albert and Peter Rosskopf, and that he might as well make the most of it and earn his money with cheerfulness.

In a word, they finally bullied the old fellow into submission, and when the morning came he set about preparing for the suicide, as he considered it, with sighs and mutterings and ominous shakings of the head.

You know the condition of the castle now,—nothing but scorched walls and crumbling piles of fallen masonry. Well, at the time I tell you of, the keep was still partially preserved. It was finally burned out only a few years ago by some wicked boys who came over from Jenbach to have a good time. But when the ghost hunters came, though the two lower floors had fallen into the crypt, the third floor remained. The peasants said it could not fall, but that it would stay until the Day of Judgment, because it was in the room above that the wicked Count Albert sat watching the flames destroy the great castle and his imprisoned guests, and where he finally hung himself in a suit of armor that had belonged to his mediæval ancestor, the first Count Kropfsberg.

No one dared touch him, and so he hung there for twelve years, and all the time venturesome boys and daring men used to creep up the turret steps and stare awfully through the chinks in the door at that ghostly mass of steel that held within itself the body of a murderer and suicide, slowly returning to the dust from which it was made. Finally it disappeared, none knew whither, and for another dozen years the room stood empty but for the old furniture and the rotting hangings.

So, when the two men climbed the stairway to the haunted room, they found a very different state of things from what exists now. The room was absolutely as it was left the night Count Albert burned the castle, except that all trace of the suspended suit of armor and its ghastly contents had vanished.

No one had dared to cross the threshold, and I suppose that for forty years no living thing had entered that dreadful room.

On one side stood a vast canopied bed of black wood, the damask hangings of which were covered with mold and mildew. All the clothing of the bed was in perfect order, and on it lay a book, open, and face downward. The only other furniture in the room consisted of several old chairs, a carved oak chest, and a big inlaid table covered with books and papers, and on one corner two or three bottles with dark solid sediment at the bottom, and a glass, also dark with the dregs of wine that had been poured out almost half a century before.

The tapestry on the walls was green with mold, but hardly torn or otherwise defaced, for although the heavy dust of forty years lay on everything the room had been preserved from further harm. No spider web was to be seen, no trace of nibbling mice, not even a dead moth or fly on the sills of the diamond-paned windows; life seemed to have shunned the room utterly and finally.

The men looked at the room curiously, and, I am sure, not without some feelings of awe and unacknowledged fear; but, whatever they may have felt of instinctive shrinking, they said nothing, and quickly set to work to make the room passably inhabitable. They decided to touch nothing that had not absolutely to be changed, and therefore they made for themselves a bed in one corner with the mattress and linen from the inn. In the great fireplace they piled a lot of wood on the caked ashes of a fire dead for forty years, turned the old chest into a table, and laid out on it all their arrangements for the evening's amusement: food, two or three bottles of wine, pipes and tobacco, and the chessboard that was their inseparable travelling companion.

All this they did themselves. The innkeeper would not even come within the walls of the outer court. He insisted that he had washed his hands of the whole affair, the silly dunderheads might go to their death their own way. He would not aid and abet them. One of the stable boys brought the basket of food and the wood and the bed up the winding stone stairs, to be sure, but neither money nor prayers nor threats would bring him within the walls of the accursed place, and he stared fearfully at the hare-brained boys as they worked around the dead old room preparing for the night that was coming so fast.

At length everything was in readiness, and after a final visit to the inn for dinner Rupert and Otto started at sunset for the Keep. Half the village went with them, for Peter Rosskopf had babbled the whole story to an open-mouthed crowd of wondering men and women, and as to an execution the awe-struck crowd followed the two boys dumbly, curious to see if they surely would put their plan into execution.

But none went farther than the outer doorway of the stairs, for it was already growing twilight. In absolute silence they watched the two foolhardy youths with their lives in their hands enter the terrible Keep, standing like a tower in the midst of the piles of stones that had once formed walls joining it with the mass of the castle beyond.

When a moment later a light showed itself in the high windows above, they sighed resignedly and went their ways, to wait stolidly until morning should come and prove the truth of their fears and warnings.

In the meantime the ghost hunters built a huge fire, lighted their many candles, and sat down to await developments. Rupert afterwards told my uncle that they really felt no fear whatever, only a contemptuous curiosity, and they ate their supper with good appetite and an unusual relish. It was a long evening. They played many games of chess, waiting for midnight. Hour passed after hour, and nothing occurred to interrupt the monotony of the evening. Ten, eleven, came and went,—it was almost midnight. They piled more wood in the fireplace, lighted new candles, looked to their pistols—and waited.

The clocks in the village struck twelve; the sound coming muffled through the high, deep-embrasured windows. Nothing happened, nothing to break the heavy silence; and with a feeling of disappointed relief they looked at each other and acknowledged that they had met another rebuff.

Finally they decided that there was no use in sitting up and boring themselves any longer, they had much better rest; so Otto threw himself down on the mattress, falling almost immediately asleep.

Rupert sat a little longer, smoking, and watching the stars creep along behind the shattered glass and the bent leads of the lofty windows; watching the fire fall together, and the strange shadows move mysteriously on the moldering walls. The iron hook in the oak beam, that crossed the ceiling midway, fascinated him, not with fear, but morbidly. So, it was from that hook that for twelve years, twelve long years of changing summer and winter, the body of Count Albert, murderer and suicide, hung in its strange casing of mediæval steel; moving a little at first, and turning gently while the fire died out on the hearth, while the ruins of the castle grew cold, and horrified peasants sought for the bodies of the score of gay, reckless, wicked guests whom Count Albert had gathered in Kropfsberg for a last debauch, gathered to their terrible and untimely death.

What a strange and fiendish idea it was, the young, handsome noble who had ruined himself and his family in the society of the splendid debauchees, gathering them all together, men and women who had known only love and pleasure, for a glorious and awful riot of luxury, and then, when they were all dancing in the great ballroom, locking the doors and burning the whole castle about them, the while he sat in the great keep listening to their screams of agonized fear, watching the fire sweep from wing to wing until the whole mighty mass was one enormous and awful pyre, and then, clothing himself in his great-great-grandfather's armor, hanging himself in the midst of the ruins of what had been a proud and noble castle. So ended a great family, a great house.

But that was forty years ago.

He was growing drowsy; the light flickered and flared in the fireplace; one by one the candles went out; the shadows grew thick in the room. Why did that great iron hook stand out so plainly?

Why did that dark shadow dance and quiver so mockingly behind it?—why—But he ceased to wonder at anything. He was asleep.

It seemed to him that he woke almost immediately; the fire still burned, though low and fitfully on the hearth. Otto was sleeping, breathing quietly and regularly; the shadows had gathered close around him, thick and murky; with every passing moment the light died in the fireplace; he felt stiff with cold. In the utter silence he heard the clock in the village strike two. He shivered with a sudden and irresistible feeling of fear, and abruptly turned and looked towards the hook in the ceiling.

Yes, it was there, he knew that It would be. It seemed quite natural, he would have been disappointed had he seen nothing; but now he knew that the story was true, knew that he was wrong, and that the dead do sometimes return to earth, for there, in the fast-deepening shadow, hung the black mass of wrought steel, turning a little now and then, with the light flickering on the tarnished and rusty metal.

He watched it quietly; he hardly felt afraid it was rather a sentiment of sadness and fatality that filled him, of gloomy forebodings of something unknown, unimaginable. He sat and watched the thing disappear in the gathering dark, his hand on his pistol as it lay by him on the great chest. There was no sound but the regular breathing of the sleeping boy on the mattress.

It had grown absolutely dark; a bat fluttered against the broken glass of the window. He wondered if he was growing mad, for—he hesitated to acknowledge it to himself—he heard music; far, curious music, a strange and luxurious dance, very faint, very vague, but unmistakable.

Like a flash of lightning came a jagged line of fire down the blank wall opposite him, a line that remained, that grew wider, that let a pale cold light into the room, showing him now all its details, —the empty fireplace, where a thin smoke rose in a spiral from a bit of charred wood, the mass of the great bed, and, in the very middle, black against the curious brightness, the armored man, or ghost, or devil, standing, not suspended, beneath the rusty hook. And with the rending of the wall the music grew more distinct, though sounding still very, very far away.

Count Albert raised his mailed hand and beckoned to him; then turned, and stood in the riven wall.

Without a word, Rupert rose and followed him, his pistol in hand.

Count Albert passed through the mighty wall and disappeared in the unearthly light. Rupert followed mechanically. He felt the crushing of the mortar beneath his feet, the roughness of the jagged wall where he rested his hand to steady himself.

The Keep rose absolutely isolated among the ruins, yet on passing through the wall Rupert found himself in a long, uneven corridor, the floor of which was warped and sagging, while the walls were covered on one side with big faded portraits of an inferior quality, like those in the corridor that connects the Pitti and Uffizzi in Florence.

Before him moved the figure of Count Albert,—a black silhouette in the ever-increasing light. And always the music grew stronger and stranger, a mad, evil, seductive dance that bewitched even while it disgusted.

In a final blaze of vivid, intolerable light, in a burst of hellish music that might have come from Bedlam, Rupert stepped from the corridor into a vast and curious room where at first he saw nothing, distinguished nothing but a mad, seething whirl of sweeping figures, white, in a white room, under white light, Count Albert standing before him, the only dark object to be seen. As his eyes grew accustomed to the fearful brightness, he knew that he was looking on a dance such as the damned might see in hell, but such as no living man had ever seen before.

Around the long, narrow hall, under the fearful light that came from nowhere, but was omnipresent, swept a rushing stream of unspeakable horrors, dancing insanely, laughing, gibbering hideously; the dead of forty years. White, polished skeletons, bare of flesh and vesture, skeletons clothed in the dreadful rags of dried and rattling sinews, the tags of tattering grave-clothes flaunting behind them.

These were the dead of many years ago. Then the dead of more recent times, with yellow bones showing only here and there, the long and insecure hair of their hideous heads writhing in the beating air. Then green and gray horrors, bloated and shapeless, stained with earth or dripping with spattering water; and here and there white, beautiful things, like chiseled ivory, the dead of yesterday, locked it may be, in the mummy arms of rattling skeletons.

Round and round the cursed room, a swaying, swirling maelstrom of death, while the air grew thick with miasma, the floor foul with shreds of shrouds, and yellow parchment, clattering bones, and wisps of tangled hair.

And in the very midst of this ring of death, a sight not for words nor for thought, a sight to blast forever the mind of the man who looked upon it: a leaping, writhing dance of Count Albert's victims, the score of beautiful women and reckless men who danced to their awful death while the castle burned around them, charred and shapeless now, a living charnel-house of nameless horror.

Count Albert, who had stood silent and gloomy, watching the dance of the damned, turned to Rupert, and for the first time spoke.

"We are ready for you now; dance!"

A prancing horror, dead some dozen years, perhaps, flaunted from the rushing river of the dead, and leered at Rupert with eyeless skull.

"Dance!"

Rupert stood frozen, motionless.

"Dance!"

His hard lips moved. "Not if the devil came from hell to make me."

Count Albert swept his vast two-handed sword into the foetid air while the tide of corruption paused in its swirling, and swept down on Rupert with gibbering grins.

The room, and the howling dead, and the black portent before him circled dizzily around, as with a last effort of departing consciousness he drew his pistol and fired full in the face of Count Albert.

* * *

Perfect silence, perfect darkness; not a breath, not a sound: the dead stillness of a long-sealed tomb. Rupert lay on his back, stunned, helpless, his pistol clenched in his frozen hand, a smell of powder in the black air. Where was he? Dead? In hell? He reached his hand out cautiously; it fell on dusty boards. Outside, far away, a clock struck three. Had he dreamed? Of course; but how ghastly a dream! With chattering teeth he called softly,—"Otto!"

There was no reply, and none when he called again and again. He staggered weakly to his feet, groping for matches and candles. A panic of abject terror came on him; the matches were gone!

He turned towards the fireplace: a single coal glowed in the white ashes. He swept a mass of papers and dusty books from the table, and with trembling hands cowered over the embers, until he succeeded in lighting the dry tinder. Then he piled the old books on the blaze, and looked fearfully around.

No: It was gone,—thank God for that; the hook was empty.

But why did Otto sleep so soundly; why did he not awake?

He stepped unsteadily across the room in the flaring light of the burning books, and knelt by the mattress.

* * *

So they found him in the morning, when no one came to the inn from Kropfsberg Keep, and the quaking Peter Rosskopf arranged a relief party;—found him kneeling beside the mattress where Otto lay, shot in the throat and quite dead.

M. R. James
(1862-1936)

Similar to Ralph Adams Cram in America, M. R. James belonged to the Ivy League of England. He was provost of King's College, Cambridge for thirteen years and then Eaton College for eighteen years.

His tenure at those colleges didn't come until many years after he penned "Lost Hearts" (1895), which is the best ghost story he wrote prior to the turn of the century given its especially fiendish ending and tight writing style. It would later be seem to set the recurring foundation of his later ghost stories.

In his professional life, James was referred to as a "medievalist," which is a fancy way of saying his scholarly focus was on medieval history. For purposes of constructing a ghost story, his background was a welcome fit as he fashioned many of these stories with a four-legged foundation: (1) a moldering English village as the setting; (2) a protagonist who is a scholar of English history; (3) the protagonist comes across an ancient secret in an old manuscript or historical artifact; and (4) a ghostly creature is reanimated as a result.

The formula worked quiet well for James. Four collections of his popular ghost and supernatural stories were published during his lifetime: *Ghost Stories of an Antiquary* (1904), *More Ghost Stories of an Antiquary* (1911), *A Thin Ghost and Others* (1919), and *A Warning to the Curious and Other Ghost Stories* (1925).

"Lost Hearts" was found in the earliest collection before the cares and reserve of the universities overtook him. It was first published in the December 1895 issue of the venerable *Pall Mall*

Magazine,[1] which published original stories from luminaries such as Joseph Conrad, Jack London, and Rudyard Kipling.

Montague Summers called "Lost Hearts" one of James's "best stories" while he deemed James to be "among the greatest . . . of modern exponents of the supernatural in fiction."[2]

---

[1] "Lost Hearts," M. R. James, *Pall Mall Magazine*, 1895, pgs. 639-47

[2] *The Supernatural Omnibus: Being a Collection of Stories of Apparitions, Witchcraft, Werewolves, Diabolism, Necromancy, Satanism, Divination, Sorcery, Goety, Voodo, Possession, Occult, Doom and Destiny*, Montague Summers, 1931, pg. 1

Lost Hearts
1895

IT WAS, AS far as I can ascertain, in September of the year 1811 that a postchaise[1] drew up before the door of Aswarby Hall,[2] in the heart of Lincolnshire.[3]

The little boy who was the only passenger in the chaise, and who jumped out as soon as it had stopped, looked about him with the keenest curiosity during the short interval that elapsed between the ringing of the bell and the opening of the hall door.

He saw a tall, square, red-brick house, built in the reign of Anne;[4] a stone-pillared porch had been added in the purer classical style of 1790;[5] the windows of the house were many, tall and narrow, with small panes and thick white woodwork. A pediment, pierced with a round window, crowned the front. There were wings to right and left, connected by curious glazed galleries, supported by colonnades, with the central block. These wings plainly contained the stables and offices of the house. Each was surmounted by an ornamental cupola with a gilded vane.[6]

An evening light shone on the building, making the window-panes glow like so many fires. Away from the Hall in front stretched a flat park studded with oaks and fringed with firs, which stood out against the sky. The clock in the church-tower, buried in trees on the edge of the park, only its golden weathercock catching the light, was striking six, and the sound came gently beating down the wind. It was altogether a pleasant impression, though tinged with the sort of melancholy appropriate to an evening in early autumn, that was conveyed to the mind of the boy who was standing in the porch waiting for the door to open to him.

He had just come from Warwickshire, and some six months ago had been left an orphan. Now, owing to the generous and

---

[1] An enclosed horse-drawn carriage having four wheels

[2] Large English country house demolished in 1951 due to military occupation after World War II and owned through the years by the Hervey, Carres, and Whichcote families, "Aswarby Hall," Lincstothepast.com, 2016

[3] Rural farming county with Aswarby parish that had only 142 residents during 1891, which is 4 years before "Lost Hearts" was published, and three farms; *Kelly's Directory of Lincolnshire with the Port of Hull and Neighborhood*, E. R. Kelly, 1885, pg. 674

[4] Queen Anne (1665-1714) ruled over Great Britain from 1707-1714

[5] Porch on a flat roof of the house

[6] Weather vane

unexpected offer of his elderly cousin, Mr. Abney, he had come to live at Aswarby. The offer was unexpected, because all who knew anything of Mr. Abney looked upon him as a somewhat austere recluse, into whose steady-going household the advent of a small boy would import a new and, it seemed, incongruous element. The truth is that very little was known of Mr. Abney's pursuits or temper.

The Professor of Greek at Cambridge had been heard to say that no one knew more of the religious beliefs of the later pagans than did the owner of Aswarby. Certainly his library contained all the then available books bearing on the Mysteries,[7] the Orphic poems,[8] the worship of Mithras,[9] and the Neo-Platonists.[10]

In the marble-paved hall stood a fine group of Mithras slaying a bull, which had been imported from the Levant[11] at great expense by the owner. He had contributed a description of it to the *Gentleman's Magazine,*[12] and he had written a remarkable series of articles in the *Critical Museum*[13] on the superstitions of the Romans of the Lower Empire. He was looked upon, in fine, as a man wrapped up in his books, and it was a matter of great surprise among his neighbors that he should ever have heard of his orphan cousin, Stephen Elliott, much more that he should have volunteered to make him an inmate of Aswarby Hall.

Whatever may have been expected by his neighbors, it is certain that Mr. Abney—the tall, the thin, the austere—seemed inclined to give his young cousin a kindly reception. The moment the front-door was opened he darted out of his study, rubbing his hands with delight.

'How are you, my boy?—how are you? How old are you?' said he—'that is, you are not too much tired, I hope, by your journey to eat your supper?'

'No, thank you, sir,' said Master Elliott; 'I am pretty well.'

'That's a good lad,' said Mr. Abney. 'And how old are you, my boy?'

It seemed a little odd that he should have asked the question twice in the first two minutes of their acquaintance.

'I'm twelve years old next birthday, sir,' said Stephen.

'And when is your birthday, my dear boy? Eleventh of September, eh? That's well—that's very well. Nearly a year hence,

---

[7] Likely a reference to the Eleusinian Mysteries, which consisted of secret religious rites performed by various cults

[8] In Greek mythology Orpheus traveled to Hell and returned with religious hymns and poems

[9] Secret religions of the ancient Romans that focused on the deity Mithras

[10] Formed a belief in using spiritualism to enhance the soul

[11] Vast area of Arabic, Greek and Turkish speaking countries in the eastern Mediterranean

[12] A London magazine founded in 1731 that published news and literary articles for nearly 200 years

[13] A made-up magazine

isn't it? I like—ha, ha!—I like to get these things down in my book. Sure it's twelve? Certain?'

'Yes, quite sure, sir.'

'Well, well! Take him to Mrs. Bunch's room, Parkes, and let him have his tea—supper—whatever it is.'

'Yes, sir,' answered the staid Mr. Parkes; and conducted Stephen to the lower regions.

Mrs. Bunch was the most comfortable and human person whom Stephen had as yet met in Aswarby. She made him completely at home; they were great friends in a quarter of an hour: and great friends they remained. Mrs. Bunch had been born in the neighborhood some fifty-five years before the date of Stephen's arrival, and her residence at the Hall was of twenty years' standing. Consequently, if anyone knew the ins and outs of the house and the district, Mrs. Bunch knew them; and she was by no means disinclined to communicate her information.

Certainly there were plenty of things about the Hall and the Hall gardens which Stephen, who was of an adventurous and inquiring turn, was anxious to have explained to him. 'Who built the temple at the end of the laurel walk? Who was the old man whose picture hung on the staircase, sitting at a table, with a skull under his hand?'

These and many similar points were cleared up by the resources of Mrs. Bunch's powerful intellect. There were others, however, of which the explanations furnished were less satisfactory.

One November evening Stephen was sitting by the fire in the housekeeper's room reflecting on his surroundings.

'Is Mr. Abney a good man, and will he go to heaven?' he suddenly asked, with the peculiar confidence which children possess in the ability of their elders to settle these questions, the decision of which is believed to be reserved for other tribunals.

'Good?—bless the child!' said Mrs. Bunch. 'Master's as kind a soul as ever I see! Didn't I never tell you of the little boy as he took in out of the street, as you may say, this seven years back? and the little girl, two years after I first come here?'

'No. Do tell me all about them, Mrs. Bunch—now this minute!'

'Well,' said Mrs. Bunch, 'the little girl I don't seem to recollect so much about. I know master brought her back with him from his walk one day, and give orders to Mrs. Ellis, as was housekeeper then, as she should be took every care with. And the pore child hadn't no one belonging to her—she telled me so her own self—and here she lived with us a matter of three weeks it might be; and then, whether she were somethink of a gipsy in her blood or what not, but one morning she out of her bed afore any of us had opened a eye and neither track nor yet trace of her have I set eyes on since. Master was wonderful put about, and had all the ponds dragged; but it's my belief she was had away by them gipsies, for there was singing round the house for as much as an hour the night she went, and Parkes, he declare as he heard them a-calling in the woods all that afternoon. Dear, dear! a hodd child she was, so silent in her ways and all, but I was wonderful taken up with her, so domesticated she was—surprising.'

'And what about the little boy?' said Stephen.

'Ah, that pore boy!' sighed Mrs. Bunch. 'He were a foreigner—Jevanny he called hisself—and he come a-tweaking his 'urdy-gurdy[14] round and about the drive one winter day, and master 'ad him in that minute, and ast all about where he came from, and how old he was, and how he made his way, and where was his relatives, and all as kind as heart could wish. But it went the same way with him. They're a hunruly lot, them foreign nations, I do suppose, and he was off one fine morning just the same as the girl. Why he went and what he done was our question for as much as a year after; for he never took his 'urdy-gurdy, and there it lays on the shelf.'

The remainder of the evening was spent by Stephen in miscellaneous cross-examination of Mrs. Bunch and in efforts to extract a tune from the hurdy-gurdy.

That night he had a curious dream. At the end of the passage at the top of the house, in which his bedroom was situated, there was an old disused bathroom. It was kept locked, but the upper half of the door was glazed, and, since the muslin curtains which used to hang there had long been gone, you could look in and see the lead-lined bath affixed to the wall on the right hand, with its head towards the window.

On the night of which I am speaking, Stephen Elliott found himself, as he thought, looking through the glazed door. The moon was shining through the window, and he was gazing at a figure which lay in the bath.

His description of what he saw reminds me of what I once beheld myself in the famous vaults of St. Michan's Church in Dublin, which possess the horrid property of preserving corpses from decay for centuries.[15] A figure inexpressibly thin and pathetic, of a dusty leaden color, enveloped in a shroud-like garment, the thin lips crooked into a faint and dreadful smile, the hands pressed tightly over the region of the heart.

As he looked upon it, a distant, almost inaudible moan seemed to issue from its lips, and the arms began to stir. The terror of the sight forced Stephen backwards, and he awoke to the fact that he was indeed standing on the cold boarded floor of the passage in the full light of the moon. With a courage which I do not think can be common among boys of his age, he went to the door of the bathroom to ascertain if the figure of his dream were really there. It was not, and he went back to bed.

---

[14] Hurdy-gurdy is a small stringed folk instrument
[15] Gothic church in Ireland containing underground crypts with remains mummified by the natural limestone deposits in the earth, both M. R. James and Bram Stoker are believed to have visited the crypts

Mrs. Bunch was much impressed next morning by his story, and went so far as to replace the muslin curtain over the glazed door of the bathroom. Mr. Abney, moreover, to whom he confided his experiences at breakfast, was greatly interested, and made notes of the matter in what he called 'his book.'

The spring equinox was approaching, as Mr. Abney frequently reminded his cousin, adding that this had been always considered by the ancients to be a critical time for the young: that Stephen would do well to take care of himself, and to shut his bedroom window at night; and that Censorinus had some valuable remarks on the subject.[16] Two incidents that occurred about this time made an impression upon Stephen's mind.

The first was after an unusually uneasy and oppressed night that he had passed—though he could not recall any particular dream that he had had.

The following evening Mrs. Bunch was occupying herself in mending his nightgown.

'Gracious me, Master Stephen!' she broke forth rather irritably, 'how do you manage to tear your nightdress all to flinders this way? Look here, sir, what trouble you do give to poor servants that have to darn and mend after you!'

There was indeed a most destructive and apparently wanton series of slits or scorings in the garment, which would undoubtedly require a skillful needle to make good. They were confined to the left side of the chest—long, parallel slits, about six inches in length, some of them not quite piercing the texture of the linen. Stephen could only express his entire ignorance of their origin: he was sure they were not there the night before.

'But,' he said, 'Mrs. Bunch, they are just the same as the scratches on the outside of my bedroom door; and I'm sure I never had anything to do with making *them*?'

Mrs. Bunch gazed at him open-mouthed, then snatched up a candle, departed hastily from the room, and was heard making her way upstairs. In a few minutes she came down.

'Well,' she said, 'Master Stephen, it's a funny thing to me how them marks and scratches can 'a' come there—too high up for any cat or dog to 'ave made 'em, much less a rat: for all the world like a Chinaman's fingernails, as my uncle in the tea-trade used to tell us of when we was girls together. I wouldn't say nothing to master, not if I was you, Master Stephen, my dear; and just turn the key of the door when you go to your bed.'

'I always do, Mrs. Bunch, as soon as I've said my prayers.'

'Ah, that's a good child: always say your prayers, and then no one can't hurt you.'

---

[16] Censorinus was a Roman historian and grammarian whose text *De Die Natale* speaks of all durations of time

Herewith Mrs. Bunch addressed herself to mending the injured nightgown, with intervals of meditation, until bedtime. This was on a Friday night in March, 1812.[17]

On the following evening the usual duet of Stephen and Mrs. Bunch was augmented by the sudden arrival of Mr. Parkes, the butler, who as a rule kept himself rather *to* himself in his own pantry. He did not see that Stephen was there: he was, moreover, flustered and less slow of speech than was his wont.

'Master may get up his own wine, if he likes, of an evening,' was his first remark. 'Either I do it in the daytime or not at all, Mrs. Bunch. I don't know what it may be: very like it's the rats, or the wind got into the cellars; but I'm not so young as I was, and I can't go through with it as I have done.'

'Well, Mr. Parkes, you know it is a surprising place for the rats, is the Hall.'

'I'm not denying that, Mrs. Bunch; and, to be sure, many a time I've heard the tale from the men in the shipyards about the rat that could speak. I never laid no confidence in that before; but tonight, if I'd demeaned myself to lay my ear to the door of the further bin, I could pretty much have heard what they was saying.'

'Oh, there, Mr. Parkes, I've no patience with your fancies! Rats talking in the wine-cellar indeed!'

'Well, Mrs. Bunch, I've no wish to argue with you: all I say is, if you choose to go to the far bin, and lay your ear to the door, you may prove my words this minute.'

'What nonsense you do talk, Mr. Parkes —not fit for children to listen to! Why, you'll be frightening Master Stephen there out of his wits.'

'What! Master Stephen?' said Parkes, awaking to the consciousness of the boy's presence. 'Master Stephen knows well enough when I'm a-playing a joke with you, Mrs. Bunch.'

In fact, Master Stephen knew much too well to suppose that Mr. Parkes had in the first instance intended a joke. He was interested, not altogether pleasantly, in the situation; but all his questions were unsuccessful in inducing the butler to give any more detailed account of his experiences in the wine-cellar.

We have now arrived at March 24, 1812.[18] It was a day of curious experiences for Stephen: a windy, noisy day, which filled the house and the gardens with a restless impression. As Stephen stood by the fence of the grounds, and looked out into the park, he felt as if an endless procession of unseen people were sweeping past him on the wind, borne on resistlessly and aimlessly, vainly striving to stop themselves, to catch at something that might arrest their flight and bring them once again into contact with the living

---

[17] The second Friday in March of 1812 was Friday the 13th in the Gregorian calendar

[18] Under the Julian calendar March 24th is the 365th and last day of the year, which was first adopted by England in the 12th century A.D. and was replaced by the Gregorian calendar in 1752

world of which they had formed a part. After luncheon that day Mr. Abney said:

'Stephen, my boy, do you think you could manage to come to me tonight as late as eleven o'clock in my study? I shall be busy until that time, and I wish to show you something connected with your future life which it is most important that you should know. You are not to mention this matter to Mrs. Bunch nor to anyone else in the house; and you had better go to your room at the usual time.'

Here was a new excitement added to life: Stephen eagerly grasped at the opportunity of sitting up till eleven o'clock. He looked in at the library door on his way upstairs that evening, and saw a brazier,[19] which he had often noticed in the corner of the room, moved out before the fire; an old silver-gilt cup stood on the table, filled with red wine, and some written sheets of paper lay near it. Mr. Abney was sprinkling some incense on the brazier from a round silver box as Stephen passed, but did not seem to notice his step.

The wind had fallen, and there was a still night and a full moon. At about ten o'clock Stephen was standing at the open window of his bedroom, looking out over the country. Still as the night was, the mysterious population of the distant moonlit woods was not yet lulled to rest. From time to time strange cries as of lost and despairing wanderers sounded from across the mere. They might be the notes of owls or water-birds, yet they did not quite resemble either sound. *Were not they coming nearer?*

Now they sounded from the nearer side of the water, and in a few moments they seemed to be floating about among the shrubberies. Then they ceased; but just as Stephen was thinking of shutting the window and resuming his reading of *Robinson Crusoe*, he caught sight of two figures standing on the gravelled terrace that ran along the garden side of the Hall—the figures of a boy and girl, as it seemed; they stood side by side, looking up at the windows. Something in the form of the girl recalled irresistibly his dream of the figure in the bath. The boy inspired him with more acute fear.

Whilst the girl stood still, half smiling, with her hands clasped over her heart, the boy, a thin shape, with black hair and ragged clothing, raised his arms in the air with an appearance of menace and of unappeasable hunger and longing. The moon shone upon his almost transparent hands, and Stephen saw that the nails were fearfully long and that the light shone through them. As he stood with his arms thus raised, he disclosed a terrifying spectacle. On the left side of his chest there opened a black and gaping rent; and there fell upon Stephen's brain, rather than upon his ear, the impression of one of those hungry and desolate cries that he had heard resounding over the woods of Aswarby all that evening. In another moment this dreadful pair had moved swiftly and noiselessly over the dry gravel, and he saw them no more.

---

[19] Portable metallic heater in which lighted wood or coals were placed

Inexpressibly frightened as he was, he determined to take his candle and go down to Mr. Abney's study, for the hour appointed for their meeting was near at hand. The study or library opened out of the front-hall on one side, and Stephen, urged on by his terrors, did not take long in getting there. To effect an entrance was not so easy. It was not locked, he felt sure, for the key was on the outside of the door as usual. His repeated knocks produced no answer. Mr. Abney was engaged: he was speaking. *What! why did he try to cry out? and why was the cry choked in his throat? Had he, too, seen the mysterious children?* But now everything was quiet, and the door yielded to Stephen's terrified and frantic pushing.

*****

On the table in Mr. Abney's study certain papers were found which explained the situation to Stephen Elliott when he was of an age to understand them. The most important sentences were as follows:

'It was a belief very strongly and generally held by the ancients—of whose wisdom in these matters I have had such experience as induces me to place confidence in their assertions—that by enacting certain processes, which to us moderns have something of a barbaric complexion, a very remarkable enlightenment of the spiritual faculties in man may be attained: that, for example, by absorbing the personalities of a certain number of his fellow-creatures, an individual may gain a complete ascendancy over those orders of spiritual beings which control the elemental forces of our universe.

'It is recorded of Simon Magus[20] that he was able to fly in the air, to become invisible, or to assume any form he pleased, by the agency of the soul of a boy whom, to use the libelous phrase employed by the author of the Clementine Recognitions, he had "murdered."[21] I find it set down, moreover, with considerable detail in the writings of Hermes Trismegistus,[22] that similar happy results may be produced by the absorption of the hearts of not less than three human beings below the age of twenty-one years. To the testing of the truth of this receipt I have devoted the greater part of the last twenty years, selecting as the *corpora vilia*[23] of my experiment such persons as could conveniently be removed without occasioning a sensible gap in society. The first step I effected by the removal of one Phoebe Stanley, a girl of gipsy extraction, on March 24, 1792. The second, by the removal of a wandering Italian lad,

---

[20] A Samaritan religious figure reported to have sorcerylike powers of levitation in the *Acts of Peter* and the *Acts of Peter and Paul* of the Biblical apocrypha

[21] Reference to the anonymous author of the *Clementine Recognitions and Homilies* whose date of authorship is also unknown

[22] Fictitious Greek author of the *Hermetic Corpus* texts that tell of sorcery

[23] Person suitable only for experimentation or for the particular experiment

named Giovanni Paoli, on the night of March 23, 1805.[24] The final "victim"—to employ a word repugnant in the highest degree to my feelings—must be my cousin, Stephen Elliott. His day must be this March 24, 1812.

'The best means of effecting the required absorption is to remove the heart from the *living* subject, to reduce it to ashes, and to mingle them with about a pint of some red wine, preferably port. The remains of the first two subjects, at least, it will be well to conceal: a disused bathroom or wine-cellar will be found convenient for such a purpose. Some annoyance may be experienced from the psychic portion of the subjects, which popular language dignifies with the name of ghosts. But the man of philosophic temperament—to whom alone the experiment is appropriate— will be little prone to attach importance to the feeble efforts of these beings to wreak their vengeance on him. I contemplate with the liveliest satisfaction the enlarged and emancipated existence which the experiment, if successful, will confer on me; not only placing me beyond the reach of human justice (so called), but eliminating to a great extent the prospect of death itself.'

*****

Mr. Abney was found in his chair, his head thrown back, his face stamped with an expression of rage, fright, and mortal pain. In his left side was a terrible lacerated wound, exposing the heart. There was no blood on his hands, and a long knife that lay on the table was perfectly clean. A savage wild-cat might have inflicted the injuries. The window of the study was open, and it was the opinion of the coroner that Mr. Abney had met his death by the agency of some wild creature.

But Stephen Elliott's study of the papers I have quoted led him to a very different conclusion.

---

[24] Night of full moon in old calendars

Joseph Le Fanu
(1814-1873)

No author had a bigger impact during the middle part of the nineteenth century on supernatural fiction than Irishman Joseph Thomas Sheridan Le Fanu. His female vampire story "Carmilla" (1872) highly influenced Bram Stoker when chiseling the foundations of *Dracula* and it is still a literary force to be reckoned with today.

Le Fanu studied law at Trinity College and began submitting short stories for publication to various magazines. His first was "The Ghost and the Bonesetter" (1838). The *Dublin Almanac* lists a "Joseph T. S. Le Fanu, barrister" having an office at Warrington Place during 1847 where he also lived.[1] In 1861 Le Fanu abandoned the practice of law and became owner of the *Dublin University Magazine*, which was the premier Irish magazine of its day.

His ghost stories influenced M. R. James who unabashedly placed Le Fanu "in the first rank as a writer of ghost stories."[2] James acknowledged how well Le Fanu set the scene of the story, which is a key component of any frightening ghost story.

---

[1] *The Dublin Almanac and General Register of Ireland, for the Year of Our Lord 1847*, pg. 817

[2] Prologue to *Madame Crowl's Ghost and Other Tales of Mystery*, M. R. James, 1923

Montague Summers called Le Fanu "the supreme master of the supernatural."[3]

He was such an excellent supernatural story writer that Le Fanu is the only author to have stories in *four* of the best supernatural collections during the nineteenth century: A "Strange Event in the Life of Schalken the Painter" (1839),[4] "Green Tea" (1872),[5] "Camilla" (1872),[6] and "The Familiar" (1872), which is provided next.

The latter is an unrelenting ghost story that is actually a longer version of "The Watcher" published by Le Fanu in 1851. He commonly revised earlier stories and published them under an entirely new title. "The Familiar" was no exception. The appearance of the owl at the end of the story is *diaboli ex machina*, for which Le Fanu can be forgiven due to the chilling ghostly tale surrounding the cameo of the feathered beast.

"The Familiar" appeared after "Green Tea" in Le Fanu's 1872 short story collection *In a Glass Darkly*. Both are supposedly taken from the journals of Dr. Hesselius. These are two of the finest atmospheric tales of protagonists who supposedly have nervous conditions that make them see evil spirits.

In the first it may be the consumption of tainted green tea from China and in this one . . .

---

[3] *The Supernatural Omnibus: Being a Collection of Stories of Apparitions, Witchcraft, Werewolves, Diabolism, Necromancy, Satanism, Divination, Sorcery, Goety, Voodo, Possession, Occult, Doom and Destiny, Montague Summers, 1931, pg. 1*

[4] *Best Vampire Short Stories 1800-1849: A BlooDeath[tm] Vampire Anthology*, 2012, pg. 101

[5] *Best Horror Short Stories 1850-1899: A 6a66le[tm] Horror Anthology*, 2016, pg. 69

[6] *Best Vampire Short Stories 1850-1899: A BlooDeath[tm] Vampire Anthology*, 2017, pg. 187

The Familiar
1872

Prologue

OUT OF ABOUT two hundred and thirty cases, more or less nearly akin to that I have entitled "Green Tea," I select the following, which I call "The Familiar." To this MS. Doctor Hesselius, has, after his wont, attached some sheets of letter-paper, on which are written, in his hand nearly as compact as print, his own remarks upon the case.

He says—"In point of conscience, no more unexceptionable narrator, than the venerable Irish Clergyman who has given me this paper, on Mr. Barton's case, could have been chosen. The statement is, however, medically imperfect. The report of an intelligent physician, who had marked its progress, and attended the patient, from its earlier stages to its close, would have supplied what is wanting to enable me to pronounce with confidence. I should have been acquainted with Mr. Barton's probable hereditary pre-dispositions; I should have known, possibly, by very early indications, something of a remoter origin of the disease than can now be ascertained.

"In a rough way, we may reduce all similar cases to three distinct classes. They are founded on the primary distinction between the subjective and the objective. Of those whose senses are alleged to be subject to supernatural impressions—some are simply visionaries, and propagate the illusions of which they complain, from diseased brain or nerves. Others are, unquestionably, infested by, as we term them, spiritual agencies, exterior to themselves. Others, again, owe their sufferings to a mixed condition. The interior sense, it is true, is opened; but it has been and continues open by the action of disease. This form of disease may, in one sense, be compared to the loss of the scarf-skin, and a consequent exposure of surfaces for whose excessive sensitiveness, nature has provided a muffling. The loss of this covering is attended by an habitual impassability, by influences against which we were intended to be guarded. But in the case of the brain, and the nerves immediately connected with its functions and its sensuous impressions, the cerebral circulation undergoes periodically that vibratory disturbance, which, I believe, I have satisfactorily examined and demonstrated, in my MS. Essay, *A. 17*. This vibratory disturbance differs, as I there prove, essentially from the congestive disturbance, the phenomena of which are examined in *A. 19*. It is, when excessive, invariably accompanied by *illusions*.

"Had I seen Mr. Barton, and examined him upon the points, in his case, which need elucidation, I should have without difficulty referred those phenomena to their proper disease. My diagnosis is now, necessarily, conjectural."

Thus writes Doctor Hesselius; and adds a great deal which is of interest only to a scientific physician. The Narrative of the Rev. Thomas Herbert, which furnishes all that is known of the case, will be found in the chapters that follow.

Chapter I
Footsteps

I WAS A young man at the time, and intimately acquainted with some of the actors in this strange tale; the impression which its incidents made on me, therefore, were deep, and lasting. I shall now endeavor, with precision, to relate them all, combining, of course, in the narrative, whatever I have learned from various sources, tending, however imperfectly, to illuminate the darkness which involves its progress and termination.

Somewhere about the year 1794, the younger brother of a certain baronet, whom I shall call Sir James Barton, returned to Dublin. He had served in the navy with some distinction, having commanded one of His Majesty's frigates during the greater part of the American war.[1] Captain Barton was apparently some two or three-and-forty years of age. He was an intelligent and agreeable companion when he pleased it, though generally reserved, and occasionally even moody.

In society, however, he deported himself as a man of the world, and a gentleman. He had not contracted any of the noisy brusqueness sometimes acquired at sea; on the contrary, his manners were remarkably easy, quiet, and even polished. He was in person about the middle size, and somewhat strongly formed— his countenance was marked with the lines of thought, and on the whole wore an expression of gravity and melancholy; being, however, as I have said, a man of perfect breeding, as well as of good family, and in affluent circumstances, he had, of course, ready access to the best society of Dublin, without the necessity of any other credentials.

In his personal habits Mr. Barton was un-expensive. He occupied lodgings in one of the *then* fashionable streets in the south side of the town—kept but one horse and one servant—and though a reputed free-thinker, yet lived an orderly and moral life— indulging neither in gaming, drinking, nor any other vicious pursuit—living very much to himself, without forming intimacies,

---

[1] American Revolutionary War (1775-1783) between American and Great Britain

or choosing any companions, and appearing to mix in gay society rather for the sake of its bustle and distraction, than for any opportunities it offered of interchanging thought or feeling with its votaries.

Barton was therefore pronounced a saving, prudent, unsocial sort of fellow, who bid fair to maintain his celibacy alike against stratagem and assault, and was likely to live to a good old age, die rich, and leave his money to a hospital. It was now apparent, however, that the nature of Mr. Barton's plans had been totally misconceived. A young lady, whom I shall call Miss Montague, was at this time introduced into the gay world, by her aunt, the Dowager Lady L——.

Miss Montague was decidedly pretty and accomplished, and having some natural cleverness, and a great deal of gaiety, became for a while a reigning toast. Her popularity, however, gained her, for a time, nothing more than that unsubstantial admiration which, however, pleasant as an incense to vanity, is by no means necessarily antecedent to matrimony—for, unhappily for the young lady in question, it was an understood thing, that beyond her personal attractions, she had no kind of earthly provision.

Such being the state of affairs, it will readily be believed that no little surprise was consequent upon the appearance of Captain Barton as the avowed lover of the penniless Miss Montague. His suit prospered, as might have been expected, and in a short time it was communicated by old Lady L—— to each of her hundred-and-fifty particular friends in succession, that Captain Barton had actually tendered proposals of marriage, with her approbation, to her niece, Miss Montague, who had, moreover, accepted the offer of his hand, conditionally upon the consent of her father, who was then upon his homeward voyage from India, and expected in two or three weeks at the furthest.

About this consent there could be no doubt—the delay, therefore, was one merely of form—they were looked upon as absolutely engaged, and Lady L——, with a rigor of old-fashioned decorum with which her niece would, no doubt, gladly have dispensed, withdrew her thenceforward from all further participation in the gaieties of the town. Captain Barton was a constant visitor, as well as a frequent guest at the house, and was permitted all the privileges of intimacy which a betrothed suitor is usually accorded. Such was the relation of parties, when the mysterious circumstances which darken this narrative first begun to unfold themselves.

Lady L—— resided in a handsome mansion at the north side of Dublin, and Captain Barton's lodgings, as we have already said, were situated at the south. The distance intervening was considerable, and it was Captain Barton's habit generally to walk home without an attendant, as often as he passed the evening with the old lady and her fair charge.

His shortest way in such nocturnal walks, lay, for a considerable space, through a line of street which had as yet merely been laid out, and little more than the foundations of the houses constructed.

One night, shortly after his engagement with Miss Montague had commenced, he happened to remain unusually late, in company with her and Lady L——. The conversation had turned upon the evidences of revelation, which he had disputed with the callous skepticism of a confirmed infidel. What were called "French principles," had in those days found their way a good deal into fashionable society, especially that portion of it which professed allegiance to Whiggism,[2] and neither the old lady nor her charge were so perfectly free from the taint, as to look upon Mr. Barton's views as any serious objection to the proposed union.

The discussion had degenerated into one upon the supernatural and the marvelous, in which he had pursued precisely the same line of argument and ridicule. In all this, it is but truth to state, Captain Barton was guilty of no affectation—the doctrines upon which he insisted, were, in reality, but, too truly the basis of his own fixed belief, if so it might be called; and perhaps not the least strange of the many strange circumstances connected with my narrative, was the fact, that the subject of the fearful influences I am about to describe, was himself, from the deliberate conviction of years, an utter disbeliever in what are usually termed preternatural agencies.

It was considerably past midnight when Mr. Barton took his leave, and set out upon his solitary walk homeward. He had now reached the lonely road, with its unfinished dwarf walls tracing the foundations of the projected row of houses on either side—the moon was shining mistily, and its imperfect light made the road he trod but additionally dreary—that utter silence which has in it something indefinably exciting, reigned there, and made the sound of his steps, which alone broke it, unnaturally loud and distinct.

He had proceeded thus some way, when he, on a sudden, heard other footfalls, pattering at a measured pace, and, as it seemed, about two score steps behind him. The suspicion of being dogged is at all times unpleasant; it is, however, especially so in a spot so lonely; and this suspicion became so strong in the mind of Captain Barton, that he abruptly turned about to confront his pursuer, but, though there was quite sufficient moonlight to disclose any object upon the road he had traversed, no form of any kind was visible there.

The steps he had heard could not have been the reverberation of his own, for he stamped his foot upon the ground, and walked briskly up and down, in the vain attempt to awake an echo; though by no means a fanciful person, therefore he was at last fain to charge the sounds upon his imagination, and treat them as an illusion. Thus satisfying himself, he resumed his walk, and before he had proceeded a dozen paces, the mysterious footfall was again

---

[2] A political movement, spawned in the seventeenth century, that sought a strong British parliament formed by the people and weak king

audible from behind, and this time, as if with the special design of showing that the sounds were not the responses of an echo—the steps sometimes slackened nearly to a halt, and sometimes hurried for six or eight strides to a run, and again abated to a walk.

Captain Barton, as before, turned suddenly round, and with the same result—no object was visible above the deserted level of the road. He walked back over the same ground, determined that, whatever might have been concerted him, it should not escape his search—the endeavor, however, was unrewarded.

In spite of all his skepticism, he felt something like a superstitious fear stealing fast upon him, and with these unwonted and uncomfortable sensations, he once more turned and pursued his way. There was no repetition of these haunting sounds, until he had reached the point where he had last stopped to retrace his steps—here they were resumed—and with sudden starts of running, which threatened to bring the unseen pursuer up to the alarmed pedestrian.

Captain Barton arrested his course; as formerly—the unaccountable nature of the occurrence filled him with vague and disagreeable sensations—and yielding to the excitement that was gaining upon him, he shouted sternly, "Who goes there?"

The sound of one's own voice, thus exerted, in utter solitude, and followed by total silence, has in it something unpleasantly dismaying, and he felt a degree of nervousness which, perhaps, from no cause had he ever known before. To the very end of this solitary street the steps pursued him—and it required a strong effort of stubborn pride on his part, to resist the impulse that prompted him every moment to run for safety at the top of his speed. It was not until he had reached his lodging, and sate by his own fireside, that he felt sufficiently reassured to rearrange and reconsider in his own mind the occurrences which had so discomposed him. So little a matter, after all, is sufficient to upset the pride of skepticism and vindicate the old simple laws.

CHAPTER II
The Watcher

Mr. Barton was next morning sitting at a late breakfast, reflecting upon the incidents of the previous night, with more of inquisitiveness than awe, so speedily do gloomy impressions upon the fancy disappear under the cheerful influence of day, when a letter just delivered by the postman was placed upon the table before him.

There was nothing remarkable in the address of this missive, except that it was written in a hand which he did not know— perhaps it was disguised—for the tall narrow characters were sloped backward; and with the self-inflicted suspense which we often see practiced in such cases, he puzzled over the inscription for a full minute before he broke the seal.

When he did so, he read the following words, written in the same hand:—

Mr. Barton, late captain of the Dolphin, *is warned of danger. He will do wisely to avoid——street [here the locality of his last night's adventure was named]—if he walks there as usual he will meet with something unlucky—let him take warning, once for all, for he has reason to dread*

THE WATCHER.

Captain Barton read and reread this strange effusion; in every light and in every direction he turned it over and over; he examined the paper on which it was written, and scrutinized the handwriting once more. Defeated here, he turned to the seal; it was nothing but a patch of wax, upon which the accidental impression of a thumb was imperfectly visible.

There was not the slightest mark, or clue of any kind, to lead him to even a guess as to its possible origin. The writer's object seemed a friendly one, and yet he subscribed himself as one whom he had "reason to dread." Altogether the letter, its author, and its real purpose were to him an inexplicable puzzle, and one, moreover, unpleasantly suggestive, in his mind, of other associations connected with his last night's adventure.

In obedience to some feeling—perhaps of pride—Mr. Barton did not communicate, even to his intended bride, the occurrences which I have just detailed. Trifling as they might appear, they had in reality most disagreeably affected his imagination, and he cared not to disclose, even to the young lady in question, what she might possibly look upon as evidences of weakness.

The letter might very well be but a hoax, and the mysterious footfall but a delusion or a trick. But although he affected to treat the whole affair as unworthy of a thought, it yet haunted him pertinaciously, tormenting him with perplexing doubts, and depressing him with undefined apprehensions. Certain it is, that for a considerable time afterwards he carefully avoided the street indicated in the letter as the scene of danger. It was not until about a week after the receipt of the letter which I have transcribed, that anything further occurred to remind Captain Barton of its contents, or to counteract the gradual disappearance from his mind of the disagreeable impressions then received.

He was returning one night, after the interval I have stated, from the theatre, which was then situated in Crow-street, and having there seen Miss Montague and Lady L—— into their carriage, he loitered for some time with two or three acquaintances.

With these, however, he parted close to the college, and pursued his way alone. It was now fully one o'clock, and the streets were quite deserted. During the whole of his walk with the companions from whom he had just parted, he had been at times painfully aware of the sound of steps, as it seemed, dogging them on their way.

Once or twice he had looked back, in the uneasy anticipation that he was again about to experience the same mysterious annoyances which had so disconcerted him a week before, and earnestly hoping that he might *see* some form to account naturally for the sounds. But the street was deserted—no one was visible. Proceeding now quite alone upon his homeward way, he grew really nervous and uncomfortable, as he became sensible, with increased distinctness, of the well-known and now absolutely dreaded sounds.

By the side of the dead wall which bounded the college park, the sounds followed, recommencing almost simultaneously with his own steps. The same unequal pace—sometimes slow, sometimes for a score yards or so, quickened almost to a run—was audible from behind him.

Again and again he turned; quickly and stealthily he glanced over his shoulder—almost at every half-dozen steps; but no one was visible. The irritation of this intangible and unseen pursuit became gradually all but intolerable; and when at last he reached his home, his nerves were strung to such a pitch of excitement that he could not rest, and did not attempt even to lie down until after the daylight had broken.

He was awakened by a knock at his chamber-door, and his servant entering, handed him several letters which had just been received by the penny post.[3] One among them instantly arrested his attention—a single glance at the direction aroused him thoroughly He at once recognized its character, and read as follows:–

> *You may as well think, Captain Barton, to escape from your own shadow as from me; do what you may, I will see you as often as I please, and you shall see me, for I do not want to hide myself, as you fancy. Do not let it trouble your rest, Captain Barton; for, with a good conscience, what need you fear from the eye of*
>
> *THE WATCHER.*

It is scarcely necessary to dwell upon the feelings that accompanied a perusal of this strange communication. Captain Barton was observed to be unusually absent and out of spirits for several days afterwards; but no one divined the cause.

Whatever he might think as to the phantom steps which followed him, there could be no possible illusion about the letters he had received; and, to say the least, their immediate sequence upon the mysterious sounds which had haunted him, was an odd

---

[3] A postal system established in Ireland during 1765 where all envelopes and packages under one pound in weight shipped for one penny

coincidence. The whole circumstance was, in his own mind, vaguely and instinctively connected with certain passages in his past life, which, of all others, he hated to remember.

It happened, however, that in addition to his own approaching nuptials, Captain Barton had just then—fortunately, perhaps, for himself—some business of an engrossing kind connected with the adjustment of a large and long-litigated claim upon certain properties. The hurry and excitement of business had its natural effect in gradually dispelling the gloom which had for a time occasionally oppressed him, and in a little while his spirits had entirely recovered their accustomed tone.

During all this time, however, he was, now and then, dismayed by indistinct and half-heard repetitions of the same annoyance, and that in lonely places, in the day-time as well as after nightfall. These renewals of the strange impressions from which he had suffered so much, were, however, desultory and faint, insomuch that often he really could not, to his own satisfaction, distinguish between them and the mere suggestions of an excited imagination. One evening he walked down to the House of Commons with a Member, an acquaintance of his and mine.

This was one of the few occasions upon which I have been in company with Captain Barton. As we walked down together, I observed that he became absent and silent, and to a degree that seemed to argue the pressure of some urgent and absorbing anxiety.

I afterwards learned that during the whole of our walk, he had heard the well-known footsteps tracking him as we proceeded. This, however, was the last time he suffered from this phase of the persecution, of which he was already the anxious victim. A new and a very different one was about to be presented.

CHAPTER III
An Advertisement

Of the new series of impressions which were afterwards gradually to work out his destiny, I that evening witnessed the first; and but for its relation to the train of events which followed, the incident would scarcely have been now remembered by me.

As we were walking in at the passage from College-Green, a man, of whom I remember only that he was short in stature, looked like a foreigner, and wore a kind of fur travelling-cap, walked very rapidly, and as if under fierce excitement, directly towards us, muttering to himself, fast and vehemently the while. This odd-looking person walked straight toward Barton, who was foremost of the three, and halted, regarding him for a moment or two with a look of maniacal menace and fury; and then turning about as abruptly, he walked before us at the same agitated pace, and disappeared at a side passage.

I do distinctly remember being a good deal shocked at the countenance and bearing of this man, which indeed irresistibly impressed me with an undefined sense of danger, such as I have never felt before or since from the presence of anything human; but these sensations were, on my part, far from amounting to anything so disconcerting as to flurry or excite me—I had seen only a singularly evil countenance, agitated, as it seemed, with the excitement of madness.

I was absolutely astonished, however, at the effect of this apparition upon Captain Barton. I knew him to be a man of proud courage and coolness in real danger—a circumstance which made his conduct upon this occasion the more conspicuously odd. He recoiled a step or two as the stranger advanced, and clutched my arm in silence, with what seemed to be a spasm of agony or terror; and then, as the figure disappeared, shoving me roughly back, he followed it for a few paces, stopped in great disorder, and sat down upon a form. I never beheld a countenance more ghastly and haggard.

"For God's sake, Barton, what is the matter?" said ——, our companion, really alarmed at his appearance. "You're not hurt, are you?—or unwell? What is it?"

"What did he say?—I did not hear it—what was it?" asked Barton, wholly disregarding the question.

"Nonsense," said ——, greatly surprised; "who cares what the fellow said. You are unwell, Barton—decidedly unwell; let me call a coach."

"Unwell! No—not unwell," he said, evidently making an effort to recover his self-possession; "but, to say the truth, I am fatigued—a little overworked—and perhaps over anxious. You know I have been in chancery,[4] and the winding up of a suit is always a nervous affair. I have felt uncomfortable all this evening; but I am better now. Come, come—shall we go on?"

"No, no. Take my advice, Barton, and go home; you really do need rest you are looking quite ill. I really do insist on your allowing me to see you home," replied his friend.

I seconded ——'s advice, the more readily as it was obvious that Barton was not himself disinclined to be persuaded. He left us, declining our offered escort. I was not sufficiently intimate with —— to discuss the scene we had both just witnessed. I was, however, convinced from his manner in the few commonplace comments and regrets we exchanged, that he was just as little satisfied as I with the extempore plea of illness with which he had accounted for the strange exhibition, and that we were both agreed in suspecting some lurking mystery in the matter.

I called next day at Barton's lodgings, to enquire for him, and learned from the servant that he had not left his room since his return the night before; but that he was not seriously indisposed, and hoped to be out in a few days. That evening he sent for Dr. R—

---

[4] Chancery Court was a court of equity where civil complaints were decided

—, then in large and fashionable practice in Dublin, and their interview was, it is said, an odd one.

He entered into a detail of his own symptoms in an abstracted and desultory way, which seemed to argue a strange want of interest in his own cure, and, at all events, made it manifest that there was some topic engaging his mind of more engrossing importance than his present ailment. He complained of occasional palpitations and headache.

Doctor R——, asked him among other questions, whether there was any irritating circumstance or anxiety then occupying his thoughts. This he denied quickly and almost peevishly; and the physician thereupon declared his opinion, that there was nothing amiss except some slight derangement of the digestion, for which he accordingly wrote a prescription, and was about to withdraw, when Mr. Barton, with the air of a man who recollects a topic which had nearly escaped him, recalled him.

"I beg your pardon, Doctor, but I really almost forgot; will you permit me to ask you two or three medical questions—rather odd ones, perhaps, but a wager depends upon their solution, you will, I hope, excuse my unreasonableness."

The physician readily undertook to satisfy the inquirer. Barton seemed to have some difficulty about opening the proposed interrogatories, for he was silent for a minute, then walked to his bookcase, and returned as he had gone; at last he sat down, and said—"You'll think them very childish questions, but I can't recover my wager without a decision; so I must put them. I want to know first about lockjaw. If a man actually has had that complaint, and appears to have died of it—so much so, that a physician of average skill pronounces him actually dead—may he, after all, recover?"

The physician smiled, and shook his head.

"But—but a blunder may be made," resumed Barton. "Suppose an ignorant pretender to medical skill; may *he* be so deceived by any stage of the complaint, as to mistake what is only a part of the progress of the disease, for death itself?"

"No one who had ever seen death," answered he, "could mistake it in a case of lockjaw."

Barton mused for a few minutes. "I am going to ask you a question, perhaps, still more childish; but first, tell me, are the regulations of foreign hospitals, such as that of, let us say, Naples, very lax and bungling. May not all kinds of blunders and slips occur in their entries of names, and so forth?"

Doctor R—— professed his incompetence to answer that query.

"Well, then, Doctor, here is the last of my questions. You will, probably, laugh at it; but it must out, nevertheless. Is there any disease, in all the range of human maladies, which would have the effect of perceptibly, contracting the stature, and the whole frame —causing the man to shrink in all his proportions, and yet to preserve his exact resemblance to himself in every particular— with the one exception, his height and bulk; *any* disease, mark—no matter how rare—how little believed in, generally—which could possibly result in producing such an effect?"

The physician replied with a smile, and a very decided negative. "Tell me, then," said Barton, abruptly, "if a man be in reasonable fear of assault from a lunatic who is at large, can he not procure a warrant for his arrest and detention?"

"Really that is more a lawyer's question than one in my way," replied Dr. R——, "but I believe, on applying to a magistrate, such a course would be directed."

The physician then took his leave; but, just as he reached the hall-door, remembered that he had left his cane upstairs, and returned. His reappearance was awkward, for a piece of paper, which he recognized as his own prescription, was slowly burning upon the fire, and Barton sitting close by with an expression of settled gloom and dismay.

Doctor R—— had too much tact to observe what presented itself; but he had seen quite enough to assure him that the mind, and not the body, of Captain Barton was in reality the seat of suffering.

A few days afterwards, the following advertisement appeared in the Dublin newspapers.

> If Sylvester Yelland, formerly a foremastman on board his Majesty's frigate *Dolphin*, or his nearest of kin, will apply to Mr. Hubert Smith, attorney, at his office, Dame Street, he or they may hear of something greatly to his or their advantage. Admission may be had at any hour up to twelve o'clock at night, should parties desire to avoid observation; and the strictest secrecy, as to all communications intended to be confidential, shall be honorably observed.

The *Dolphin*, as I have mentioned, was the vessel which Captain Barton had commanded; and this circumstance, connected with the extraordinary exertions made by the circulation of hand-bills, &c., as well as by repeated advertisements, to secure for this strange notice the utmost possible publicity, suggested to Dr. R—— the idea that Captain Barton's extreme uneasiness was somehow connected with the individual to whom the advertisement was addressed, and he himself the author of it. This, however, it is needless to add, was no more than a conjecture. No information whatsoever, as to the real purpose of the advertisement was divulged by the agent, nor yet any hint as to who his employer might be.

CHAPTER IV
He Talks with a Clergyman

Mr. Barton, although he had latterly begun to earn for himself the character of an hypochondriac, was yet very far from deserving it. Though by no means lively, he had yet, naturally, what are termed "even spirits," and was not subject to undue depressions. He soon, therefore, began to return to his former habits; and one of the earliest symptoms of this healthier tone of spirits was, his appearing at a grand dinner of the Freemasons,[5] of which worthy fraternity he was himself a brother.

Barton, who had been at first gloomy and abstracted, drank much more freely than was his wont—possibly with the purpose of dispelling his own secret anxieties—and under the influence of good wine, and pleasant company, became gradually (unlike himself) talkative, and even noisy.

It was under this unwonted excitement that he left his company at about half-past ten o'clock; and, as conviviality is a strong incentive to gallantry, it occurred to him to proceed forthwith to Lady L——'s and pass the remainder of the evening with her and his destined bride.

Accordingly, he was soon at —— street, and chatting gaily with the ladies. It is not to be supposed that Captain Barton had exceeded the limits which propriety prescribes to good fellowship— he had merely taken enough wine to raise his spirits, without, however, in the least degree unsteadying his mind, or affecting his manners.

With this undue elevation of spirits had supervened an entire oblivion or contempt of those undefined apprehensions which had for so long weighed upon his mind, and to a certain extent estranged him from society; but as the night wore away, and his artificial gaiety began to flag, these painful feelings gradually intruded themselves again, and he grew abstracted and anxious as heretofore.

He took his leave at length, with an unpleasant foreboding of some coming mischief, and with a mind haunted with a thousand mysterious apprehensions, such as, even while he acutely felt their pressure, he, nevertheless, inwardly strove, or affected to contemn. It was this proud defiance of what he regarded as his own weakness, which prompted him upon the present occasion to that course which brought about the adventure I am now about to relate.

Mr. Barton might have easily called a coach,[6] but he was conscious that his strong inclination to do so proceeded from no cause other than what he desperately persisted in representing to himself to be his own superstitious tremors. He might also have returned home by a *route* different from that against which he had been warned by his mysterious correspondent; but for the same reason he dismissed this idea also, and with a dogged and half desperate resolution to force matters to a crisis of some kind, if there were any reality in the causes of his former suffering, and if not, satisfactorily to bring their delusiveness to the proof, he

---

[5] A secret religious society
[6] Horse-drawn taxi

determined to follow precisely the course which he had trodden upon the night so painfully memorable in his own mind as that on which his strange persecution commenced.

Though, sooth to say, the pilot who for the first time steers his vessel under the muzzles of a hostile battery, never felt his resolution more severely tasked than did Captain Barton as he breathlessly pursued this solitary path—a path which, spite of every effort of skepticism and reason, he felt to be infested by some (as respected *him)* malignant being.

He pursued his way steadily and rapidly, scarcely breathing from intensity of suspense; he, however, was troubled by no renewal of the dreaded footsteps, and was beginning to feel a return of confidence, as more than three-fourths of the way being accomplished with impunity, he approached the long line of twinkling oil lamps which indicated the frequented streets. This feeling of self-congratulation was, however, but momentary.

The report of a musket[7] at some hundred yards behind him, and the whistle of a bullet close to his head, disagreeably and startlingly dispelled it.

His first impulse was to retrace his steps in pursuit of the assassin; but the road on either side was, as we have said, embarrassed by the foundations of a street, beyond which extended waste fields, full of rubbish and neglected lime and brick-kilns,[8] and all now as utterly silent as though no sound had ever disturbed their dark and unsightly solitude. The futility of, singlehanded, attempting, under such circumstances, a search for the murderer, was apparent, especially as no sound, either of retreating steps or any other kind, was audible to direct his pursuit.

With the tumultuous sensations of one whose life has just been exposed to a murderous attempt, and whose escape has been the narrowest possible, Captain Barton turned again; and without, however, quickening his pace actually to a run, hurriedly pursued his way.

He had turned, as I have said, after a pause of a few seconds, and had just commenced his rapid retreat, when on a sudden he met the well-remembered little man in the fur cap.

The encounter was but momentary. The figure was walking at the same exaggerated pace, and with the same strange air of menace as before; and as it passed him, he thought he heard it say, in a furious whisper, "Still alive—still alive!"

The state of Mr. Barton's spirits began now to work a corresponding alteration in his health and looks, and to such a degree that it was impossible that the change should escape general remark. For some reasons, known but to himself, he took

---

[7] Early form of rifle

[8] Drying kilns for making lime mortar and bricks, which were typically made of ceramic in the late nineteenth century and easily cracked or broken

no step whatsoever to bring the attempt upon his life, which he had so narrowly escaped, under the notice of the authorities; on the contrary, he kept it jealously to himself; and it was not for many weeks after the occurrence that he mentioned it, and then in strict confidence, to a gentleman, whom the torments of his mind at last compelled him to consult.

Spite of his blue devils, however, poor Barton, having no satisfactory reason to render to the public for any undue remissness in the attentions exacted by the relation subsisting between him and Miss Montague was obliged to exert himself, and present to the world a confident and cheerful bearing.

The true source of his sufferings, and every circumstance connected with them, he guarded with a reserve so jealous, that it seemed dictated by at least a suspicion that the origin of his strange persecution was known to himself, and that it was of a nature which, upon his own account, he could not or dared not disclose.

The mind thus turned in upon itself, and constantly occupied with a haunting anxiety which it dared not reveal or confide to any human breast, became daily more excited, and, of course, more vividly impressible, by a system of attack which operated through the nervous system; and in this state he was destined to sustain, with increasing frequency, the stealthy visitations of that apparition which from the first had seemed to possess so terrible a hold upon his imagination.

It was about this time that Captain Barton called upon the then celebrated preacher, Dr. ——, with whom he had a slight acquaintance, and an extraordinary conversation ensued.

The divine was seated in his chambers in college, surrounded with works upon his favorite pursuit, and deep in theology, when Barton was announced.

There was something at once embarrassed and excited in his manner, which, along with his wan and haggard countenance, impressed the student with the unpleasant consciousness that his visitor must have recently suffered terribly indeed, to account for an alteration so striking—almost shocking.

After the usual interchange of polite greeting, and a few commonplace remarks, Captain Barton, who obviously perceived the surprise which his visit had excited, and which

Doctor —— was unable wholly to conceal, interrupted a brief pause by remarking—"This is a strange call, Doctor ——, perhaps scarcely warranted by an acquaintance so slight as mine with you. I should not under ordinary circumstances have ventured to disturb you; but my visit is neither an idle nor impertinent intrusion. I am sure you will not so account it, when I tell you how afflicted I am."

Doctor —— interrupted him with assurances such as good breeding suggested, and Barton resumed—"I am come to task your patience by asking your advice. When I say your patience, I might, indeed, say more; I might have said your humanity—your compassion; for I have been and am a great sufferer."

"My dear sir," replied the churchman, "it will, indeed, afford me infinite gratification if I can give you comfort in any distress of mind; but—you know——"

"I know what you would say," resumed Barton, quickly; "I am an unbeliever, and, therefore, incapable of deriving help from religion; but don't take that for granted. At least you must not assume that, however unsettled my convictions may be, I do not feel a deep—a very deep—interest in the subject. Circumstances have lately forced it upon my attention, in such a way as to compel me to review the whole question in a more candid and teachable spirit, I believe, than I ever studied it in before."

"Your difficulties, I take it for granted, refer to the evidences of revelation," suggested the clergyman.

"Why—no—not altogether; in fact I am ashamed to say I have not considered even my objections sufficiently to state them connectedly; but—but there is one subject on which I feel a peculiar interest."

He paused again, and Doctor —— pressed him to proceed.

"The fact is," said Barton, "whatever may be my uncertainty as to the authenticity of what we are taught to call revelation, of one fact I am deeply and horribly convinced, that there does exist beyond this a spiritual world—a system whose workings are generally in mercy hidden from us—a system which may be, and which is sometimes, partially and terribly revealed. I am sure—I *know,*" continued Barton, with increasing excitement, "that there is a God—a dreadful God—and that retribution follows guilt, in ways the most mysterious and stupendous—by agencies the most inexplicable and terrific;—there is a spiritual system—great God, how I have been convinced!—a system malignant, and implacable, and omnipotent, under whose persecutions I am, and have been, suffering the torments of the damned!—yes, sir—yes—the fires and frenzy of hell!"

As Barton spoke, his agitation became so vehement that the Divine was shocked, and even alarmed. The wild and excited rapidity with which he spoke, and, above all, the indefinable horror, that stamped his features, afforded a contrast to his ordinary cool and unimpassioned self-possession striking and painful in the last degree.

CHAPTER V
Mr. Barton States His Case

"My dear sir," said Doctor ——, after a brief pause, "I fear you have been very unhappy, indeed; but I venture to predict that the depression under which you labor will be found to originate in purely physical causes, and that with a change of air, and the aid of a few tonics, your spirits will return, and the tone of your mind be once more cheerful and tranquil as heretofore. There was, after all, more truth than we are quite willing to admit in the classic theories which assigned the undue predominance of any one affection of the mind, to the undue action or torpidity of one or other of our bodily organs. Believe me, that a little attention to diet, exercise, and the other essentials of health, under competent direction, will make you as much yourself as you can wish."

"Doctor ———," said Barton, with something like a shudder, *"I cannot* delude myself with such a hope. I have no hope to cling to but one, and that is, that by some other spiritual agency more potent than that which tortures me, *it* may be combated, and I delivered. If this may not be, I am lost—now and forever lost."

"But, Mr. Barton, you must remember," urged his companion, "that others have suffered as you have done, and—"

"No, no, no," interrupted he, with irritability—"no, sir, I am not a credulous—far from a superstitious man. I have been, perhaps, too much the reverse—too skeptical, too slow of belief; but unless I were one whom no amount of evidence could convince, unless I were to condemn the repeated, the *perpetual* evidence of my own senses, I am now—now at last constrained to believe—I have no escape from the conviction—the overwhelming certainty—that I am haunted and dogged, go where I may, by—by a DEMON!"

There was a preternatural energy of horror in Barton's face, as, with its damp and deathlike lineaments turned towards his companion, he thus delivered himself.

"God help you, my poor friend," said Dr. ———, much shocked, "God help you; for, indeed, you *are* a sufferer, however your sufferings may have been caused."

"Ay, ay, God help me," echoed Barton, sternly; "but *will* He help me—will He help me?"

"Pray to Him—pray in an humble and trusting spirit," said he.

"Pray, pray," echoed he again; "I can't pray—I could as easily move a mountain by an effort of my will.[9] I have not belief enough to pray; there is something within me that will not pray. You prescribe impossibilities—literal impossibilities."

"You will not find it so, if you will but try," said Doctor ———.

"Try! I *have* tried, and the attempt only fills me with confusion; and, sometimes, terror; I have tried in vain, and more than in vain. The awful, unutterable idea of eternity and infinity oppresses and maddens my brain whenever my mind approaches the contemplation of the Creator; I recoil from the effort scared. I tell you, Doctor ——— if I am to be saved, it must be by other means. The idea of an eternal Creator is to me intolerable—my mind cannot support it."

---

[9] Biblical reference to Mathew 17:20 "And Jesus said unto them, Because of your unbelief: for verily I say unto you, If ye have faith as a grain of mustard seed, ye shall say unto this mountain, Remove hence to yonder place; and it shall remove; and nothing shall be impossible unto you." King James version

"Say, then, my dear sir," urged he, "say how you would have me serve you—what you would learn of me—what I can do or say to relieve you?"

"Listen to me first," replied Captain Barton, with a subdued air, and an effort to suppress his excitement, "listen to me while I detail the circumstances of the persecution under which my life has become all but intolerable—a persecution which has made me fear *death* and the world beyond the grave as much as I have grown to hate existence."

Barton then proceeded to relate the circumstances which I have already detailed, and then continued: "This has now become habitual—an accustomed thing. I do not mean the actual seeing him in the flesh—thank God, *that* at least is not permitted daily. Thank God, from the ineffable horrors of that visitation I have been mercifully allowed intervals of repose, though none of security; but from the consciousness that a malignant spirit is following and watching me wherever I go, I have never, for a single instant, a temporary respite. I am pursued with blasphemies, cries of despair and appalling hatred. I hear those dreadful sounds called after me as I turn the corners of the streets; they come in the nighttime, while I sit in my chamber alone; they haunt me everywhere, charging me with hideous crimes, and—great God!—threatening me with coming vengeance and eternal misery. Hush! do you hear *that?*" he cried with a horrible smile of triumph; "there—there, will that convince you?"

The clergyman felt a chill of horror steal over him, while, during the wail of a sudden gust of wind, he heard, or fancied he heard, the half articulate sounds of rage and derision mingling in the sough.

"Well, what do you think of *that?*" at length Barton cried, drawing a long breath through his teeth.

"I heard the wind," said Doctor ——. "What should I think of it—what is there remarkable about it?"

"The prince of the powers of the air,"[10] muttered Barton, with a shudder.

"Tut, tut! my dear sir," said the student, with an effort to reassure himself; for though it was broad daylight, there was nevertheless something disagreeably contagious in the nervous excitement under which his visitor so miserably suffered. "You must not give way to those wild fancies; you must resist these impulses of the imagination."

"Ay, ay; 'resist the devil and he will flee from thee,'"[11] said Barton, in the same tone; "but *how* resist him? ay, there it is—there is the rub. *What—what* am I to do? What *can* I do?"

---

[10] Reference to Satan as found in Ephesians 2:2 "Wherein in time past ye walked according to the course of this world, according to the prince of the power of the air, the spirit that now worketh in the children of disobedience." King James version

[11] Biblical reference to James 4:7 "Submit yourselves therefore to God. Resist the devil, and he will flee from you." King James version

"My dear sir, this *is* fancy," said the man of folios; "you are your own tormentor."

"No, no, sir—fancy has no part in it," answered Barton, somewhat sternly. "Fancy! was it that made *you,* as well as me, hear, but this moment, those accents of hell? Fancy, indeed! No, no."

"But you have seen this person frequently," said the ecclesiastic;[12] "why have you not accosted or secured him? Is it not a little precipitate, to say no more, to assume, as you have done, the existence of preternatural agency, when, after all, everything may be easily accountable, if only proper means were taken to sift the matter."

"There are circumstances connected with this—this *appearance,*" said Barton, "which it is needless to disclose, but which to *me* are proof of its horrible nature. I know that the being that follows me is not human—I say I *know* this; I could prove it to your own conviction." He paused for a minute, and then added, "And as to accosting it, I dare not, I could not; when I see it I am powerless; I stand in the gaze of death, in the triumphant presence of infernal power and malignity. My strength, and faculties, and memory, all forsake me. O God, I fear, sir, you know not what you speak of Mercy, mercy; heaven have pity on me!"

He leaned his elbow on the table, and passed his hand across his eyes, as if to exclude some image of horror, muttering the last words of the sentence he had just concluded, again and again.

"Doctor ——," he said, abruptly raising himself, and looking full upon the clergyman with an imploring eye, "I know you will do for me whatever may be done. You know now fully the circumstances and the nature of my affliction. I tell you I cannot help myself; I cannot hope to escape; I am utterly passive. I conjure you, then, to weigh my case well, and if anything may be done for me by vicarious supplication—by the intercession of the good—or by any aid or influence whatsoever, I implore of you, I adjure you in the name of the Most High, give me the benefit of that influence— deliver me from the body of this death. Strive for me, pity me; I know you will; you cannot refuse this; it is the purpose and object of my visit. Send me away with some hope, however little, some faint hope of ultimate deliverance, and I will nerve myself to endure, from hour to hour, the hideous dream into which my existence has been transformed."

Doctor —— assured him that all he could do was to pray earnestly for him, and that so much he would not fail to do. They parted with a hurried and melancholy valediction.

Barton hastened to the carriage that awaited him at the door, drew down the blinds, and drove away, while Doctor —— returned to his chamber, to ruminate at leisure upon the strange interview which had just interrupted his studies.

---

[12] Of the Christian church with Ecclesiastes being a book in the Christian Bible

CHAPTER VI
Seen Again

It was not to be expected that Captain Barton's changed and eccentric habits should long escape remark and discussion. Various were the theories suggested to account for it.

Some attributed the alteration to the pressure of secret pecuniary embarrassments; others to a repugnance to fulfil an engagement into which he was presumed to have too precipitately entered; and others, again, to the supposed incipiency of mental disease, which latter, indeed, was the most plausible as well as the most generally, received, of the hypotheses circulated in the gossip of the day.

From the very commencement of this change, at first so gradual in its advances, Miss Montague had of course been aware of it. The intimacy involved in their peculiar relation, as well as the near interest which it inspired afforded, in her case, a like opportunity and motive for the successful exercise of that keen and penetrating observation peculiar to her sex.

His visits became, at length, so interrupted, and his manner, while they lasted, so abstracted, strange, and agitated, that Lady L——, after hinting her anxiety and her suspicions more than once, at length distinctly stated her anxiety, and pressed for an explanation. The explanation was given, and although its nature at first relieved the worst solicitudes of the old lady and her niece, yet the circumstances which attended it, and the really dreadful consequences which it obviously indicated, as regarded the spirits, and indeed the reason of the now wretched man, who made the strange declaration, were enough, upon little reflection, to fill their minds with perturbation and alarm.

General Montague, the young lady's father, at length arrived. He had himself slightly known Barton, some ten or twelve years previously, and being aware of his fortune and connections, was disposed to regard him as an unexceptionable and indeed a most desirable match for his daughter. He laughed at the story of Barton's supernatural visitations, and lost no time in calling upon his intended son-in-law.

"My dear Barton," he continued, gaily, after a little conversation, "my sister tells me that you are a victim to blue devils,[13] in quite a new and original shape."

Barton changed countenance, and sighed profoundly.

---

[13] "A slang or colloquial phrase for dejection, hypochondria or lowness of spirits," *The Imperial Dictionary of the English Language: A Complete Encyclopedic Lexicon, Literary, Scientific, and Technological*, John Ogilvie, Vol. I, 1885, pg. 294

"Come, come; I protest this will never do," continued the General; "you are more like a man on his way to the gallows than to the altar. These devils have made quite a saint of you."

Barton made an effort to change the conversation.

"No, no, it won't do," said his visitor laughing; "I am resolved to say what I have to say upon this magnificent mock mystery of yours. You must not be angry, but really it is too bad to see you at your time of life, absolutely frightened into good behavior, like a naughty child by a bugaboo, and as far as I can learn, a very contemptible one. Seriously, I have been a good deal annoyed at what they tell me; but at the same time thoroughly convinced that there is nothing in the matter that may not cleared up, with a little attention and management, within a week at furthest."

"Ah, General, you do not know—" he began.

"Yes, but I do know quite enough to warrant my confidence," interrupted the soldier, "don't I know that all your annoyance proceeds from the occasional appearance of al certain little man in a cap and greatcoat, with a red vest and a bad face, who follows you about, and pops upon you at corners of lanes, and throws you into ague fits. Now, my dear fellow, I'll make it my business to *catch* this mischievous little mountebank,[14] and either beat him to a jelly with my own hands, or have him whipped through the town, at the cart's-tail,[15] before a month passes."

"If *you* knew what I knew," said Barton, with gloomy agitation, "you would speak very differently. Don't imagine that I am so weak as to assume, without proof the most overwhelming, the conclusion to which I have been forced—the proofs are here, locked up here." As he spoke he tapped upon his breast, and with an anxious sigh continued to walk up and down the room.

"Well, well, Barton," said his visitor, "I'll wager a rump and a dozen[16] I collar the ghost, and convince even you before many days are over."

He was running on in the same strain when he was suddenly arrested, and not a little shocked, by observing Barton, who had approached the window, stagger slowly back, like one who had received a stunning blow; his arm extended toward the street—his face and his very lips white as ashes—while he muttered, "There—by heaven—there—there!"

General Montague started mechanically to his feet, and from the window of the drawing room, saw a figure corresponding as well as his hurry would permit him to discern, with the description of the person, whose appearance so persistently disturbed the repose of his friend.

---

[14] Troublemaker
[15] Drug behind a cart
[16] An Irish bet of a rump of beef and a dozen clarets of wine, or a rump of steak and a dozen oysters, see *Dictionary of Phrase and Fable*, E. Cobham Brewer, 1894, pg. 1084

The figure was just turning from the rails of the area upon which it had been leaning, and, without waiting to see more, the old gentleman snatched his cane and hat, and rushed down the stairs and into the street, in the furious hope of securing the person, and punishing the audacity of the mysterious stranger.

He looked round him, but in vain, for any trace of the person he had himself distinctly seen. He ran breathlessly to the nearest corner, expecting to see from thence the retiring figure, but no such form was visible. Back and forward, from crossing to crossing, he ran, at fault, and it was not until the curious gaze and laughing countenances of the passers-by reminded him of the absurdity of his pursuit, that he checked his hurried pace, lowered his walking cane from the menacing altitude which he had mechanically given it, adjusted his hat, and walked composedly back again, inwardly vexed and flurried.

He found Barton pale and trembling in every joint; they both remained silent, though under emotions very different. At last Barton whispered, "You saw it?"

"*It*—him—someone—you mean—to be sure I did," replied Montague, testily. "But where is the good or the harm of seeing him? The fellow runs like a lamp-lighter.[17] I wanted to *catch* him, but he had stole away before I could reach the hall-door. However, it is no great matter; next time, I dare say, I'll do better; and egad, if I once come within reach of him, I'll introduce his shoulders to the weight of my cane."

Notwithstanding General Montague's undertakings and exhortations, however, Barton continued to suffer from the self-same unexplained cause; go how, when, or where he would, he was still constantly dogged or confronted by the being who had established over him so horrible an influence.

Nowhere and at no time was he secure against the odious appearance which haunted him with such diabolic perseverance. His depression, misery, and excitement became more settled and alarming every day, and the mental agonies that ceaselessly preyed upon him, began at last so sensibly to affect his health, that Lady L—— and General Montague succeeded, without, indeed, much difficulty, in persuading him to try a short tour on the Continent, in the hope that an entire change of scene would, at all events, have the effect of breaking through the influences of local association, which the more skeptical of his friends assumed to be by no means inoperative in suggesting and perpetuating what they conceived to be a mere form of nervous illusion.

General Montague indeed was persuaded that the figure which haunted his intended son-in-law was by no means the creation of his imagination, but, on the contrary, a substantial form of flesh and blood, animated by a resolution, perhaps with some

---

[17] Person who would light the many gas lights of a town at dusk and who extremely quick at the operation

murderous object in perspective, to watch and follow the unfortunate gentleman.

Even this hypothesis was not a very pleasant one; yet it was plain that if Barton could ever be convinced that there was nothing preternatural in the phenomenon which he had hitherto regarded in that light, the affair would lose all its terrors in his eyes, and wholly cease to exercise upon his health and spirits the baleful influence which it had hitherto done. He therefore reasoned, that if the annoyance were actually escaped by mere locomotion and change of scene, it obviously could not have originated in any supernatural agency.

CHAPTER VII
Flight

Yielding to their persuasions, Barton left Dublin for England, accompanied by General Montague. They posted rapidly to London, and thence to Dover, whence they took the packet with a fair wind for Calais.

The General's confidence in the result of the expedition on Barton's spirits had risen day by day, since their departure from the shores of Ireland; for to the inexpressible relief and delight of the latter, he had not since then, so much as even once fancied a repetition of those impressions which had, when at home, drawn him gradually down to the very depths of despair.

This exemption from what he had begun to regard as the inevitable condition of his existence, and the sense of security which began to pervade his mind, were inexpressibly delightful; and in the exultation of what he considered his deliverance, he indulged in a thousand happy anticipations for a future into which so lately he had hardly dared to look; and in short, both he and his companion secretly congratulated themselves upon the termination of that persecution which had been to its immediate victim a source *of* such unspeakable agony.

It was a beautiful day, and a crowd of idlers stood upon the jetty to receive the packet, and enjoy the bustle of the new arrivals.[18] Montague walked a few paces in advance of his friend, and as he made his way through the crowd, a little man touched his arm, and said to him, in a broad provincial *patois*—"Monsieur is walking too fast; he will lose his sick comrade in the throng, for, by my faith, the poor gentleman seems to be fainting."

Montague turned quickly, and observed that Barton did indeed look deadly pale. He hastened to his side. "My dear fellow, are you ill?" he asked anxiously.

The question was unheeded and twice, repeated, ere Barton stammered—"I saw him—by—, I saw him!"

---

[18] Pier where people would gather to receive packages sent from distant locals

"*Him!*—the wretch—who—where now?—where is he?" cried Montague, looking around him.

"I saw him—but he is gone," repeated Barton, faintly. "But where—where? For God's sake speak," urged Montague, vehemently.

"It is but this moment—here," said he.

"But what did he look like—what had he on—what did he wear—quick, quick," urged his excited companion, ready to dart among the crowd and collar the delinquent on the spot.

"He touched your arm—he spoke to you—he pointed to me. God be merciful to me, there is no escape," said Barton, in the low, subdued tones of despair.

Montague had already bustled away in all the flurry of mingled hope and rage; but though the singular *personnel* of the stranger who had accosted him was vividly impressed upon his recollection, he failed to discover among the crowd even the slightest resemblance to him.

After a fruitless search, in which he enlisted the services of several of the bystanders, who aided all the more zealously, as they believed he had been robbed, he at length, out of breath and baffled, gave over the attempt.

"Ah, my friend, it won't do," said Barton, with the faint voice and bewildered, ghastly look of one who had been stunned by some mortal shock; "there is no use in contending; whatever it is, the dreadful association between me and it, is now established—I shall never escape—never!"

"Nonsense, nonsense, my dear Barton; don't talk so," said Montague with something at once of irritation and dismay; "you must not, I say; we'll jockey the scoundrel yet; never mind, I say—never mind."

It was, however, but labor lost to endeavor henceforward to inspire Barton with one ray of hope; he became desponding. This intangible, and, as it seemed, utterly inadequate influence was fast destroying his energies of intellect, character, and health.

His first object was now to return to Ireland, there, as he believed, and now almost hoped, speedily to die. To Ireland accordingly he came and one of the first faces he saw upon the shore, was again that of his implacable and dreaded attendant.

Barton seemed at last to have lost not only all enjoyment and every hope in existence, but all independence of will besides. He now submitted himself passively to the management of the friends most nearly interested in his welfare. With the apathy of entire despair, he implicitly assented to whatever measures they suggested and advised; and as a last resource, it was determined to remove him to a house of Lady L——'s, in the neighborhood of Clontarf, where, with the advice of his medical attendant, who persisted in his opinion that the whole train of consequences resulted merely from some nervous derangement, it was resolved that he was to confine himself, strictly to the house, and to make use only of those apartments which commanded a view of an enclosed yard, the gates of which were to be kept jealously locked.

Those precautions would certainly secure him against the casual appearance of any living form, that his excited imagination might possibly confound with the spectre which, as it was contended, his fancy recognized in every figure that bore even a distant or general resemblance to the peculiarities with which his fancy had at first invested it.

A month or six weeks' absolute seclusion under these conditions, it was hoped might, by interrupting the series of these terrible impressions, gradually dispel the predisposing apprehensions, and the associations which had confirmed the supposed disease, and rendered recovery hopeless.

Cheerful society and that of his friends was to be constantly supplied, and on the whole, very sanguine expectations were indulged in, that under the treatment thus detailed, the obstinate hypochondria of the patient might at length give way.

Accompanied, therefore, by Lady L——, General Montague and his daughter—his own affianced bride—poor Barton—himself never daring to cherish a hope of his ultimate emancipation from the horrors under which his life was literally wasting away—took possession of the apartments, whose situation protected him against the intrusions, from which he shrank with such unutterable terror.

After a little time, a steady persistence in this system began to manifest its results, in a very marked though gradual improvement, alike in the health and spirits of the invalid. Not, indeed, that anything at all approaching complete recovery was yet discernible. On the contrary, to those who had not seen him since the commencement of his strange sufferings, such an alteration would have been apparent as might well have shocked them.

The improvement, however, such as it was, was welcomed with gratitude and delight, especially by the young lady, whom her attachment to him, as well as her now singularly painful position, consequent on his protracted illness, rendered an object scarcely one degree less to be commiserated than himself. A week passed—a fortnight—a month—and yet there had been no recurrence of the hated visitation.

The treatment had, so far forth, been followed by complete success. The chain of associations was broken. The constant pressure upon the overtasked spirits had been removed, and, under these comparatively favorable circumstances, the sense of social community with the world about him, and something of human interest, if not of enjoyment, began to reanimate him.

It was about this time that Lady L—— who, like most old ladies of the day, was deep in family receipts, and a great pretender to medical science, dispatched her own maid to the kitchen garden, with a list of herbs, which were there to be carefully culled, and brought back to her housekeeper for the purpose stated. The handmaiden, however, returned with her task scarce half completed, and a good deal flurried and alarmed.

Her mode of accounting for her precipitate retreat and evident agitation was odd, and, to the old lady, startling.

CHAPTER VIII
Softened

It appeared that she had repaired to the kitchen garden, pursuant to her mistress's directions, and had there begun to make the specified election among the rank and neglected herbs which crowded one corner of the enclosure, and while engaged in this pleasant labor, she carelessly sang a fragment of an old song, as she said, "to keep herself company."

She was, however, interrupted by an ill-natured laugh; and, looking up, she saw through the old thorn hedge, which surrounded the garden, a singularly ill-looking little man, whose countenance wore the stamp of menace and malignity, standing close to her, at the other side of the hawthorn screen.[19]

She described herself as utterly unable to move or speak, while he charged her with a message for Captain Barton; the substance of which she distinctly remembered to have been to the effect, that he, Captain Barton, must come abroad as usual, and show himself to his friends, out of doors, or else prepare for a visit in his own chamber.

On concluding this brief message, the stranger had, with a threatening air, got down into the outer ditch, and, seizing the hawthorn stems in his hands, seemed on the point of climbing through the fence—a feat which might have been accomplished without much difficulty. Without, of course, awaiting this result, the girl—throwing down her treasures of thyme and rosemary—had turned and run, with the swiftness of terror, to the house. Lady L—— commanded her, on pain of instant dismissal, to observe an absolute silence respecting all that passed of the incident which related to Captain Barton; and, at the same time, directed instant search to be made by her men, in the garden and the fields adjacent.

This measure, however, was as usual, unsuccessful, and, filled with undefinable misgivings, Lady L—— communicated the incident to her brother. The story, however, until long afterwards, went no further, and, of course, it was jealously guarded from Barton, who continued to amend, though slowly. Barton now began to walk occasionally in the courtyard which I have mentioned, and which being enclosed by a high wall, commanded no view beyond its own extent.

Here he, therefore, considered himself perfectly secure; and, but for a careless violation of orders by one of the grooms, he might

---

[19] Hawthorn shrub hedge

have enjoyed, at least for some time longer, his much-prized immunity.

Opening upon the public road, this yard was entered by a wooden gate, with a wicket in it, and was further defended by an iron gate upon the outside. Strict orders had been given to keep both carefully locked; but, spite of these, it had happened that one day, as Barton was slowly pacing this narrow enclosure, in his accustomed walk, and reaching the further extremity, was turning to retrace his steps, he saw the boarded wicket[20] ajar, and the face of his tormentor immovably looking at him through the iron bars. For a few seconds he stood riveted to the earth—breathless and bloodless—in the fascination of that dreaded gaze, and then fell helplessly insensible, upon the pavement.

There he was found a few minutes afterwards, and conveyed to his room—the apartment which he was never afterwards to leave alive. Henceforward a marked and unaccountable change was observable in the tone of his mind.

Captain Barton was now no longer the excited and despairing man he had been before; a strange alteration had passed upon him—an unearthly tranquility reigned in his mind—it was the anticipated stillness of the grave.

"Montague, my friend, this struggle is nearly ended now," he said, tranquilly, but with a look of fixed and fearful awe. "I have, at last, some comfort from that world of spirits, from which my punishment has come. I now know that my sufferings will soon be over."

Montague pressed him to speak on.

"Yes," said he, in a softened voice, "my punishment is nearly ended. From sorrow, perhaps I shall never, in time or eternity, escape; but my *agony* is almost over. Comfort has been revealed to me, and what remains of my allotted struggle I will bear with submission—even with hope."

"I am glad to hear you speak so tranquilly, my dear Barton," said Montague; "peace and cheer of mind are all you need to make you what you were."

"No, no—I never can be that," said he mournfully. "I am no longer fit for life. I am soon to die. I am to see *him* but once again, and then all is ended."

"He said so, then?" suggested Montague.

"*He?*—No, no; good tidings could scarcely come through him; and these were good and welcome; and they came so solemnly and sweetly—with unutterable love and melancholy, such as I could not—without saying more than is needful, or fitting, of other long past scenes and persons—fully explain to you."

As Barton said this he shed tears.

"Come, come," said Montague, mistaking the source of his emotions, "you must not give way. What is it, after all, but a pack of dreams and nonsense; or, at worst, the practices of a scheming

---

[20] Gate

rascal that enjoys his power of playing upon your nerves, and loves to exert it—a sneaking vagabond that owes you a grudge, and pays it off this way, not daring to try a more manly one."

"A grudge, indeed, he owes me—you say rightly," said Barton, with a sudden shudder; "a grudge as you call it. Oh, my God! when the justice of Heaven permits the Evil one to carry out a scheme of vengeance—when its execution is committed to the lost and terrible victim of sin, who owes his own ruin to the man, the very man, whom he is commissioned to pursue—then, indeed, the torments and terrors of hell are anticipated on earth. But heaven has dealt mercifully with me—hope has opened to me at last; and if death could come without the dreadful sight I am doomed to see, I would gladly close my eyes this moment upon the world. But though death is welcome, I shrink with an agony you cannot understand— an actual frenzy of terror—from the last encounter with that—that DEMON, who has drawn me thus to the verge of the chasm, and who is himself to plunge me down. I am to see him again—once more—but under circumstances unutterably more terrific than ever."

As Barton thus spoke, he trembled so violently that Montague was really alarmed at the extremity of his sudden agitation, and hastened to lead him back to the topic which had before seemed to exert so tranquillizing an effect upon his mind.

"It was not a dream," he said, after a time; "I was in a different state—I felt differently and strangely; and yet it was all as real, as clear, and vivid, as what I now see and hear—it was a reality."

"And what *did* you see and hear?" urged his companion.

"When I wakened from the swoon I fell into on seeing *him,*" said Barton, continuing as if he had not heard the question, "it was slowly, very slowly—I was lying by the margin of a broad lake, with misty hills all round, and a soft, melancholy, rose-colored light illuminated it all. It was unusually sad and lonely, and yet more beautiful than any earthly scene.

"My head was leaning on the lap of a girl, and she was singing a song, that told, I know not how—whether by words or harmonies—of all my life—all that is past, and all that is still to come; and with the song the old feelings that I thought had perished within me came back, and tears flowed from my eyes— partly for the song and its mysterious beauty, and partly for the unearthly sweetness of her voice; and yet I knew the voice—oh! how well; and I was spellbound as I listened and looked at the solitary scene, without stirring, almost without breathing—and, alas! alas! without turning my eyes toward the face that I knew was near me, so sweetly powerful was the enchantment that held me.

"And so, slowly, the song and scene grew fainter, and fainter, to my senses, till all was dark and still again. And then I awoke to this world, as you saw, comforted, for I knew that I was forgiven much."

Barton wept again long and bitterly. From this time, as we have said, the prevailing tone of his mind was one of profound and tranquil melancholy. This, however, was not without its interruptions. He was thoroughly impressed with the conviction that he was to experience another and a final visitation, transcending in horror all he had before experienced.

From this anticipated and unknown agony, he often shrank in such paroxysms of abject terror and distraction, as filled the whole household with dismay and superstitious panic. Even those among them who affected to discredit the theory of preternatural agency, were often in their secret souls visited during the silence of night with qualms and apprehensions, which they would not have readily confessed; and none of them attempted to dissuade Barton from the resolution on which he now systematically acted, of shutting himself up in his own apartment.

The window-blinds of this room were kept jealously down; and his own man was seldom out of his presence, day or night, his bed being placed in the same chamber. This man was an attached and respectable servant; and his duties, in addition to those ordinarily imposed upon valets, but which Barton's independent habits generally dispensed with, were to attend carefully to the simple precautions by means of which his master hoped to exclude the dreaded intrusion of the "Watcher."

And, in addition to attending to those arrangements, which amounted merely to guarding against the possibility of his master's being, through any unscreened window or open door, exposed to the dreaded influence, the valet was never to suffer him to be alone—total solitude, even for a minute, had become to him now almost as intolerable as the idea of going abroad into the public ways—it was an instinctive anticipation of what was coming.

CHAPTER IX
Requiescat

It is needless to say, that under these circumstances, no steps were taken toward the fulfilment of that engagement into which he had entered. There was quite disparity enough in point of years, and indeed of habits, between the young lady and Captain Barton, to have precluded anything like very vehement or romantic attachment on her part. Though grieved and anxious, therefore, she was very far from being heartbroken.

Miss Montague, however, devoted much of her time to the patient but fruitless attempt to cheer the unhappy invalid. She read for him, and conversed with him; but it was apparent that whatever exertions he made, the endeavor to escape from the one ever waking fear that preyed upon him, was utterly and miserably unavailing.

Young ladies are much given to the cultivation of pets; and among those who shared the favor of Miss Montague was a fine old owl, which the gardener, who caught him napping among the ivy of a ruined stable, had dutifully presented to that young lady.

The caprice which regulates such preferences was manifested in the extravagant favor with which this grim and ill-favored bird was at once distinguished by his mistress; and, trifling as this whimsical circumstance may seem, I am forced to mention it, inasmuch as it is connected, oddly enough, with the concluding scene of the story.

Barton, so far from sharing in this liking for the new favorite, regarded it from the first with an antipathy as violent as it was utterly unaccountable. Its very vicinity was unsupportable to him. He seemed to hate and dread it with a vehemence absolutely laughable, and, which, to those who have never witnessed the exhibition of antipathies of this kind, would seem all but incredible.

With these few words of preliminary explanation, I shall proceed to state the particulars of the last scene in this strange series of incidents.

It was almost two o'clock one winter's night, and Barton was, as usual at that hour, in his bed; the servant we have mentioned occupied a smaller bed in the same room, and a light was burning.

The man was on a sudden aroused by his master, "I can't get it out of my head that that accursed bird has got out somehow, and is lurking in some corner of the room. I have been dreaming about him. Get up, Smith, and look about; search for him. Such hateful dreams!"

The servant rose, and examined the chamber, and while engaged in so doing, he heard the well-known sound, more like a long-drawn gasp than a hiss, with which these birds from their secret haunts affright the quiet of the night.[21]

This ghostly indication of its proximity—for the sound proceeded from the passage upon which Barton's chamber-door opened—determined the search of the servant, who, opening the door, proceeded a step or two forward for the purpose of driving the bird away.

He had however, hardly entered the lobby, when the door behind him slowly swung to under the impulse, as it seemed, of some gentle current of air; but as immediately over the door there was a kind of window, intended in the day time to aid in lighting the passage, and through which at present the rays of the candle were issuing, the valet could see quite enough for his purpose.

As he advanced he heard his master—who, lying in a well-curtained bed, had not, as it seemed, perceived his exit from the room, call him by name, and direct him to place the candle on the table by his bed.

The servant, who was now some way in the long passage, and not liking to raise his voice for the purpose of replying, lest he

---

[21] "[M]arkers of the flying or noise of foules: as they which prognosticate death by the croaking of Ravens, or the hideous crying of Owles in the night," *Anatomie of Sorcerie: Wherein the Wicked Impietie of Charmers, Inchanters, and Such Like, is Discovered and Confuted*, James Mason, 1612, pg. 85

should startle the sleeping inmates of the house, began to walk hurriedly and softly back again, when, to his amazement, he heard a voice in the interior of the chamber answering calmly, and actually saw, through the window which overtopped the door, that the light was slowly shifting, as if carried across the room in answer to his master's call.

Palsied by a feeling akin to terror, yet not unmingled with curiosity, he stood breathless and listening at the threshold, unable to summon resolution to push open the door and enter. Then came a rustling of the curtains, and a sound like that of one who in a low voice hushes a child to rest, in the midst of which he heard Barton say, in a tone of stifled horror—"Oh, God—oh, my God!" and repeat the same exclamation several times.

Then ensued a silence, which again was broken by the same strange soothing sound; and at last there burst forth, in one swelling peal, a yell of agony so appalling and hideous, that, under some impulse of ungovernable horror, the man rushed to the door, and with his whole strength strove to force it open.

Whether it was that, in his agitation, he had himself but imperfectly turned the handle, or that the door was really secured upon the inside, he failed to effect an entrance; and as he tugged and pushed, yell after yell rang louder and wilder through the chamber, accompanied all the while by the same hushed sounds.

Actually freezing with terror, and scarce knowing what he did, the man turned and ran down the passage, wringing his hands in the extremity of horror and irresolution. At the stair-head he was encountered by General Montague, scared and eager, and just as they met the fearful sounds had ceased.

"What is it? Who—where is your master?" said Montague with the incoherence of extreme agitation. "Has anything—for God's sake is anything wrong?"

"Lord have mercy on us, it's all over," said the man staring wildly towards his master's chamber. "He's dead, sir, I'm sure he's dead."

Without waiting for inquiry or explanation, Montague, closely followed by the servant, hurried to the chamber-door, turned the handle, and pushed it open.

As the door yielded to his pressure, the ill-omened bird of which the servant had been in search, uttering its spectral warning, started suddenly from the far side of the bed, and flying through the doorway close over their heads, and extinguishing, in his passage, the candle which Montague carried, crashed through the skylight that overlooked the lobby, and sailed away into the darkness of the outer space.

"There it is, God bless us," whispered the man, after a breathless pause.

"Curse that bird," muttered the General, startled by the suddenness of the apparition, and unable to conceal his discomposure.

"The candle is moved," said the man, after another breathless pause, pointing to the candle that still burned in the room; "see, they put it by the bed."

"Draw the curtains, fellow, and don't stand gaping there," whispered Montague, sternly.

The man hesitated.

"Hold this, then," said Montague, impatiently thrusting the candlestick into the servant's hand, and himself advancing to the bedside, he drew the curtains apart.

The light of the candle, which was still burning at the bedside, fell upon a figure huddled together, and half upright, at the head of the bed. It seemed as though it had slunk back as far as the solid paneling would allow, and the hands were still clutched in the bedclothes.

"Barton, Barton, *Barton!*" cried the General, with a strange mixture of awe and vehemence. He took the candle, and held it so that it shone full upon the face. The features were fixed, stern, and white; the jaw was fallen; and the sightless eyes, still open, gazed vacantly forward toward the front of the bed.

"God Almighty he's dead," muttered the General, as he looked upon this fearful spectacle.

They both continued to gaze upon it in silence for a minute or more.

"And cold, too," whispered Montague, withdrawing his hand from that of the dead man.

"And see, see—may I never have life, sir," added the man, after a another pause, with a shudder, "but there was something else on the bed with him. Look there—look there—see that, sir."

As the man thus spoke, he pointed to a deep indenture, as if caused by a heavy pressure, near the foot of the bed.

Montague was silent.

"Come, sir, come away, for God's sake," whispered the man, drawing close up to him, and holding fast by his arm, while he glanced fearfully round; "what good can be done here now—come away, for God's sake!"

At this moment they heard the steps of more than one approaching, and Montague, hastily desiring the servant to arrest their progress, endeavored to loose the rigid grip with which the fingers of the dead man were clutched in the bedclothes, and drew, as well as he was able, the awful figure into a reclining posture; then closing the curtains carefully upon it, he hastened himself to meet those persons that were approaching.

It is needless to follow the personages so slightly connected with this narrative, into the events of their afterlife; it is enough to say, that no clue to the solution of these mysterious occurrences was ever after discovered; and so long an interval having now passed since the event which I have just described concluded this strange history, it is scarcely to be expected that time can throw any new lights upon its dark and inexplicable outline.

Until the secrets of the earth shall be no longer hidden, therefore, these transactions must remain shrouded in their original obscurity.

The only occurrence in Captain Barton's former life to which reference was ever made, as having any possible connection with the sufferings with which his existence closed, and which he himself seemed to regard as working out a retribution for some grievous sin of his past life, was a circumstance which not for several years after his death was brought to light.

The nature of this disclosure was painful to his relatives, and discreditable to his memory. It appeared that some six years before Captain Barton's final return to Dublin, he had formed, in the town of Plymouth, a guilty attachment, the object of which was the daughter of one of the ship's crew under his command.

The father had visited the frailty of his unhappy child with extreme harshness, and even brutality, and it was said that she had died heartbroken. Presuming upon Barton's implication in her guilt, this man had conducted himself toward him with marked insolence, and Barton retaliated this, and what he resented with still more exasperated bitterness—his treatment of the unfortunate girl—by a systematic exercise of those terrible and arbitrary severities which the regulations of the navy placed at the command of those who are responsible for its discipline.

The man had at length made his escape, while the vessel was in port at Naples, but died, as it was said, in an hospital in that town, of the wounds inflicted in one of his recent and sanguinary punishments. Whether these circumstances in reality bear, or not, upon the occurrences of Barton's afterlife, it is, of course, impossible to say.

It seems, however more than probable that they were at least, in his own mind, closely associated with them. But however the truth may be, as to the origin and motives of this mysterious persecution, there can be no doubt that, with respect to the agencies by which it was accomplished, absolute and impenetrable mystery is like to prevail until the day of doom.

POSTSCRIPT BY THE EDITOR

The preceding narrative is given in the *ipsissima verba*[22] of the good old clergyman, under whose hand it was delivered to Dr. Hesselius. Notwithstanding the occasional stiffness and redundancy of his sentences, I thought it better to reserve to myself the power of assuring the reader, that in handing to the printer, the M.S. of a statement of marvelous, the Editor has not altered one letter of the original text.—[Ed. Papers of Dr. Hesselius.]

---

[22] In the voice

Rosa Mulholland
(1841-1921)

Rosa Mulholland was as Irish a writer as they come. She was born in Belfast and later moved to Dublin where she lived at 48 Upper Gardiner Street. She was the daughter of a doctor and grew up hearing ghost stories around many an Irish fireplace.

Not only did Mulholland enjoy a good supernatural story, she liked to write them, too. She published *The Wicked Woods of Tooberevil* (1872), *The Walking Trees and Other Tales* (1885), and the gothic *Banshee Castle* (1895).

Early in her career she dabbled in illustrations and poetry before Charles Dickens took a liking to her short stories and published a few of her early works in his serialized magazine *Household Words*, a predecessor to *All the Year Round*.

At the age of twenty-five, Mulholland struck literary gold when Dickens asked her to write a story for his "To Be Taken" series of stories. It was then, in 1865, when she published "Not to be Taken at Bedtime," a tale of a maddening charm and a house called the Devil's Inn.

At the time, prescription drugs and health tonics were all the rage in London. Frequent advertisements told consumers that some were to be taken at night or after dinner or after exercise. There was a drug for everything. Sound familiar? Dickens played off the popularity of drugs by titling a group of short stories in the form of an advertisement under "Dr. Marigold's Prescriptions."

DOCTOR MARIGOLD'S PRESCRIPTIONS.

THE EXTRA CHRISTMAS NUMBER OF **ALL THE YEAR ROUND.**

CONDUCTED BY CHARLES DICKENS.

CONTAINING THE AMOUNT OF TWO ORDINARY NUMBERS.

CHRISTMAS, 1865.	Price **4d.**

INDEX.

On December 12, 1865, Dickens published in *All the Year Round* the following group of disparate short stories with similar titles: "To Be Taken Immediately" an introduction by Charles Dickens, "Not to Be Taken At Bed-time" by Rosa Mulholland, "To Be Taken at the Dinner-Table" by Dickens's son-in-law Charles Allston Collins, "Not to Be Taken for Granted" by Hesba Stretton (pseudonym of Sarah Smith), "To Be Taken In Water" by Walter Thornbury, "To Be Taken with a Grain of Salt," which was later called "The Trial for Murder" by Charles Dickens, "To Be Taken and Tried" by Carloine Leigh Smith, and "To Be Taken For Life."

A quarter of a century later, Mulholland penned her seminal ghost story "The Haunted Organist of Hurly Burly" in *The Irish Monthly* of 1886.[1] The story was later included in her anthology of 1890 titled *The Haunted Organist of Hurly Burly and Other Stories*. It contained a number of good supernatural stories including "The Ghost at the Rath," "The Hungry Death," "A Strange Love Story," and "The Ghost of Wildwood Chase."

"The Haunted Organist of Hurly Burly" will sear your memory and never be forgotten. It makes one wonder if Mulholland was subjected to long hours of organ practice as a girl.

---

[1] *The Irish Monthly: A Magazine of General Literature*, Vol. XIV, "The Haunted Organist of Hurly Burly," Rosa Mulholland, September 1886, pgs. 457-469

The Haunted Organist of Hurly Burly
1886

THERE HAD BEEN a thunderstorm in the village of Hurly Burly.[1] Every door was shut, every dog in his kennel, every rut and gutter a flowing river after the deluge of rain that had fallen.

Up at the great house, a mile from the town, the rooks were calling to one another about the fright they had been in, the fawns in the deer-park were venturing their timid heads from behind the trunks of trees, and the old woman at the gate-lodge had risen from her knees, and was putting back her prayer-book on the shelf. In the garden, July roses, unwieldy with their full-blown richness, and saturated with rain, hung their heads heavily to the earth; others, already fallen, lay flat upon their blooming faces on the path, where Bess, Mistress Hurly's maid, would find them, when going on her morning quest of roseleaves for her lady's potpourri.

Ranks of white lilies, just brought to perfection by today's sun, lay dabbled in the mire of flooded mold. Tears ran down the amber cheeks of the plums on the south wall, and not a bee had ventured out of the hives, though the scent of the air was sweet enough to tempt the laziest drone. The sky was still lurid behind the boles of the upland oaks, but the birds had begun to dive in and out of the ivy that wrapped up the home of the Hurlys of Hurly Burly.

This thunderstorm took place more than half a century ago, and we must remember that Mistress Hurly was dressed in the fashion of that time as she crept out from behind the squire's chair, now that the lightning was over, and, with many nervous glances towards the window, sat down before her husband, the tea-urn, and the muffins.

We can picture her fine lace cap, with its peachy ribbons, the frill on the hem of her cambric gown just touching her ankles, the embroidered clocks on her stockings, the rosettes on her shoes, but not so easily the lilac shade of her mild eyes, the satin skin, which still kept its delicate bloom, though wrinkled with advancing age, and the pale, sweet, puckered mouth, that time and sorrow had made angelic while trying vainly to deface its beauty.

The squire was as rugged as his wife was gentle, his skin as brown as hers was white, his grey hair as bristling as hers was glossed; the years had ploughed his face into ruts and channels; a

---

[1] Fictitious place and term that means a confused state

bluff, choleric,[2] noisy man he had been; but of late a dimness had come on his eyes, a hush on his loud voice, and a check on the spring of his hale step.

He looked at his wife often, and very often she looked at him. She was not a tall woman, and he was only a head higher.

They were a quaintly well-matched couple, despite their differences. She turned to you with nervous sharpness and revealed her tender voice and eye; he spoke and glanced roughly, but the turn of his head was courteous. Of late they fitted one another better than they had ever done in the heyday of their youthful love. A common sorrow had developed a singular likeness between them.

In former years the cry from the wife had been, 'Don't curb my son too much!' and from the husband, 'You ruin the lad with softness.' But now the idol that had stood between them was removed, and they saw each other better.

The room in which they sat was a pleasant old-fashioned drawing-room, with a general spider-legged character about the fittings; spinnet[3] and guitar in their places, with a great deal of copied music beside them; carpet, tawny wreaths on the pale blue; blue flutings on the walls, and faint gilding on the furniture.

A huge urn, crammed with roses, in the open bay-window, through which came delicious airs from the garden, the twittering of birds settling to sleep in the ivy close by, and occasionally the pattering of a flight of raindrops, swept to the ground as a bough bent in the breeze. The urn on the table was ancient silver, and the china rare. There was nothing in the room for luxurious ease of the body, but everything of delicate refinement for the eye.

There was a great hush all over Hurly Burly, except in the neighborhood of the rooks. Every living thing had suffered from heat for the past month, and now, in common with all Nature, was receiving the boon of refreshed air in silent peace. The mistress and master of Hurly Burly shared the general spirit that was abroad, and were not talkative over their tea.

'Do you know,' said Mistress Hurly, at last, 'when I heard the first of the thunder beginning I thought it was—it was—' The lady broke down, her lips trembling, and the peachy ribbons of her cap stirring with great agitation.

'Pshaw!' cried the old squire, making his cup suddenly ring upon the saucer, 'we ought to have forgotten that. Nothing has been heard for three months.'

At this moment a rolling sound struck upon the ears of both. The lady rose from her seat trembling, and folded her hands together, while the tea-urn flooded the tray.

'Nonsense, my love,' said the squire; 'that is the noise of wheels. Who can be arriving?'

---

[2] Mean tempered
[3] Small harpsichord or piano

'Who, indeed?' murmured the lady, reseating herself in agitation.

Presently pretty Bess of the rose-leaves appeared at the door in a flutter of blue ribbons.

'Please, madam, a lady has arrived, and says she is expected. She asked for her apartment, and I put her into the room that was got ready for Miss Calderwood. And she sends her respects to you, madam, and she'll be down with you presently.'

The squire looked at his wife, and his wife looked at the squire.

'It is some mistake,' murmured madam. 'Some visitor for Calderwood[4] or the Grange.[5] It is very singular.'

Hardly had she spoken when the door again opened, and the stranger appeared—a small creature, whether girl or woman it would be hard to say—dressed in a scanty black silk dress, her narrow shoulders covered with a white muslin pelerine. Her hair was swept up to the crown of her head, all but a little fringe hanging over her low forehead within an inch of her brows. Her face was brown and thin, eyes black and long, with blacker settings, mouth large, sweet, and melancholy. She was all head, mouth, and eyes; her nose and chin were nothing.

This visitor crossed the floor hastily, dropped a courtesy in the middle of the room, and approached the table, saying abruptly, with a soft Italian accent:

'Sir and madam, I am here. I am come to play your organ.'

'The organ!' gasped Mistress Hurly.

'The organ!' stammered the squire.

'Yes, the organ,' said the little stranger lady, playing on the back of a chair with her fingers, as if she felt notes under them. 'It was but last week that the handsome signor, your son, came to my little house, where I have lived teaching music since my English father and my Italian mother and brothers and sisters died and left me so lonely.'

Here the fingers left off drumming, and two great tears were brushed off, one from each eye with each hand, child's fashion. But the next moment the fingers were at work again, as if only whilst they were moving the tongue could speak.

'The noble signor, your son,' said the little woman, looking trustfully from one to the other of the old couple, while a bright blush shone through her brown skin, 'he often came to see me before that, always in the evening, when the sun was warm and yellow all through my little studio, and the music was swelling my

---

[4] Fictitious inn for the story, yet in Essex County there was a Calderwood Inn run by Lilias Calderrwood, see *Letters and Journals of Mrs. Calderwood of Polton from England, Holland and the Low Countries in 1756*, Alexander Fergusson, 1884, pg. 45

[5] The town of Hamilton was originally an "obscure village" called The Grange that had a Grange Inn, see *The Church in Victoria During the Episcopate of the Right Reverend Charles Perry First Bishop of Melbourne Prelate of the Order of St. Michael and St. George*, George Goodman, 1892, pg. 210

heart, and I could play out grand with all my soul; then he used to come and say,

"Hurry, little Lisa, and play better, better still. I have work for you to do by-and-by." Sometimes he said, "Brava!" and sometimes he said "Eccellentissima!" but one night last week he came to me and said, "It is enough. Will you swear to do my bidding, whatever it may be?"

'Here the black eyes fell. And I said, "Yes."

'And he said, "Now you are my betrothed."

'And I said, "Yes."

'And he said, "Pack up your music, little Lisa, and go off to England to my English father and mother, who have an organ in their house which must be played upon. If they refuse to let you play, tell them I sent you, and they will give you leave. You must play all day, and you must get up in the night and play. You must never tire. You are my betrothed, and you have sworn to do my work."

'I said, "Shall I see you there, signor?"

'And he said, "Yes, you shall see me there."

'I said, "I will keep my vow, Signor."

'And so, sir and madam, I am come.'

The soft foreign voice left off talking, the fingers left off thrumming on the chair, and the little stranger gazed in dismay at her auditors, both pale with agitation.

'You are deceived. You make a mistake,' said they in one breath.

'Our son—' began Mistress Hurly, but her mouth twitched, her voice broke, and she looked piteously towards her husband.

'Our son,' said the squire, making an effort to conquer the quavering in his voice, 'our son is long dead.'

'Nay, nay,' said the little foreigner. 'If you have thought him dead have good cheer, dear sir and madam. He is alive; he is well, and strong, and handsome. But one, two, three, four, five' (on the fingers) 'days ago he stood by my side.'

'It is some strange mistake, some wonderful coincidence!' said the mistress and master of Hurly Burly.

'Let us take her to the gallery,' murmured the mother of this son who was thus dead and alive.

'There is yet light to see the pictures. She will not know his portrait.'

The bewildered wife and husband led their strange visitor away to a long gloomy room at the west side of the house, where the faint gleams from the darkening sky still lingered on the portraits of the Hurly family.

'Doubtless he is like this,' said the squire, pointing to a fair-haired young man with a mild face, a brother of his own who had been lost at sea.

But Lisa shook her head, and went softly on tiptoe from one picture to another, peering into the canvas, and still turning away troubled. But at last a shriek of delight startled the shadowy chamber.

'Ah, here he is! See, here he is, the noble signor, the beautiful signor, not half so handsome as he looked five days ago, when talking to poor little Lisa! Dear sir and madam, you are now content. Now take me to the organ, that I may commence to do his bidding at once.'

The mistress of Hurly Burly clung fast by her husband's arm. 'How old are you, girl?' she said faintly.

'Eighteen,' said the visitor impatiently, moving towards the door.

'And my son has been dead for twenty years!' said his mother, and swooned on her husband's breast.

'Order the carriage at once,' said Mistress Hurly, recovering from her swoon; 'I will take her to Margaret Calderwood. Margaret will tell her the story. Margaret will bring her to reason. No, not tomorrow; I cannot bear tomorrow, it is so far away. We must go tonight.'

The little signora thought the old lady mad, but she put on her cloak again obediently, and took her seat beside Mistress Hurly in the Hurly family coach. The moon that looked in at them through the pane as they lumbered along was not whiter than the aged face of the squire's wife, whose dim faded eyes were fixed upon it in doubt and awe too great for tears or words. Lisa, too, from her corner gloated upon the moon, her black eyes shining with passionate dreams.

A carriage rolled away from the Calderwood door as the Hurly coach drew up at the steps.

Margaret Calderwood had just returned from a dinner-party, and at the open door a splendid figure was standing, a tall woman dressed in brown velvet, the diamonds on her bosom glistening in the moonlight that revealed her, pouring, as it did, over the house from eaves to basement. Mistress Hurly fell into her outstretched arms with a groan, and the strong woman carried her aged friend, like a baby, into the house. Little Lisa was overlooked, and sat down contentedly on the threshold to gloat awhile longer on the moon, and to thrum imaginary sonatas on the doorstep.

There were tears and sobs in the dusk, moonlit room into which Margaret Calderwood carried her friend. There was a long consultation, and then Margaret, having hushed away the grieving woman into some quiet corner, came forth to look for the little dark-faced stranger, who had arrived, so unwelcome, from beyond the seas, with such wild communication from the dead.

Up the grand staircase of handsome Calderwood the little woman followed the tall one into a large chamber where a lamp burned, showing Lisa, if she cared to see it, that this mansion of Calderwood was fitted with much greater luxury and richness than was that of Hurly Burly. The appointments of this room announced it the sanctum of a woman who depended for the interest of her life upon resources of intellect and taste.

Lisa noticed nothing but a morsel of biscuit that was lying on a plate. 'May I have it?' said she eagerly. 'It is so long since I have eaten. I am hungry.'

Margaret Calderwood gazed at her with a sorrowful, motherly look, and, parting the fringing hair on her forehead, kissed her. Lisa, staring at her in wonder, returned the caress with ardor.

Margaret's large fair shoulders, Madonna face, and yellow braided hair, excited a rapture within her. But when food was brought her, she flew to it and ate.

'It is better than I have ever eaten at home!' she said gratefully.

And Margaret Calderwood murmured, 'She is physically healthy, at least.'

'And now, Lisa,' said Margaret Calderwood, 'come and tell me the whole history of the grand signor who sent you to England to play the organ.'

Then Lisa crept in behind a chair, and her eyes began to burn and her fingers to thrum, and she repeated word for word her story as she had told it at Hurly Burly.

When she had finished, Margaret Calderwood began to pace up and down the floor with a very troubled face. Lisa watched her, fascinated, and, when she bade her listen to a story which she would relate to her, folded her restless hands together meekly, and listened.

'Twenty years ago, Lisa, Mr. and Mrs. Hurly had a son. He was handsome, like that portrait you saw in the gallery, and he had brilliant talents. He was idolized by his father and mother, and all who knew him felt obliged to love him. I was then a happy girl of twenty. I was an orphan, and Mrs. Hurly, who had been my mother's friend, was like a mother to me. I, too, was petted and caressed by all my friends, and I was very wealthy; but I only valued admiration, riches—every good gift that fell to my share— just in proportion as they seemed of worth in the eyes of Lewis Hurly. I was his affianced wife, and I loved him well.

'All the fondness and pride that were lavished on him could not keep him from falling into evil ways, nor from becoming rapidly more and more abandoned to wickedness, till even those who loved him best despaired of seeing his reformation. I prayed him with tears, for my sake, if not for that of his grieving mother, to save himself before it was too late. But to my horror I found that my power was gone, my words did not even move him; he loved me no more. I tried to think that this was some fit of madness that would pass, and still clung to hope. At last his own mother forbade me to see him.'

Here Margaret Calderwood paused, seemingly in bitter thought, but resumed:

'He and a party of his boon companions, named by themselves the "Devil's Club," were in the habit of practicing all kinds of unholy pranks in the country. They had midnight carousings on the tombstones in the village graveyard; they carried away helpless old men and children, whom they tortured by making believe to bury them alive; they raised the dead and placed them sitting round the tombstones at a mock feast.

'On one occasion there was a very sad funeral from the village. The corpse was carried into the church, and prayers were read over the coffin, the chief mourner, the aged father of the dead man, standing weeping by. In the midst of this solemn scene the organ suddenly pealed forth a profane tune, and a number of voices shouted a drinking chorus.

'A groan of execration burst from the crowd, the clergyman turned pale and closed his book, and the old man, the father of the dead, climbed the altar steps, and, raising his arms above his head, uttered a terrible curse. He cursed Lewis Hurly to all eternity, he cursed the organ he played, that it might be dumb henceforth, except under the fingers that had now profaned it, which, he prayed, might be forced to labor upon it till they stiffened in death. And the curse seemed to work, for the organ stood dumb in the church from that day, except when touched by Lewis Hurly.

'For a bravado he had the organ taken down and conveyed to his father's house, where he had it put up in the chamber where it now stands. It was also for a bravado that he played on it every day. But, by-and-by, the amount of time which he spent at it daily began to increase rapidly.

'We wondered long at this whim, as we called it, and his poor mother thanked God that he had set his heart upon an occupation which would keep him out of harm's way. I was the first to suspect that it was not his own will that kept him hammering at the organ so many laborious hours, while his boon companions tried vainly to draw him away.

'He used to lock himself up in the room with the organ, but one day I hid myself among the curtains, and saw him writhing on his seat, and heard him groaning as he strove to wrench his hands from the keys, to which they flew back like a needle to a magnet. It was soon plainly to be seen that he was an involuntary slave to the organ; but whether through a madness that had grown within himself, or by some supernatural doom, having its cause in the old man's curse, we did not dare to say.

'By-and-by there came a time when we were wakened out of our sleep at nights by the rolling of the organ. He wrought now night and day. Food and rest were denied him. His face got haggard, his beard grew long, his eyes started from their sockets. His body became wasted, and his cramped fingers like the claws of a bird. He groaned piteously as he stooped over his cruel toil. All save his mother and I were afraid to go near him. She, poor, tender woman, tried to put wine and food between his lips, while the tortured fingers crawled over the keys; but he only gnashed his teeth at her with curses, and she retreated from him in terror, to pray. At last, one dreadful hour, we found him a ghastly corpse on the ground before the organ.

'From that hour the organ was dumb to the touch of all human fingers. Many, unwilling to believe the story, made persevering endeavors to draw sound from it, in vain. But when the darkened empty room was locked up and left, we heard as loud as ever the well-known sounds humming and rolling through the walls.

'Night and day the tones of the organ boomed on as before. It seemed that the doom of the wretched man was not yet fulfilled, although his tortured body had been worn out in the terrible struggle to accomplish it. Even his own mother was afraid to go near the room then.

'So the time went on, and the curse of this perpetual music was not removed from the house. Servants refused to stay about the place. Visitors shunned it. The squire and his wife left their home for years, and returned; left it, and returned again, to find their ears still tortured and their hearts wrung by the unceasing persecution of terrible sounds.

'At last, but a few months ago, a holy man was found, who locked himself up in the cursed chamber for many days, praying and wrestling with the demon. After he came forth and went away the sounds ceased, and the organ was heard no more. Since then there has been peace in the house. And now, Lisa, your strange appearance and your strange story convince us that you are a victim of a ruse of the Evil One. Be warned in time, and place yourself under the protection of God, that you may be saved from the fearful influences that are at work upon you. Come—'

Margaret Calderwood turned to the corner where the stranger sat, as she had supposed, listening intently. Little Lisa was fast asleep, her hands spread before her as if she played an organ in her dreams.

Margaret took the soft brown face to her motherly breast, and kissed the swelling temples, too big with wonder and fancy.

'We will save you from a horrible fate!' she murmured, and carried the girl to bed.

In the morning Lisa was gone. Margaret Calderwood, coming early from her own chamber, went into the girl's room and found the bed empty.

She is just such a wild thing, thought Margaret, *as would rush out at sunrise to hear the larks!* and she went forth to look for her in the meadows, behind the beech hedges and in the home park.

Mistress Hurly, from the breakfast-room window, saw Margaret Calderwood, large and fair in her white morning gown, coming down the garden-path between the rose bushes, with her fresh draperies dabbled by the dew, and a look of trouble on her calm face. Her quest had been unsuccessful. The little foreigner had vanished.

A second search after breakfast proved also fruitless, and towards evening the two women drove back to Hurly Burly together. There all was panic and distress. The squire sat in his study with the doors shut, and his hands over his ears. The servants, with pale faces, were huddled together in whispering groups. The haunted organ was pealing through the house as of old.

Margaret Calderwood hastened to the fatal chamber, and there, sure enough, was Lisa, perched upon the high seat before the organ, beating the keys with her small hands, her slight figure swaying, and the evening sunshine playing about her weird head.

Sweet unearthly music she wrung from the groaning heart of the organ—wild melodies, mounting to rapturous heights and falling to mournful depths. She wandered from Mendelssohn to Mozart, and from Mozart to Beethoven.

Margaret stood fascinated awhile by the ravishing beauty of the sounds she heard, but, rousing herself quickly, put her arms round the musician and forced her away from the chamber. Lisa returned next day, however, and was not so easily coaxed from her post again.

Day after day she labored at the organ, growing paler and thinner and more weird-looking as time went on.

'I work so hard,' she said to Mrs. Hurly. 'The signor, your son, is he pleased? Ask him to come and tell me himself if he is pleased.'

Mistress Hurly got ill and took to her bed. The squire swore at the young foreign baggage, and roamed abroad. Margaret Calderwood was the only one who stood by to watch the fate of the little organist. The curse of the organ was upon Lisa; it spoke under her hand, and her hand was its slave.

At last she announced rapturously that she had had a visit from the brave signor, who had commended her industry, and urged her to work yet harder. After that she ceased to hold any communication with the living. Time after time Margaret Calderwood wrapped her arms about the frail thing, and carried her away by force, locking the door of the fatal chamber.

But locking the chamber and burying the key were of no avail. The door stood open again, and Lisa was laboring on her perch.

One night, wakened from her sleep by the well-known humming and moaning of the organ, Margaret dressed hurriedly and hastened to the unholy room. Moonlight was pouring down the staircase and passages of Hurly Burly. It shone on the marble bust of the dead Lewis Hurly, that stood in the niche above his mother's sitting-room door.

The organ room was full of it when Margaret pushed open the door and entered—full of the pale green moonlight from the window, mingled with another light, a dull lurid glare which seemed to center round a dark shadow, like the figure of a man standing by the organ, and throwing out in fantastic relief the slight form of Lisa writhing, rather than swaying, back and forward, as if in agony. The sounds that came from the organ were broken and meaningless, as if the hands of the player lagged and stumbled on the keys.

Between the intermittent chords low moaning cries broke from Lisa, and the dark figure bent towards her with menacing gestures. Trembling with the sickness of supernatural fear, yet strong of will, Margaret Calderwood crept forward within the lurid light, and was drawn into its influence. It grew and intensified upon her, it dazzled and blinded her at first; but presently, by a daring effort of will, she raised her eyes, and beheld Lisa's face convulsed with torture in the burning glare, and bending over her the figure and the features of Lewis Hurly!

Smitten with horror, Margaret did not even then lose her presence of mind. She wound her strong arms around the wretched girl and dragged her from her seat and out of the influence of the lurid light, which immediately paled away and vanished. She carried her to her own bed, where Lisa lay, a wasted wreck, raving about the cruelty of the pitiless signor who would not see that she was laboring her best. Her poor cramped hands kept beating the coverlet, as though she were still at her agonizing task.

Margaret Calderwood bathed her burning temples, and placed fresh flowers upon her pillow.

She opened the blinds and windows, and let in the sweet morning air and sunshine, and then, looking up at the newly awakened sky with its fair promise of hope for the day, and down at the dewy fields, and afar off at the dark green woods with the purple mists still hovering about them, she prayed that a way might be shown her by which to put an end to this curse. She prayed for Lisa, and then, thinking that the girl rested somewhat, stole from the room. She thought that she had locked the door behind her.

She went downstairs with a pale, resolved face, and, without consulting anyone, sent to the village for a bricklayer. Afterwards she sat by Mistress Hurly's bedside, and explained to her what was to be done. Presently she went to the door of Lisa's room, and hearing no sound, thought the girl slept, and stole away.

By-and-by she went downstairs, and found that the bricklayer had arrived and already begun his task of building up the organ-room door. He was a swift workman, and the chamber was soon sealed safely with stone and mortar.

Having seen this work finished, Margaret Calderwood went and listened again at Lisa's door; and still hearing no sound, she returned, and took her seat at Mrs. Hurly's bedside once more. It was towards evening that she at last entered her room to assure herself of the comfort of Lisa's sleep. But the bed and room were empty.

Lisa had disappeared.

Then the search began, upstairs and downstairs, in the garden, in the grounds, in the fields and meadows. No Lisa.

Margaret Calderwood ordered the carriage and drove to Calderwood to see if the strange little Will-o'-the-wisp might have made her way there; then to the village, and to many other places in the neighborhood which it was not possible she could have reached. She made enquiries everywhere; she pondered and puzzled over the matter.

In the weak, suffering state that the girl was in, how far could she have crawled?

After two days' search, Margaret returned to Hurly Burly. She was sad and tired, and the evening was chill. She sat over the fire wrapped in her shawl when little Bess came to her, weeping behind her muslin apron.

'If you'd speak to Mistress Hurly about it, please, ma'am,' she said.

'I love her dearly, and it breaks my heart to go away, but the organ haven't done yet, ma'am, and I'm frightened out of my life, so I can't stay.'

'Who has heard the organ, and when?' asked Margaret Calderwood, rising to her feet.

'Please, ma'am, I heard it the night you went away—the night after the door was built up!'

'And not since?'

'No, ma'am,' hesitatingly, 'not since. Hist! hark, ma'am! Is not that like the sound of it now?'

'No,' said Margaret Calderwood; 'it is only the wind.'

But pale as death she flew down the stairs and laid her ear to the yet damp mortar of the newly built wall. All was silent. There was no sound but the monotonous sough of the wind in the trees outside. Then Margaret began to dash her soft shoulder against the strong wall, and to pick the mortar away with her white fingers, and to cry out for the bricklayer who had built up the door.

It was midnight, but the bricklayer left his bed in the village, and obeyed the summons to Hurly Burly. The pale woman stood by and watched him undo all his work of three days ago, and the servants gathered about in trembling groups, wondering what was to happen next.

What happened next was this: When an opening was made the man entered the room with a light, Margaret Calderwood and others following. A heap of something dark was lying on the ground at the foot of the organ. Many groans arose in the fatal chamber.

Here was little Lisa dead!

When Mistress Hurly was able to move, the squire and his wife went to live in France, where they remained till their death. Hurly Burly was shut up and deserted for many years. Lately it has passed into new hands. The organ has been taken down and banished, and the room is a bedchamber, more luxuriously furnished than any in the house. But no one sleeps in it twice.

Margaret Calderwood was carried to her grave the other day, a very aged woman.

Charles Dickens
(1812-1870)

"Charles Dickens was born near Portsmouth, England, February 7, 1812. Early on he developed a fondness for reading, and when only nine years old had read *Don Quixote, Gil Bias, Robinson Crusoe,* and several of the early English novels."[1]

Though ghosts played small parts in Dickens's novels, they featured prominently in many of his short stories. At a young age ghost stories left an indelible mark on his mind. Mary Weller, the nursemaid to Dickens and his siblings, never missed a chance to tell them horrifying stories. Her favorite was "Captain Murderer."

The Captain brought out a silver pie-dish of immense capacity, and the Captain brought out flour, and butter, and eggs, and all things needful, except the inside of the pie; of materials for the staple of the pie itself, the Captain brought out none. Then said the lovely bride, "Dear Captain Murderer, what pie is this to be?" He replied, "A meat pie." Then said the lovely bride, "Dear Captain Murderer, I see no meat." The Captain humorously retorted, "Look in the glass." She looked in the glass, but still she saw no meat, and then the Captain roared with laughter, and, suddenly frowning and drawing his sword, bid her roll out the crust. So she rolled out the crust, dropping large tears upon it all the time because he was so

---

[1] *The Story of Little Nell from Old Curiosity Shop,* Anonymous Introduction, 1897, pg. 4

cross, and when she had lined the dish with crust and had cut the crust all ready to fit the top, the Captain called out, *"I* see the meat in the glass!" And the bride looked up at the glass, just in time to see the Captain cutting her head off; and he chopped her in pieces, and peppered her, and salted her, and put her in the pie, and sent it to the baker's, and eat it all, and picked the bones.[2]

Not so fondly, Dickens remembered Mary Weller when he was an adult: "Hundreds of times did I hear this legend of Captain Murderer, in my early youth, and added hundreds of times was there a mental compulsion upon me in bed to peep in at his window as the dark twin peeped, and to revisit his horrible house, and look at him in his blue and spotty and screaming stage, as he reached from floor to ceiling and from wall to wall. The young woman who brought me acquainted with Captain Murderer had a fiendish enjoyment of my terrors, and used to begin, I remember— as a sort of introductory overture—by clawing the air with both hands, and uttering a long, low, hollow groan. So acutely did I suffer from this ceremony in combination with this infernal Captain, that I sometimes used to plead I thought I was hardly strong enough and old enough to hear the story again just yet. But she never spared me one word of it, and indeed commended the awful chalice to my lips as the only preservative known to science against 'The Black Cat'—a weird and glaring-eyed supernatural Tom, who was reputed to prowl about the world by night, sucking the breath of infancy, and who was endowed with a special thirst (as I was given to understand) for mine. This female bard—may she have been repaid my debt of obligation to her in the matter of nightmares and perspirations!"[3]

The year after Dickens published his "To Be Taken" series of stories on December 12, 1865, which centered around times to take medicine, he published his "Branch Line" series that focused on the theme of a set of railroad lines at Mugby Junction.

---

[2] *The Uncommercial Traveler, Hard Times, and the Mystery of Edwin Drood,* Charles Dickens, 1876, pg.67
[3] *The Uncommercial Traveler, Hard Times, and the Mystery of Edwin Drood,* Charles Dickens, 1876, pg. 68

MUGBY JUNCTION.

THE EXTRA CHRISTMAS NUMBER OF **ALL THE YEAR ROUND.**

CONDUCTED BY CHARLES DICKENS.

CONTAINING THE AMOUNT OF TWO ORDINARY NUMBERS.

CHRISTMAS, 1866.   Price **4d.**

INDEX.

Unlike the "To Be Taken" series, however, Dickens penned most of the stories in this collection, including the haunting ghost story "No. 1 Branch Line. The Signalman," which will make you never look at a train the same way again.

No. 1 Branch Line: The Signalman
1865

"HALLOA! BELOW THERE!"

When he heard a voice thus calling to him, he was standing at the door of his box,[1] with a flag in his hand, furled round its short pole.[2] One would have thought, considering the nature of the ground, that he could not have doubted from what quarter the voice came; but instead of looking up to where I stood on the top of the steep cutting nearly over his head, he turned himself about, and looked down the Line.

There was something remarkable in his manner of doing so, though I could not have said for my life what. But I know it was remarkable enough to attract my notice, even though his figure was foreshortened and shadowed, down in the deep trench, and mine was high above him, so steeped in the glow of an angry sunset, that I had shaded my eyes with my hand before I saw him at all.

"Halloa! Below!"

From looking down the Line, he turned himself about again, and, raising his eyes, saw my figure high above him.

"Is there any path by which I can come down and speak to you?"

He looked up at me without replying, and I looked down at him without pressing him too soon with a repetition of my idle question. Just then there came a vague vibration in the earth and air, quickly changing into a violent pulsation, and an oncoming rush that caused me to start back, as though it had a force to draw me down. When such vapor as rose to my height from this rapid train had passed me, and was skimming away over the landscape, I looked down again, and saw him refurling the flag he had shown while the train went by.

I repeated my inquiry.

After a pause, during which he seemed to regard me with fixed attention, he motioned with his rolled-up flag towards a point on my level, some two or three hundred yards distant. I called down to him, "All right!" and made for that point. There, by dint of looking closely about me, I found a rough zigzag descending path notched out, which I followed.

---

[1] Small booth called a "signal box" where signal workers stayed between the running of trains to keep warm

[2] Early signal workers used flags to signal train drivers

The cutting was extremely deep, and unusually precipitate. It was made through a clammy stone, that became oozier and wetter as I went down. For these reasons, I found the way long enough to give me time to recall a singular air of reluctance or compulsion with which he had pointed out the path.

When I came down low enough upon the zigzag descent to see him again, I saw that he was standing between the rails on the way by which the train had lately passed, in an attitude as if he were waiting for me to appear. He had his left hand at his chin, and that left elbow rested on his right hand, crossed over his breast. His attitude was one of such expectation and watchfulness that I stopped a moment, wondering at it.

I resumed my downward way, and stepping out upon the level of the railroad, and drawing nearer to him, saw that he was a dark, sallow man, with a dark beard and rather heavy eyebrows. His post was in as solitary and dismal a place as ever I saw.

On either side, a dripping-wet wall of jagged stone, excluding all view but a strip of sky; the perspective one way only a crooked prolongation of this great dungeon; the shorter perspective in the other direction terminating in a gloomy red light, and the gloomier entrance to a black tunnel, in whose massive architecture there was a barbarous, depressing, and forbidding air. So little sunlight ever found its way to this spot, that it had an earthy, deadly smell; and so much cold wind rushed through it, that it struck chill to me, as if I had left the natural world.

Before he stirred, I was near enough to him to have touched him. Not even then removing his eyes from mine, he stepped back one step, and lifted his hand.

This was a lonesome post to occupy (I said), and it had riveted my attention when I looked down from up yonder. A visitor was a rarity, I should suppose; not an unwelcome rarity, I hoped? In me, he merely saw a man who had been shut up within narrow limits all his life, and who, being at last set free, had a newly-awakened interest in these great works. To such purpose I spoke to him; but I am far from sure of the terms I used; for, besides that I am not happy in opening any conversation, there was something in the man that daunted me.

He directed a most curious look towards the red light near the tunnel's mouth, and looked all about it, as if something were missing from it, and then looked at me.

That light was part of his charge? Was it not?

He answered in a low voice,—"Don't you know it is?"

The monstrous thought came into my mind, as I perused the fixed eyes and the saturnine face, that this was a spirit, not a man. I have speculated since, whether there may have been infection in his mind.

In my turn, I stepped back. But in making the action, I detected in his eyes some latent fear of me. This put the monstrous thought to flight.

"You look at me," I said, forcing a smile, "as if you had a dread of me."

"I was doubtful," he returned, "whether I had seen you before."

"Where?"

He pointed to the red light he had looked at.

"There?" I said.

Intently watchful of me, he replied (but without sound), "Yes."

"My good fellow, what should I do there? However, be that as it may, I never was there, you may swear."

"I think I may," he rejoined. "Yes; I am sure I may."

His manner cleared, like my own. He replied to my remarks with readiness, and in well-chosen words. Had he much to do there? Yes; that was to say, he had enough responsibility to bear; but exactness and watchfulness were what was required of him, and of actual work—manual labor—he had next to none.

To change that signal, to trim those lights, and to turn this iron handle now and then, was all he had to do under that head.[3] Regarding those many long and lonely hours of which I seemed to make so much, he could only say that the routine of his life had shaped itself into that form, and he had grown used to it. He had taught himself a language down here,—if only to know it by sight, and to have formed his own crude ideas of its pronunciation, could be called learning it. He had also worked at fractions and decimals, and tried a little algebra; but he was, and had been as a boy, a poor hand at figures.

Was it necessary for him when on duty always to remain in that channel of damp air, and could he never rise into the sunshine from between those high stone walls? Why, that depended upon times and circumstances. Under some conditions there would be less upon the Line than under others, and the same held good as to certain hours of the day and night. In bright weather, he did choose occasions for getting a little above these lower shadows; but, being at all times liable to be called by his electric bell, and at such times listening for it with redoubled anxiety, the relief was less than I would suppose.

He took me into his box, where there was a fire, a desk for an official book in which he had to make certain entries,[4] a telegraphic instrument with its dial, face, and needles,[5] and the little bell of which he had spoken. On my trusting that he would excuse the remark that he had been well educated, and (I hoped I might say without offence) perhaps educated above that station, he observed

---

[3] Signal workers had to monitor trains that passed their signal box, which rang a bell upon approach, and could only be sure that the train had fully passed when the red signal light was seen again; they also had to ratchet long handles in the signal box to move parts of the track so the train could move in a different direction

[4] The Train Register Book was where the signal worker logged each passing train, time, and its line

[5] Train drivers could communicate with the signal worker via telegraphic codes and vice versa

that instances of slight incongruity in such wise would rarely be found wanting among large bodies of men; that he had heard it was so in workhouses, in the police force, even in that last desperate resource, the army; and that he knew it was so, more or less, in any great railway staff.

He had been, when young (if I could believe it, sitting in that hut,—he scarcely could), a student of natural philosophy, and had attended lectures; but he had run wild, misused his opportunities, gone down, and never risen again. He had no complaint to offer about that. He had made his bed, and he lay upon it. It was far too late to make another.

All that I have here condensed he said in a quiet manner, with his grave dark regards divided between me and the fire. He threw in the word, "Sir," from time to time, and especially when he referred to his youth,—as though to request me to understand that he claimed to be nothing but what I found him.

He was several times interrupted by the little bell, and had to read off messages, and send replies. Once he had to stand without the door, and display a flag as a train passed, and make some verbal communication to the driver. In the discharge of his duties, I observed him to be remarkably exact and vigilant, breaking off his discourse at a syllable, and remaining silent until what he had to do was done.

In a word, I should have set this man down as one of the safest of men to be employed in that capacity, but for the circumstance that while he was speaking to me he twice broke off with a fallen color, turned his face towards the little bell when it did NOT ring, opened the door of the hut (which was kept shut to exclude the unhealthy damp), and looked out towards the red light near the mouth of the tunnel. On both of those occasions, he came back to the fire with the inexplicable air upon him which I had remarked, without being able to define, when we were so far asunder.

Said I, when I rose to leave him, "You almost make me think that I have met with a contented man."

(I am afraid I must acknowledge that I said it to lead him on.)

"I believe I used to be so," he rejoined, in the low voice in which he had first spoken; "but I am troubled, sir, I am troubled."

He would have recalled the words if he could. He had said them, however, and I took them up quickly.

"With what? What is your trouble?"

"It is very difficult to impart, sir. It is very, very difficult to speak of. If ever you make me another visit, I will try to tell you."

"But I expressly intend to make you another visit. Say, when shall it be?"

"I go off early in the morning, and I shall be on again at ten tomorrow night, sir."

"I will come at eleven."

He thanked me, and went out at the door with me. "I'll show my white light, sir," he said, in his peculiar low voice, "till you have found the way up. When you have found it, don't call out! And when you are at the top, don't call out!"

His manner seemed to make the place strike colder to me, but I said no more than, "Very well."

"And when you come down tomorrow night, don't call out! Let me ask you a parting question. What made you cry, 'Halloa! Below there!' tonight?"

"Heaven knows," said I. "I cried something to that effect—"

"Not to that effect, sir. Those were the very words. I know them well."

"Admit those were the very words. I said them, no doubt, because I saw you below."

"For no other reason?"

"What other reason could I possibly have?"

"You had no feeling that they were conveyed to you in any supernatural way?"

"No."

He wished me goodnight, and held up his light. I walked by the side of the down Line of rails (with a very disagreeable sensation of a train coming behind me) until I found the path. It was easier to mount than to descend, and I got back to my inn without any adventure.

Punctual to my appointment, I placed my foot on the first notch of the zigzag next night, as the distant clocks were striking eleven. He was waiting for me at the bottom, with his white light on.

"I have not called out," I said, when we came close together; "may I speak now?"

"By all means, sir."

"Goodnight, then, and here's my hand."

"Goodnight, sir, and here's mine."

With that we walked side by side to his box, entered it, closed the door, and sat down by the fire.

"I have made up my mind, sir," he began, bending forward as soon as we were seated, and speaking in a tone but a little above a whisper, "that you shall not have to ask me twice what troubles me. I took you for someone else yesterday evening. That troubles me."

"That mistake?"

"No. That someone else."

"Who is it?"

"I don't know."

"Like me?"

"I don't know. I never saw the face. The left arm is across the face, and the right arm is waved,—violently waved. This way."

I followed his action with my eyes, and it was the action of an arm gesticulating, with the utmost passion and vehemence, "For God's sake, clear the way!"

"One moonlight night," said the man, "I was sitting here, when I heard a voice cry, 'Halloa! Below there!' I started up, looked from that door, and saw this Someone else standing by the red light near the tunnel, waving as I just now showed you. The voice seemed hoarse with shouting, and it cried, 'Look out! Look out!' And then again, 'Halloa! Below there! Look out!' I caught up my lamp, turned it on red, and ran towards the figure, calling, 'What's wrong? What has happened? Where?' It stood just outside the blackness of the tunnel. I advanced so close upon it that I wondered at its keeping the sleeve across its eyes. I ran right up at it, and had my hand stretched out to pull the sleeve away, when it was gone."

"Into the tunnel?" said I.

"No. I ran on into the tunnel, five hundred yards. I stopped, and held my lamp above my head, and saw the figures of the measured distance,[6] and saw the wet stains stealing down the walls and trickling through the arch.

I ran out again faster than I had run in (for I had a mortal abhorrence of the place upon me), and I looked all round the red light with my own red light, and I went up the iron ladder to the gallery atop of it, and I came down again, and ran back here. I telegraphed both ways, 'An alarm has been given. Is anything wrong?' The answer came back, both ways, 'All well.'"

Resisting the slow touch of a frozen finger tracing out my spine, I showed him how that this figure must be a deception of his sense of sight; and how that figures, originating in disease of the delicate nerves that minister to the functions of the eye, were known to have often troubled patients, some of whom had become conscious of the nature of their affliction, and had even proved it by experiments upon themselves.

"As to an imaginary cry," said I, "do but listen for a moment to the wind in this unnatural valley while we speak so low, and to the wild harp it makes of the telegraph wires."

That was all very well, he returned, after we had sat listening for a while, and he ought to know something of the wind and the wires,—he who so often passed long winter nights there, alone and watching. But he would beg to remark that he had not finished.

I asked his pardon, and he slowly added these words, touching my arm—"Within six hours after the Appearance, the memorable accident on this Line happened, and within ten hours the dead and wounded were brought along through the tunnel over the spot where the figure had stood."

A disagreeable shudder crept over me, but I did my best against it. It was not to be denied, I rejoined, that this was a remarkable coincidence, calculated deeply to impress his mind. But it was unquestionable that remarkable coincidences did continually occur, and they must be taken into account in dealing with such a subject. Though to be sure I must admit, I added (for I thought I saw that he was going to bring the objection to bear upon me), men of common sense did not allow much for coincidences in making the ordinary calculations of life.

He again begged to remark that he had not finished.

---

[6] Distance markers were typically marked on tunnel walls to let train drivers know how far away the signal box was

I again begged his pardon for being betrayed into interruptions.

"This," he said, again laying his hand upon my arm, and glancing over his shoulder with hollow eyes, "was just a year ago. Six or seven months passed, and I had recovered from the surprise and shock, when one morning, as the day was breaking, I, standing at the door, looked towards the red light, and saw the spectre again." He stopped, with a fixed look at me.

"Did it cry out?"

"No. It was silent."

"Did it wave its arm?"

"No. It leaned against the shaft of the light, with both hands before the face. Like this."

Once more I followed his action with my eyes. It was an action of mourning. I have seen such an attitude in stone figures on tombs.

"Did you go up to it?"

"I came in and sat down, partly to collect my thoughts, partly because it had turned me faint. When I went to the door again, daylight was above me, and the ghost was gone."

"But nothing followed? Nothing came of this?"

He touched me on the arm with his forefinger twice or thrice giving a ghastly nod each time:—

"That very day, as a train came out of the tunnel, I noticed, at a carriage window on my side, what looked like a confusion of hands and heads, and something waved. I saw it just in time to signal the driver, Stop! He shut off, and put his brake on, but the train drifted past here a hundred and fifty yards or more. I ran after it, and, as I went along, heard terrible screams and cries. A beautiful young lady had died instantaneously in one of the compartments, and was brought in here, and laid down on this floor between us."

Involuntarily I pushed my chair back, as I looked from the boards at which he pointed to himself.

"True, sir. True. Precisely as it happened, so I tell it you."

I could think of nothing to say, to any purpose, and my mouth was very dry. The wind and the wires took up the story with a long lamenting wail.

He resumed. "Now, sir, mark this, and judge how my mind is troubled. The spectre came back a week ago. Ever since, it has been there, now and again, by fits and starts."

"At the light?"

"At the Danger-light."

"What does it seem to do?"

He repeated, if possible with increased passion and vehemence, that former gesticulation of, "For God's sake, clear the way!"

Then he went on. "I have no peace or rest for it. It calls to me, for many minutes together, in an agonized manner, 'Below there! Look out! Look out!' It stands waving to me. It rings my little bell—"

I caught at that. "Did it ring your bell yesterday evening when I was here, and you went to the door?"

"Twice."

"Why, see," said I, "how your imagination misleads you. My eyes were on the bell, and my ears were open to the bell, and if I am a living man, it did NOT ring at those times. No, nor at any other time, except when it was rung in the natural course of physical things by the station communicating with you."

He shook his head. "I have never made a mistake as to that yet, sir. I have never confused the spectre's ring with the man's. The ghost's ring is a strange vibration in the bell that it derives from nothing else, and I have not asserted that the bell stirs to the eye. I don't wonder that you failed to hear it. But I heard it."

"And did the spectre seem to be there, when you looked out?"

"It WAS there."

"Both times?"

He repeated firmly: "Both times."

"Will you come to the door with me, and look for it now?"

He bit his under lip as though he were somewhat unwilling, but arose. I opened the door, and stood on the step, while he stood in the doorway. There was the Danger-light. There was the dismal mouth of the tunnel. There were the high, wet stone walls of the cutting. There were the stars above them.

"Do you see it?" I asked him, taking particular note of his face. His eyes were prominent and strained, but not very much more so, perhaps, than my own had been when I had directed them earnestly towards the same spot.

"No," he answered. "It is not there."

"Agreed," said I.

We went in again, shut the door, and resumed our seats. I was thinking how best to improve this advantage, if it might be called one, when he took up the conversation in such a matter-of-course way, so assuming that there could be no serious question of fact between us, that I felt myself placed in the weakest of positions.

"By this time you will fully understand, sir," he said, "that what troubles me so dreadfully is the question, What does the spectre mean?"

I was not sure, I told him, that I did fully understand.

"What is its warning against?" he said, ruminating, with his eyes on the fire, and only by times turning them on me. "What is the danger? Where is the danger? There is danger overhanging somewhere on the Line. Some dreadful calamity will happen. It is not to be doubted this third time, after what has gone before. But surely this is a cruel haunting of ME. What can I do?"

He pulled out his handkerchief, and wiped the drops from his heated forehead.

"If I telegraph Danger, on either side of me, or on both, I can give no reason for it," he went on, wiping the palms of his hands. "I should get into trouble, and do no good. They would think I was mad. This is the way it would work,—Message: 'Danger! Take care!' Answer: 'What Danger? Where?' Message: 'Don't know. But, for God's sake, take care!' They would displace me. What else could they do?"

His pain of mind was most pitiable to see. It was the mental torture of a conscientious man, oppressed beyond endurance by an unintelligible responsibility involving life.

"When it first stood under the Danger-light," he went on, putting his dark hair back from his head, and drawing his hands outward across and across his temples in an extremity of feverish distress, "why not tell me where that accident was to happen,—if it must happen? Why not tell me how it could be averted,—if it could have been averted? When on its second coming it hid its face, why not tell me, instead, 'She is going to die. Let them keep her at home'? If it came, on those two occasions, only to show me that its warnings were true, and so to prepare me for the third, why not warn me plainly now? And I, Lord help me! A mere poor signal-man on this solitary station! Why not go to somebody with credit to be believed, and power to act?"

When I saw him in this state, I saw that for the poor man's sake, as well as for the public safety, what I had to do for the time was to compose his mind. Therefore, setting aside all question of reality or unreality between us, I represented to him that whoever thoroughly discharged his duty must do well, and that at least it was his comfort that he understood his duty, though he did not understand these confounding Appearances.

In this effort I succeeded far better than in the attempt to reason him out of his conviction. He became calm; the occupations incidental to his post as the night advanced began to make larger demands on his attention: and I left him at two in the morning. I had offered to stay through the night, but he would not hear of it.

That I more than once looked back at the red light as I ascended the pathway, that I did not like the red light, and that I should have slept but poorly if my bed had been under it, I see no reason to conceal. Nor did I like the two sequences of the accident and the dead girl. I see no reason to conceal that either.

But what ran most in my thoughts was the consideration how ought I to act, having become the recipient of this disclosure? I had proved the man to be intelligent, vigilant, painstaking, and exact; but how long might he remain so, in his state of mind? Though in a subordinate position, still he held a most important trust, and would I (for instance) like to stake my own life on the chances of his continuing to execute it with precision?

Unable to overcome a feeling that there would be something treacherous in my communicating what he had told me to his superiors in the Company, without first being plain with himself and proposing a middle course to him, I ultimately resolved to offer to accompany him (otherwise keeping his secret for the present) to the wisest medical practitioner we could hear of in those parts, and to take his opinion. A change in his time of duty would come round next night, he had apprised me, and he would be off an hour or two after sunrise, and on again soon after sunset. I had appointed to return accordingly.

Next evening was a lovely evening, and I walked out early to enjoy it. The sun was not yet quite down when I traversed the field-path near the top of the deep cutting. I would extend my walk for an hour, I said to myself, half an hour on and half an hour back, and it would then be time to go to my signal-man's box.

Before pursuing my stroll, I stepped to the brink, and mechanically looked down, from the point from which I had first seen him. I cannot describe the thrill that seized upon me, when, close at the mouth of the tunnel, I saw the appearance of a man, with his left sleeve across his eyes, passionately waving his right arm.

The nameless horror that oppressed me passed in a moment, for in a moment I saw that this appearance of a man was a man indeed, and that there was a little group of other men, standing at a short distance, to whom he seemed to be rehearsing the gesture he made. The Danger-light was not yet lighted. Against its shaft, a little low hut, entirely new to me, had been made of some wooden supports and tarpaulin. It looked no bigger than a bed.

With an irresistible sense that something was wrong,—with a flashing self-reproachful fear that fatal mischief had come of my leaving the man there, and causing no one to be sent to overlook or correct what he did,—I descended the notched path with all the speed I could make.

"What is the matter?" I asked the men.

"Signal-man killed this morning, sir."

"Not the man belonging to that box?"

"Yes, sir."

"Not the man I know?"

"You will recognize him, sir, if you knew him," said the man who spoke for the others, solemnly uncovering his own head, and raising an end of the tarpaulin, "for his face is quite composed."

"Oh, how did this happen, how did this happen?" I asked, turning from one to another as the hut closed in again.

"He was cut down by an engine, sir. No man in England knew his work better. But somehow he was not clear of the outer rail. It was just at broad day. He had struck the light, and had the lamp in his hand. As the engine came out of the tunnel, his back was towards her, and she cut him down. That man drove her, and was showing how it happened. Show the gentleman, Tom."

The man, who wore a rough dark dress, stepped back to his former place at the mouth of the tunnel.

"Coming round the curve in the tunnel, sir," he said, "I saw him at the end, like as if I saw him down a perspective-glass. There was no time to check speed, and I knew him to be very careful. As he didn't seem to take heed of the whistle, I shut it off when we were running down upon him, and called to him as loud as I could call."

"What did you say?"

"I said, 'Below there! Look out! Look out! For God's sake, clear the way!'"

I started.

"Ah! it was a dreadful time, sir. I never left off calling to him. I put this arm before my eyes not to see, and I waved this arm to the last; but it was no use."

Without prolonging the narrative to dwell on any one of its curious circumstances more than on any other, I may, in closing it, point out the coincidence that the warning of the Engine-Driver included, not only the words which the unfortunate Signal-man had repeated to me as haunting him, but also the words which I myself—not he—had attached, and that only in my own mind, to the gesticulation he had imitated.

Edith Nesbit
(1858-1924)

Like many authors, Edith Nesbit started out writing poetry. She was born into a large London family. When her father died, Nesbit was only four years old. His death kicked off years of moving around England for the large family as it tried to support itself without a father figure. At the age of 21, Nesbit married Hubert Bland, a bank clerk who had children with a number of different women. He agreed to care for the children, which at times left Nesbit feeling like a stranger in her own home.

In 1884, at the age of 26, Edith joined a bohemian group that called itself the Fabian Society. It was where she was introduced to such literary figures as H. G. Wells and George Bernard Shaw. They encouraged her to keep writing and less than ten years later she penned her finest ghost short story, "The Hurst of Hurstcote."

It originally appeared in the *Temple Bar: A London Magazine for Town and Country Readers* in the summer of 1893.[1] In it she offers one of the first ghost short stories written by a woman that is fictitiously narrated by a man.

Nearly twenty years before, in 1871, gothic poet Dante Gabriel Rossetti published his poem "Down Stream" that referenced the fictitious Hurstcote five times.[2] This is perhaps where Nesbit derived the name for her crumbling mansion.

In the story Nesbit skillfully posed the question as to when a soul leaves a body after a person dies? And in doing so she drew many parallels to the decaying mansion and the eventual descent of the story down into its moldering coffins.

---

[1] *Temple Bar: A London Magazine for Town and Country Readers*, Edith Nesbit, June 1893, pg. 391
[2] *The Dark Blue*, Dante Gabriel Rossetti, Vol. II, 1871, pg. 211

By the turn of the century, Nesbit focused her talents on writing children and fantasy stories, which is where she gained her primary fame as a writer.

One of her most popular fantasy story collections was *The Book of Dragons*. She penned upwards of sixty works for children, many of which were published in *The Strand* magazine.

Due to her success as a writer of children's stories, Nesbit would sadly never write another ghost story to surpass "The Hurst of Hurstcote."

Hurst of Hurstcote
1893

WE WERE AT Eton[1] together, and afterwards at Christchurch,[2] and I always got on very well with him; but somehow he was a man about whom none of the other men cared very much.

There was always something strange and secret about him; even at Eton he liked grubbing among books and trying chemical experiments, better than cricket or the boats. That sort of thing would make any boy unpopular.

At Oxford, it wasn't merely his studious ways and his love of science that went against him; it was a certain way he had of gazing at us through narrowing lids, as though he were looking at us more from the outside than any human being has a right to look at another, and a bored air of belonging to another and a higher race, whenever we talked the ordinary chatter about athletics and the Schools.

A certain paper on "Black Magic," which he read to the Essay Society,[3] filled to overflowing the cup of his College's contempt for him. I suppose no man was ever so much disliked for so little cause.

When we went down I noticed—for I knew his people at home—that the sentiment of dislike which he excited in most men was curiously in contrast to the emotions which he inspired in women. They all liked him, listened to him with rapt attention, talked of him with undisguised enthusiasm. I watched their strange infatuation with calmness for several years, but the day came when he met Kate Danvers, and then I was not calm anymore. She behaved like all the rest of the women, and to her, quite suddenly, Hurst threw the handkerchief.

He was not Hurst[4] of Hurstcote then, but his family was good, and his means not despicable, so he and she were conditionally engaged. People said it was a poor match for the beauty of the county; and her people, I know, hoped she would think better of it.

---

[1] Eaton College was founded in 1440 by Henry VI and is an English boarding school for boys

[2] Christ Church is a college of the University of Oxford

[3] William Gladstone (1809-1898) founded the Essay Society at Oxford on October 31, 1829, All Hallows' Eve

[4] Archaic term for male head of a family line

As for me—well, this is not the story of my life, but of his. I need only say that I thought him a lucky man.

I went to town to complete the studies that were to make me M.D.; Hurst went abroad, to Paris or Leipzig or somewhere, to study hypnotism, and to prepare notes for his book on "Black Magic." This came out in the autumn, and had a strange and brilliant success.

Hurst became famous, famous as men do become nowadays. His writings were asked for by all the big periodicals. His future seemed assured. In the spring they were married; I was not present at the wedding. The practice my father had bought for me in London claimed all my time.

It was more than a year after their marriage that I had a letter from Hurst.

> *Congratulate me, old man! Crowds of uncles and cousins have died, and I am Hurst of Hurstcote, which God wot I never thought to be. The place is all to pieces, but we can't live anywhere else. If you can get away about September, come down and see us. We shall be installed. I have everything now that I ever longed for—Hurstcote— cradle of our race—and all that, the only woman in the world for my wife, and but that's enough for any man, surely.—*

> *John Hurst Of Hurstcote.*

Of course I knew Hurstcote. Who doesn't? Hurstcote, which seventy years ago was one of the most perfect, as well as the finest, brick Tudor mansions in England. The Hurst who lived there seventy years ago noticed one day that his chimneys smoked, and called in a Hastings architect.

"Your chimneys," said the local man, "are beyond me, but with the timbers and lead of your castle I can build you a snug little house in the corner of your Park, much more suitable for a residence than this old brick building."

So they gutted Hurstcote, and built the new house, and faced it with stucco. All of which things you will find written in the *Guide to Sussex*.[5] Hurstcote, when I had seen it, had been the merest shell. How would Hurst make it habitable? Even if he had inherited much money with the castle, and intended to restore the building, that would be a work of years, not months. What would he do?

In September I went to see.

Hurst met me at Pevensey Station.

"Let's walk up," he said; "there's a cart to bring your traps. Eh! but it's good to see you again, Bernard."

---

[5] *Tourists' Guide to the County of Sussex*, George Frederick Chambers, 1891, which was originally published in 1877 by Chambers and subsequently updated

It was good to see him again. And to see him so changed. And so changed for good too. He was much stouter, and no longer wore the untidy ill-fitting clothes of the old days. He was rather smartly got up in grey stockings and knee-breeches, and wore a velvet shooting-jacket. But the most noteworthy change was in his face; it bore no more the eager, inquiring, half-scornful, half-tolerant look that had won him such ill-will at Oxford. His face now was the face of a man completely at peace with himself and with the world.

"How well you look!" I said, as we walked along the level winding road through the still marshes.

"How much better you mean!" he laughed.

"I know it. Bernard, you'll hardly believe it, but I am on the way to be a popular man!"

He had not lost his old knack of reading one's thoughts.

"Don't trouble yourself to find the polite answer to that," he hastened to add. "No one knows as well as I how unpopular I was—and no one knows so well why," he added in a very low voice. "However," he went on gaily, "unpopularity is a thing of the past. The folk hereabout call on us, and condole with us on our hutch. A thing of the past, as I said—but what a past it was, eh! You're the only man who ever liked me. You don't know what that's been to me many a dark day and night. When the others were—you know—it was like a hand holding mine, to think of you. I've always thought I was sure of one soul in the world to stand by me."

"Yes," I said—"Yes."

He flung his arm over my shoulder with a frank, boyish gesture of affection quite foreign to his nature as I had known it.

"And I know why you didn't come to our wedding," he went on—"but that's all right now, isn't it?"

"Yes," I said again, for indeed it was. There are brown eyes in the world, after all, as well as blue, and one pair of brown that meant Heaven to me as the blue had never done.

"That's well," Hurst answered, and we walked on in satisfied silence, till we passed across the furze-crowned ridge, and went down the hill to Hurstcote. It lies in the hollow, ringed round by its moat, its dark red walls showing the sky behind them; no welcoming sparkle of early litten candle, only the pale amber of the September evening shining through the gaunt unglazed windows.

Three planks and a rough handrail had replaced the old drawbridge. We passed across the moat, and Hurst pulled a knotted rope that hung beside the great iron-bound door. A bell clanged loudly inside. In the moment we spent there, waiting, Hurst pushed back a brier that was trailing across the arch, and let it fall outside the handrail.

"Nature is too much with us here," he said, laughing. "The clematis spends its time tripping one up or clawing at one's hair, and we are always expecting the ivy to force itself through the window and make an uninvited third at our dinner table."

Then the great door of Hurstcote Castle swung back, and there stood Kate, a thousand times sweeter and more beautiful than ever. I looked at her with momentary terror and dazzlement. She was a thousand times more beautiful than any woman with brown eyes could be. My heart almost stopped beating. "With life or death in the balance: Right!"

To be beautiful is not the same thing as to be dear, thank God. I went forward and took her hand with a free heart.

It was a pleasant fortnight I spent with them. They had had one tower completely repaired, and in its queer eight-sided rooms we lived, when we were not out among the marshes or by the blue sea at Pevensey.

Mrs. Hurst had made the rooms quaintly charming by a medley of Liberty stuffs[6] and Wardour Street furniture.[7] The grassy space within the castle walls, with its underground passages, its crumbling heaps of masonry overgrown with lush creepers, was better than any garden. There we met the fresh morning; there we lounged through lazy noons. There the grey evenings found us.

I have never seen any two married people so utterly, so undisguisedly in love as these were. I, the third, had no embarrassment in so being—for their love had in it a completeness, a childish abandonment, to which the presence of a third—a friend —was no burden. A happiness, reflected from theirs, shone on me. The days went by, dreamlike, and brought the eve of my return to London and the commonplaces of life.

We were sitting in the courtyard; Hurst had gone to the village to post some letters. A big moon was just showing over the battlements, when Mrs. Hurst shivered.

"It's late," she said, "and cold; the summer is gone. Let us go in."

So we went in to the little warm room, where a wood fire flickered on a brick hearth, and a shaded lamp was already glowing softly. Here we sat on the cushioned seat in the open window, and looked out through the lozenge panes at the gold moon and the light of her making ghosts in the white mist that rose thick and heavy from the moat.

"I am so sorry you are going," she said, presently; "but you will come and skate on the moat with us at Christmas, won't you? We mean to have a mediaeval Christmas. You don't know what that is? Neither do I, but John does. He is very, very wise."

"Yes," I answered, "he used to know many things that most men don't even dream of as possible to know."

She was silent a minute, and then shivered again. I picked up the shawl she had thrown down when we came in, and put it round her.

"Thank you! I think—don't you—that there are some things one is not meant to know, and some things one is meant *not* to know. You see the distinction?"

"I suppose so—yes."

---

6 London street having a variety of shops in the late nineteenth century
7 Famous street in Soho, London that had a number of furniture stores

"Did it never frighten you, in the old days," she went on, "to see that John would never—was always—"

"But he has given all that up now?"

"Oh yes, ever since our honeymoon. Do you know he used to mesmerize me.[8] It was horrible. And that book of his—"

"I didn't know you believed in Black Magic."

"Oh, I don't—not the least bit. I never was at all superstitious, you know. But those things always frighten me just as much as if I believed in them. And besides—I think they're wicked; but John— Ah, there he is! Let's go and meet him."

His dark figure was outlined against the sky behind the hill. She wrapped the soft shawl more closely around her, and we went out in the moonlight to meet her husband.

The next morning when I entered the room I found that it lacked its chief ornament. The sparkling white and silver breakfast accessories were there, but for the deft white hands and kindly welcoming blue eyes of my hostess I looked in vain. At ten minutes past nine Hurst came in looking horribly worried, and more like his old self than I had ever expected to see him.

"I say, old man," he said, hurriedly, "are you really set on going back to town today? Because Kate's awfully queer—I can't think what's wrong. I want you to see her after breakfast."

I reflected a minute. "I can stay if I send a wire," I said.

"I wish you would then," Hurst said, wringing my hand and turning away; "she's been off her head most of the night, talking the most astounding nonsense. You must see her after breakfast. Will you pour out the coffee?"

"I'll see her now, if you like," I said, and he led me up the winding stair to the room at the top of the tower.

I found her quite sensible, but very feverish. I wrote a prescription, and rode Hurst's mare over to Eastbourne to get it made up. When I got back she was worse. It seemed to be a sort of aggravated marsh-fever. I reproached myself with having let her sit by the open window the night before. But I remembered with some satisfaction that I had told Hurst that the place was not quite healthy. I only wished I had insisted on it more strongly.

For the first day or two I thought it was merely a touch of marsh-fever, that would pass off with no worse consequence than a little weakness; but on the third day I perceived that she would die.

Hurst met me as I came from her bedside, stood aside on the narrow landing for me to pass, and followed me down into the little sitting-room, which, deprived for three days of her presence, already bore the air of a room long deserted. He came in after me and shut the door.

"You're wrong," he said abruptly, reading my thoughts as usual; "she won't die—she can't die."

---

[8] Mesmerism was an early form of hypnotism practiced in the nineteenth century and based on the pseudo-theories of German Franz Anton Mesmer (1734-1815)

"She will," I bluntly answered, for I am no believer in that worst refinement of torture known as 'breaking bad news gently.' "Send for any other man you choose. I'll consult with the whole College of Physicians if you like. But nothing short of a miracle can save her."

"And you don't believe in miracles," he answered quietly. "I do, you see."

"My dear old fellow, don't buoy yourself up with false hopes. I know my trade; I wish I could believe I didn't! Go back to her now; you have not very long to be together."

I wrung his hand; he returned the pressure, but said almost cheerfully—

"You know your trade, old man, but there are some things you don't know. Mine, for instance—I mean my wife's constitution. Now I know that thoroughly. And you mark my words—she won't die. You might as well say *I* was not long for this world."

"*You,*" I said with a touch of annoyance; "you're good for another thirty or forty years."

"Exactly so," he rejoined quickly, "and so is she. Her life's as good as mine; you'll see, she won't die."

At dusk on the next day she died. He was with her; he had not left her since he had told me that she would not die. He was sitting by her holding her hand. She had been unconscious for some time, when suddenly she dragged her hand from his, raised herself in bed, and cried out in a tone of acutest anguish—

"John! John! Let me go! For God's sake let me go!"

Then she fell back dead.

He would not understand—would not believe; he still sat by her, holding her hand, and calling on her by every name that love could teach him. I began to fear for his brain. He would not leave her, so by-and-by I brought him a cup of coffee in which I had mixed a strong opiate.[9]

In about an hour I went back and found him fast asleep with his face on the pillow close by the face of his dead wife. The gardener and I carried him down to my bedroom, and I sent for a woman from the village. He slept for twelve hours.

When he awoke his first words were—"She is not dead! I must go to her!"

I hoped that the sight of her, pale, and beautiful, and cold, with the white asters about her, and her white hands crossed on her breast, would convince him; but no.

He looked at her and said—"Bernard, you're no fool; you know as well as I do that this is not death. Why treat it so? It is some form of catalepsy.[10] If she should awake and find herself like this the shock might destroy her reason."

---

[9] Naturally occurring drugs derived from the opium poppy that calm the nervous system

[10] A paralyzed but living state where the patient cannot move

And, to the horror of the woman from the village, he flung the asters[11] on to the floor, covered the body with blankets, and sent for hot water bottles.

I was now quite convinced that his brain was affected, and I saw plainly enough that he would never consent to take the necessary steps for the funeral.

I began to wonder whether I had not better send for another doctor, for I felt that I did not care to try the opiate again on my own responsibility, and something must be done about the funeral.

I spent a day in considering the matter—a day spent by John Hurst beside his wife's body. Then I made up my mind to try all my powers to bring him to reason, and to this end I went once more into the chamber of death.

I found Hurst talking wildly, in low whispers. He seemed to be talking to someone who was not there. He did not know me, and suffered himself to be led away. He was, in fact, in the first stage of brain fever. I actually blessed his illness, because it opened a way out of the dilemma in which I found myself. I wired for a trained nurse from town, and for the local undertaker. In a week she was buried, and John Hurst still lay unconscious and unheeding; but I did not look forward to his first renewal of consciousness.

Yet his first conscious words were not the inquiry I dreaded. He only asked whether he'd been ill long, and what had been the matter. When I had told him he just nodded and went off to sleep again.

A few evenings later I found him excited and feverish, but quite himself, mentally. I said as much to him in answer to a question which he put to me—

"There's no brain disturbance now? I'm not mad or anything?"

"No, no, my dear fellow. Everything as it should be."

"Then," he answered slowly, "I must get up and go to her."

My worst fears were realized.

In moments of intense mental strain the truth sometimes overpowers all one's better resolves. It sounds brutal, horrible. I don't know what I meant to say; what I said was—"You can't; she's buried."

He sprang up in bed, and I caught him by the shoulders. "Then it's true!" he cried, "and I'm not mad. Oh, great God in heaven, let me go to her, let me go! It's true! It's true!"

I held him fast, and spoke. "I am strong—you know that. You are weak and ill; you are quite in my power—we're old friends, and there's nothing I wouldn't do to serve you. Tell me what you mean; I will do anything you wish." This I said to soothe him.

"Let me go to her," he said again.

"Tell me all about it," I repeated. "You are too ill to go to her. I will go, if you can collect yourself and tell me why. You could not walk five yards."

He looked at me doubtfully.

---

[11] Purple flowers used to adorn the dead in the Victorian age

"You'll help me? You won't say I'm mad, and have me shut up? You'll help me?"

"Yes, yes—I swear it!" All the time I was wondering what I should do to keep him from his mad purpose.

He lay back on his pillows, white and ghastly; his thin features and sunken eyes showed hawklike above the rough growth of his four weeks' beard. I took his hand. His pulse was rapid, and his lean fingers clenched themselves round mine.

"Look here," he said, "I don't know. There aren't any words to tell you how true it is. I am not mad, I am not wandering. I am as sane as you are. Now listen, and if you've a human heart in you, you'll help me. When I married her I gave up hypnotism and all the old studies; she hated the whole business. But before I gave it up I hypnotized her, and when she was completely under my control I forbade her soul to leave its body till my time came to die."

I breathed more freely. Now I understood why he had said, "She *cannot* die."

"My dear old man," I said gently, "dismiss these fancies, and face your grief boldly. You can't control the great facts of life and death by hypnotism. She is dead; she is dead, and her body lies in its place. But her soul is with God who gave it."

"No!" he cried, with such strength as the fever had left him. "No! no! Ever since I have been ill I have seen her, every day, every night, and always wringing her hands and moaning, 'Let me go, John—let me go.'"

"Those were her last words, indeed," I said; "it is natural that they should haunt you. See, you bade her soul not leave her body. It has left it, for she is dead."

His answer came almost in a whisper, borne on the wings of a long breathless pause.

"*She is dead, but her soul has not left her body.*"

I held his hand more closely, still debating what I should do.

"She comes to me," he went on; "she comes to me continually. She does not reproach, but she implores, 'Let me go, John, let me go!' And I have no more power now; I cannot let her go, I cannot reach her; I can do nothing, nothing. Ah!" he cried, with a sudden sharp change of voice that thrilled through me to the ends of my fingers and feet: "Ah, Kate, my life, I will come to you! No, no, you shan't be left alone among the dead. I am coming, my sweet."

He reached his arms out towards the door with a look of longing and love, so really, so patently addressed to a sentient presence, that I turned sharply to see if, in truth, perhaps nothing—of course—nothing.

"She is dead," I repeated stupidly. "I was obliged to bury her."

A shudder ran through him. "I must go and see for myself," he said.

Then I knew—all in a minute—what to do. "I will go," I said; "I will open her coffin, and if she is not—is not as other dead folk, I will bring her body back to this house."

"Will you go now?" he asked, with set lips. It was nigh on midnight.

I looked into his eyes. "Yes, now," I said, "but you must swear to lie still till I return."

"I swear it." I saw I could trust him, and I went to wake the nurse. He called weakly after me, "There's a lanthorn[12] in the toolshed, and Bernard—"

"Yes, my poor old chap."

"There's a screwdriver in the sideboard drawer."

I think until he said that I really meant to go. I am not accustomed to lie, even to mad people, and I think I meant it till then.

He leaned on his elbow, and looked at me with wide eyes. "Think," he said, "what she must feel. Out of the body, and yet tied to it, all alone among the dead. Oh, make haste, make haste, for if I am not mad, and I have really fettered her soul, there is but one way!"

"And that is?"

"I must die too. Her soul can leave her body when I die."

I called the nurse, and left him. I went out, and across the wold to the church, but I did not go in. I carried the screwdriver and the lanthorn, lest he should send the nurse to see if I had taken them. I leaned on the churchyard wall, and thought of her. I had loved the woman, and I remembered it in that hour.

As soon as I dared I went back to him—remember I believed him mad—and told the lie that I thought would give him most ease.

"Well?" he said, eagerly, as I entered. I signed to the nurse to leave us.

"There is no hope," I said. "You will not see your wife again till you meet her in heaven."

I laid down the screwdriver and the lanthorn, and sat down by him.

"You have seen her?"

"Yes."

"And there's no doubt?"

"No doubt."

"Then I *am* mad; but you're a good fellow, Bernard, and I'll never forget it in this world or the next."

He seemed calmer, and fell asleep with my hand in his. His last word was a "Thank you," that cut me like a knife.

When I went into his room next morning he was gone. But on his pillow a letter lay, painfully scrawled in pencil, and addressed to me.

> *You lied. Perhaps you meant kindly. You didn't understand. She is not dead. She has been with me again. Though her soul may not leave her body, thank God it can*

---

[12] Lamp

still speak to mine. That vault—it is worse than a mere grave. Goodbye.

I ran all the way to the church, and entered by the open door. The air was chill and dank after the crisp October sunlight. The stone that closed the vault of the Hursts of Hurstcote had been raised, and was lying beside the dark gaping hole in the chancel floor.

The nurse, who had followed me, came in before I could shake off the horror that held me moveless.

We both went down into the vault. Weak, exhausted by illness and sorrow, John Hurst had yet found strength to follow his love to the grave.

I tell you he had crossed that wold alone, in the grey of the chill dawn; alone he had raised the stone and gone down to her. He had opened her coffin, and he lay on the floor of the vault with his wife's body in his arms.

He had been dead some hours.

• • • • •

The brown eyes filled with tears when I told my wife this story.

"You were quite right, he was mad," she said. "Poor things, poor lovers!"

But sometimes when I wake in the grey morning, and between waking and sleeping, I think of all those things that I must shut out from my sleeping and my waking thoughts. I wonder was I right, or was he? Was he mad, or was I idiotically incredulous?

For—and it is this thing that haunts me—when I found them dead together in the vault, she had been buried five weeks. But the body that lay in John Hurst's arms, among the moldering coffins of the Hursts of Hurstcote, was perfect and beautiful as when first he clasped her in his arms, a bride.

Bram Stoker
(1847-1912)

There was no bigger name in horror fiction during the last part of the nineteenth century than Bram Stoker, due in large part to his publication of *Dracula* in May of 1897. Stoker failed, however, to be recognized as a ghost story writer because he published few of them in comparison to the large number published by the three pillars that held up the genre: Joseph Le Fanu, Charles Dickens, and M. R. James.

Stoker was born in Dublin, Ireland. He was the third of seven children. He suffered from an unknown illness and spent most his days bedridden until he recovered at the age of seven. His confinement to bed caused him to be a dreamer at a young age. Later he attended Trinity College, Dublin where he studied mathematics. As a young man Stoker became the personal assistant to the popular stage actor Henry Irving.

Bram Stoker started his career by writing short stories. "The Crystal Cup" was his first. It was published in 1872 when Stoker was twenty-five and, oddly enough, twenty-five years before *Dracula* was published.

In later supernatural tales he was big on using animals to add mystic and terror. In "The Squaw" (1893) he used black cats to weave the most fiendish horror tale since Edgar Allan Poe's "The Black Cat" (1843) published fifty years earlier. Rats were an animal of choice in a number of his tales including, of course, "The Burial of the Rats" (1896) and his best ghost story, "The Judge's House" (1891).

The latter was published in the *Holly Leaves* issue on December 5, 1891 and first appeared in book form during 1914, two years after his death. Stoker's wife, Florence, published it in the Stoker anthology *Dracula's Guest and Other Stories*. It contained the first publication of "Dracula's Guest," a segment cut from *Dracula* due to length.

Knowing he was not a preeminent ghost story teller, Stoker appears to have paid homage to Joseph Le Fanu by naming his most famous ghost story with the identical title of the first chapter in Fanu's "Mr. Justice Harbottle" (1872), which is also a ghost story centered around a judge.

It was originally published by Le Fanu as "An Account of Some Strange Disturbances in Aungier Street" (1851). Stoker became acquainted with Le Fanu when he was the unpaid theatre critic for the *Dublin Evening Mail* in November of 1871. Le Fanu was co-owner of the magazine at the time.

Apart from certain similarities to Le Fanu's story, there is a parallel to Stoker's life. Malcolm Malcolmson, the protagonist of Stoker's tale, is a mathematics major just like Stoker was at the university, though Malcolm attends Cambridge and Stoker attended Trinity.

The fate of Malcolm was his way of issuing a dig at Cambridge math students.

The Judge's House
1891

WHEN THE TIME for his examination drew near, Malcolm Malcolmson made up his mind to go somewhere to read by himself. He feared the attractions of the seaside, and also he feared completely rural isolation, for of old he knew its charms, and so he determined to find some unpretentious little town where there would be nothing to distract him. He refrained from asking suggestions from any of his friends, for he argued that each would recommend some place of which he had knowledge, and where he had already acquaintances.

As Malcolmson wished to avoid friends he had no wish to encumber himself with the attention of friends' friends and so he determined to look out for a place for himself. He packed a portmanteau[1] with some clothes and all the books he required, and then took ticket for the first name on the local timetable which he did not know.

When at the end of three hours' journey he alighted at Benchurch.[2] He felt satisfied that he had so far obliterated his tracks as to be sure of having a peaceful opportunity of pursuing his studies. He went straight to the one inn which the sleepy little place contained, and put up for the night. Benchurch was a market town, and once in three weeks was crowded to excess, but for the reminder of the twenty-one days it was as attractive as a desert.

Malcolmson looked around the day after his arrival to try to find quarters more isolated than even so quiet an inn as "The Good Traveller"[3] afforded.

There was only one place which took his fancy, and it certainly satisfied his wildest ideas regarding quiet; in fact, quiet was not the proper word to apply to it—desolation was the only term conveying any suitable idea of its isolation. It was an old, rambling, heavy-built house of the Jacobean style,[4] with heavy gables and windows, unusually small, and set higher than was customary in such houses, and was surrounded with a high brick wall massively built.

---

[1] Precursor to the suitcase

[2] Fictitious town and perhaps a play on Dunchurch village in Warwickshire, England

[3] Fictitious inn

[4] Style of homes built during the reign of James VI of Scotland (1567-1625) that were solidly built

Indeed, on examination, it looked more like a fortified house than an ordinary dwelling.

But all these things pleased Malcolmson.

Here, he thought, *is the very spot I have been looking for, and if I can only get opportunity of using it I shall be happy.* His joy was increased when he realized beyond doubt that it was not at present inhabited.

From the post-office he got the name of the agent, who was rarely surprised at the application to rent a part of the old house. Mr. Carnford, the local lawyer and agent, was a genial old gentleman, and frankly confessed his delight at anyone being willing to live in the house.

"To tell you the truth," said he, "I should be only too happy, on behalf of the owners, to let anyone have the house rent free, for a term of years if only to accustom the people here to see it inhabited. It has been so long empty that some kind of absurd prejudice has grown up about it, and this can be best put down by its occupation—if only," he added with a sly glance at Malcolmson, "by a scholar like yourself, who wants its quiet for a time."

Malcolmson thought it needless to ask the agent about the "absurd prejudice;" he knew he would get more information, if he should require it, on that subject from other quarters. He paid his three months' rent, got a receipt, and the name of an old woman who would probably undertake to "do" for him, and came away with the keys in his pocket. He then went to the landlady of the inn, who was a cheerful and most kindly person, and asked her advice as to such stores and provisions as he would be likely to require. She threw up her hands in amazement when he told her where he was going to settle himself.

"Not in the Judge's House!" she said, and grew pale as she spoke.

He explained the locality of the house, saying that he did not know its name.

When he had finished she answered: "Aye, sure enough—sure enough the very place! It is the Judge's House sure enough."

He asked her to tell him about the place, why so called, and what there was against it. She told him that it was so called locally because it had been many years before—how long she could not say, as she was herself from another part of the country, but she thought it must have been a hundred years or more—the abode of a judge who was held in great terror on account of his harsh sentences and his hostility to prisoners at Assizes.[5]

As to what there was against the house she could not tell. She had often asked, but no one could inform her, but there was a general feeling that there was *something*, and for her own part she

---

[5] Courts that met quarterly in England and Wales, which heard the most serious cases and held the accused in mini-prisons

would not take all the money in Drinkwater's Bank[6] and stay in the house an hour by herself. Then she apologized to Malcolmson for her disturbing talk.

"It is too bad of me, sir, and you—and a young gentleman, too—if you will pardon me saying it, going to live there all alone. If you were my boy—and you'll excuse me for saying it—you wouldn't sleep there a night, not if I had to go there myself and pull the big alarm bell that's on the roof!"

The good creature was so manifestly in earnest, and was so kindly in her intentions, that Malcolmson, although amused, was touched. He told her kindly how much he appreciated her interest in him, and added:

"But, my dear Mrs. Witham, indeed you need not be concerned about me! A man who is reading for the Mathematical Tripos[7] has too much to think of to be disturbed by any of these mysterious 'somethings,' and his work is of too exact and prosaic a kind to allow of his having any order in his mind for mysteries of any kind. Harmonical Progression,[8] Permutations[9] and Combinations,[10] and Elliptic Functions[11] have sufficient mysteries for me!"

Mrs. Witham kindly undertook to see after his commissions, and he went himself to look for the old woman who had been recommended to him. When he turned to the Judge's House with her, after an interval of a couple of hours, he found Mrs. Witham herself waiting with several men and boys carrying parcels, and an upholsterer's man with a bed in a cart, for she said, though table and chairs might be all very well, a bed that hadn't been aired for maybe fifty years was not proper for young ones to lie on. She was evidently curious to see the inside of the house, and though manifestly so afraid of the 'somethings' that at the slightest sound she clutched on to Malcolmson, whom she never left for a moment, went over the whole place.

After his examination of the house, Malcolmson decided to take up his abode in the great dining-room, which was big enough to serve for all his requirements, and Mrs. Witham, with the aid of the charwoman,[12] Mrs. Dempster, proceeded to arrange matters. When the hampers were brought in and unpacked, Malcolmson saw that

---

[6] A joke about Peter Drinkwater's very profitable steam engine cotton mill started in 1789 and called the Bank Top Mill in Manchester, England that had a workforce of 500 people, see *The Life of Robert Owen*, C. Knight, 1971, pg. 35

[7] An extremely difficult math test given to undergraduate students at Cambridge University that started in 1780

[8] A sequence of fractions based on the reciprocal of the sequence number before it: $1/b$, $1/b+c$, $1/b+2c$, . . .

[9] Arranging the members of a set into a sequence

[10] Arranging the members of a set into a combination

[11] A mathematical function meromorphic on a letter where two non-zero complex numbers exist in the function

[12] House cleaner

with much kind forethought she had sent from her own kitchen sufficient provisions to last for a few days.

Before going she expressed all sorts of kind wishes, and at the door turned and said: "And perhaps, sir, as the room is big and draughty it might be well to have one of those big screens put round your bed at night—though truth to tell, I would die myself if I were to be so shut in with all kinds of—of 'things,' that put their heads round the sides or over the top, and look on me!"

The image which she had called up was too much for her nerves and she fled incontinently.

Mrs. Dempster sniffed in a superior manner as the landlady disappeared, and remarked that for her own part she wasn't afraid of all the bogies in the kingdom.

"I'll tell you what it is, sir," she said, "bogies is all kinds and sorts of things—except bogies! Rats and mice, and beetles and creaky doors, and loose slates, and broken panes, and stiff drawer handles, that stay out when you pull them and then fall down in the middle of the night. Look at the wainscot of the room! It is old—hundreds of years old! Do you think there's no rats and beetles there? And do you imagine, sir, that you won't see none of them? Rats is bogies, I tell you, and bogies is rats, and don't you get to think anything else!"

"Mrs. Dempster," said Malcolmson gravely, making her a polite bow, "you know more than a Senior Wrangler![13] And let me say that, as a mark of esteem for your indubitable soundness of head and heart, I shall, when I go, give you possession of this house, and let you stay here by yourself for the last two months of my tenancy, for four weeks will serve my purpose."

"Thank you kindly, sir!" she answered, "but I couldn't sleep away from home a night. I am in Greenhow's Charity,[14] and if I slept a night away from my rooms I should lose all I have got to live on. The rules is very strict, and there's too many watching for a vacancy for me to run any risks in the matter. Only for that, sir, I'd gladly come here and attend on you altogether during your stay."

"My good woman," said Malcolmson hastily, "I have come here on a purpose to obtain solitude, and believe me that I am grateful to the late Greenhow for having organized his admirable charity—whatever it is—that I am perforce denied the opportunity of suffering from such a form of temptation! Saint Anthony himself could not be more rigid on the point!"[15]

---

[13] Term for the highest-performing mathematics undergraduate at Cambridge

[14] Thomas Greenhow (1792-1881) was an English medical doctor who started a ward for patients under his care, see *Thomas Michael Greehow*, Monthly Chronicle of North-Country Lore and Legend, 1891, Vols. 1-5, pgs. 251-253 and was a proponent of vaccination to eradicate small pox, see *An Estimate of the True Value of Vaccination as a Security Against Small Pox*, Thomas Greenhow, 1825

[15] Saint Anthony of Padua (1195-1231) was a saint of the Catholic Church who taught the avoidance of temptation in the life of Christian

The old woman laughed harshly. "Ah, you young gentlemen," she said, "you don't fear for nought, and belike you'll get all the solitude you want here."

She set to work with her cleaning, and by nightfall, when Malcolmson returned from his walk—he always had one of his books to study as he walked—he found the room swept and tidied, a fire burning on the old hearth, the lamp lit, and the table spread for supper with Mrs. Witham's excellent fare.

"This is comfort indeed," he said, and rubbed his hands.

When he had finished his supper, and lifted the tray to the other end of the great oak dining-table, he got out his books again, put fresh wood on the fire, trimmed his lamp, and set himself down to a spell of real hard work. He went on without a pause till about eleven o'clock, when he knocked off for a bit to fix his fire and lamp, and to make himself a cup of tea.

He had always been a tea-drinker, and during his college life had sat late at work and had taken tea late. The rest was a great luxury to him, and he enjoyed it with a sense of delicious voluptuous ease. The renewed fire leaped and sparkled, and threw quaint shadows through the great old room, and as he sipped his hot tea he reveled in the sense of isolation from his kind. Then it was that he began to notice for the first time what a noise the rats were making.

Surely, he thought, *they cannot have been at it all the time I was reading. Had they been, I must have noticed it!*

Presently, when the noise increased, he satisfied himself that it was really new. It was evident that at first the rats had been frightened at the presence of a stranger, and the light of fire and lamp, but that as the time went on they had grown bolder and were now disporting themselves as was their wont.

How busy they were—and hark to the strange noises! Up and down the old wainscot, over the ceiling and under the floor they raced, and gnawed, and scratched! Malcolmson smiled to himself as he recalled to mind the saying of Mrs. Dempster, "Bogies is rats, and rats is bogies!"

The tea began to have its effect of intellectual and nervous stimulus, he saw with joy another long spell of work to be done before the night was past, and in the sense of security which it gave him, he allowed himself the luxury of a good look round the room.

He took his lamp in one hand, and went all round, wondering that so quaint and beautiful an old house had been so long neglected. The carving of the oak on the panels of the wainscot was fine, and on and round the doors and windows it was beautiful and of rare merit. There were some old pictures on the walls, but they were coated so thick with dust and dirt that he could not distinguish any detail of them, though he held his lamp as high as he could over his head.

Here and there as he went round he saw some crack or hole blocked for a moment by the face of a rat with its bright eyes glittering in the light, but in an instant it was gone, and a squeak and a scamper followed.

The thing that most struck him, however, was the rope of the great alarm bell on the roof, which hung down in a corner of the room on the right-hand side of the fireplace. He pulled up close to the hearth a great high-backed carved oak chair, and sat down to his last cup of tea.

When this was done he made up the fire, and went back to his work, sitting at the corner of the table, having the fire to his left. For a little while the rats disturbed him somewhat with their perpetual scampering, but he got accustomed to the noise as one does to the ticking of the clock or to the roar of moving water, and he became so immersed in his work that everything in the world, except the problem which he was trying to solve, passed away from him.

He suddenly looked up, his problem was still unsolved, and there was in the air that sense of the hour before the dawn, which is so dread to doubtful life. The noise of the rats had ceased. Indeed it seemed to him that it must have ceased but lately and that it was the sudden cessation which had disturbed him. The fire had fallen low, but still it threw out a deep red glow. As he looked he started in spite of his *sang froid.*[16]

There, on the great high-backed carved oak chair by the right side of the fireplace sat an enormous rat, steadily glaring at him with baleful eyes. He made a motion to it as though to hunt it away, but it did not stir. Then he made the motion of throwing something. Still it did not stir, but showed its great white teeth angrily, and its cruel eyes shone in the lamplight with an added vindictiveness.

Malcolmson felt amazed, and seizing the poker from the hearth ran at it to kill it. Before, however, he could strike it the rat, with a squeak that sounded like the concentration of hate, jumped upon the floor, and, running up the rope of the alarm bell, disappeared in the darkness beyond the range of the green-shaded lamp. Instantly, strange to say, the noisy scampering of the rats in the wainscot began again.

By this time Malcolmson's mind was quite off the problem, and as a shrill cockcrow outside told him of the approach of morning, he went to bed and to sleep.

He slept so sound that he was not even waked by Mrs. Dempster coming in to make up his room. It was only when she had tidied up the place and got his breakfast ready and tapped on the screen which closed in his bed that he woke. He was a little tired still after his night's hard work, but a strong cup of tea soon freshened him up and, taking his book, he went out for his morning walk, bringing with him a few sandwiches lest he should not care to return till dinnertime.

----

[16] Composure under the circumstances

He found a quiet walk between high elms some way outside the town, and here he spent the greater part of the day studying his Laplace. On his return he looked in to see Mrs. Witham and to thank her for her kindness. When she saw him coming through the diamond-paned bay window of her sanctum she came out to meet him and asked him in.

She looked at him searchingly and shook her head as she said: "You must not overdo it, sir. You are paler this morning than you should be. Too late hours and too hard work on the brains isn't good for any man! But tell me, sir, how did you pass the night? Well, I hope? But, my heart! sir, I was glad when Mrs. Dempster told me this morning that you were all right and sleeping sound when she went in."

"Oh, I was all right," he answered smiling. "The 'somethings' didn't worry me, as yet. Only the rats, and they had a circus, I tell you, all over the place. There was one wicked-looking old devil that sat up on my own chair by the fire, and wouldn't go till I took the poker to him, and then he ran up the rope of the alarm bell and got to somewhere up the wall or the ceiling—I couldn't see where, it was so dark."

"Mercy on us," said Mrs. Witham, "an old devil, and sitting on a chair by the fireside! Take care, sir! take care! There's many a true word spoken in jest."

"How do you mean? 'Pon my word, I don't understand."

"An old devil! The old devil, perhaps. There! sir, you needn't laugh," for Malcolmson had broken into a hearty peal. "You young folks think it easy to laugh at things that makes older ones shudder. Never mind, sir! never mind! Please God, you'll laugh all the time. It's what I wish you myself!" and the good lady beamed all over in sympathy with his enjoyment, her fears gone for a moment.

"Oh, forgive me," said Malcolmson presently. "Don't think me rude, but the idea was too much for me—that the old devil himself was on the chair last night!" And at the thought he laughed again. Then he went home to dinner.

This evening the scampering of the rats began earlier, indeed it had been going on before his arrival, and only ceased whilst his presence by its freshness disturbed them. After dinner he sat by the fire for a while and had a smoke, and then, having cleared his table, began to work as before. Tonight the rats disturbed him more than they had done on the previous night.

How they scampered up and down and under and over! How they squeaked and scratched and gnawed! How they, getting bolder by degrees, came to the mouths of their holes and to the chinks and cracks and crannies in the wainscoting till their eyes shone like tiny lamps as the firelight rose and fell. But to him, now doubtless accustomed to them, their eyes were not wicked, only their playfulness touched him.

Sometimes the boldest of them made sallies out on the floor or along the moldings of the wainscot. Now and again as they disturbed him Malcolmson made a sound to frighten them, smiting the table with his hand or giving a fierce "Hsh, hsh," so that they fled straightway to their holes.

And so the early part of the night wore on, and despite the noise Malcolmson got more and more immersed in his work.

All at once he stopped, as on the previous night, being overcome by a sudden silence. There was not the faintest sound of gnaw, or scratch, or squeak. The silence was as of the grave.

He remembered the odd occurrence of the previous night, and instinctively he looked at the chair standing close by the fireside. And then a very odd sensation thrilled through him.

There, on the great old high-backed carved oak chair beside the fireplace sat the same enormous rat, steadily glaring at him with baleful eyes.

Instinctively he took the nearest thing to his hand, a book of logarithms,[17] and flung it at it. The book was badly aimed and the rat did not stir, so again the poker performance of the previous night was repeated, and again the rat, being closely pursued, fled up the rope of the alarm bell.

Strangely, too, the departure of this rat was instantly followed by the renewal of the noise made by the general rat community. On this occasion, as on the previous one, Malcolmson could not see at what part of the room the rat disappeared, for the green shade of his lamp left the upper part of the room in darkness and the fire had burned low.

On looking at his watch he found it was close on midnight, and, not sorry for the *divertissement*, he made up his fire and made himself his nightly pot of tea. He had got through a good spell of work, and thought himself entitled to a cigarette, and so he sat on the great carved oak chair before the fire and enjoyed it.

Whilst smoking he began to think that he would like to know where the rat disappeared to, for he had certain ideas for the morrow not entirely disconnected with a rattrap. Accordingly he lit another lamp and placed it so that it would shine well into the right-hand corner of the wall by the fireplace.

Then he got all the books he had with him, and placed them handy to throw at the vermin. Finally he lifted the rope of the alarm bell and placed the end of it on the table, fixing the extreme end under the lamp. As he handled it he could not help noticing how pliable it was, especially for so strong a rope and one not in use.

You could hang a man with it, he thought to himself.

When his preparations were made he looked around, and said complacently: "There now, my friend, I think we shall learn something of you this time!"

He began his work again, and though, as before, somewhat disturbed at first by the noise of the rats, soon lost himself in his proposition and problems.

---

[17] Book containing logarithmic formulas that are the opposite of the exponent of a number

Again he was called to his immediate surroundings suddenly. This time it might not have been the sudden silence only which took his attention; there was a slight movement of the rope, and the lamp moved.

Without stirring, he looked to see if his pile of books was within range, and then cast his eye along the rope. As he looked he saw the great rat drop from the rope on the oak arm-chair and sit there glaring at him. He raised a book in his right hand, and taking careful aim, flung it at the rat. The latter, with a quick movement, sprang aside and dodged the missile. Then he took another book, and a third, and flung them one after the other at the rat, but each time unsuccessfully.

At last, as he stood with a book poised in his hand to throw, the rat squeaked and seemed afraid. This made Malcolmson more than ever eager to strike, and the book flew and struck the rat a resounding blow. It gave a terrified squeak, and turning on his pursuer a look of terrible malevolence, ran up the chair-back and made a great jump to the rope of the alarm bell and ran up it like lightning. The lamp rocked under the sudden strain, but it was a heavy one and did not topple over.

Malcolmson kept his eyes on the rat, and saw it by the light of the second lamp leap to a molding of the wainscot and disappear through a hole in one of the great pictures which hung on the wall, obscured and invisible through its coating of dirt and dust.

"I shall look up my friend's habitation in the morning," said the student, as he went over to collect his books. "The third picture from the fireplace, I shall not forget."

He picked up the books one by one, commenting on them as he lifted them. "*Conic Sections*[18] he does not mind, nor *Cycloid Oscillations*,[19] nor the *Principia*,[20] nor *Quaternions*,[21] nor *Thermodynamics*.[22] Now for a look at the book that fetched him!"

Malcolmson took it up and looked at it. As he did so he started, and a sudden pallor overspread his face. He looked round uneasily and shivered slightly, as he murmured to himself: "The Bible my mother gave me! What an odd coincidence."

He sat down to work again, and the rats in the wainscot renewed their gambols. They did not disturb him, however; somehow their presence gave him a sense of companionship. But he could not attend to his work, and after striving to master the subject on which he was engaged gave it up in despair, and went to bed as the first streak of dawn stole in through the eastern window.

---

[18] A geometry book on mathematical equations for three-dimensional cones
[19] Text on the oscillation movements of physical bodies and the Sir Isaac Newton (1642-1726) equations that govern them
[20] Three part series of books by Sir Isaac Newton (1642-1726) titled *Philosophiæ Naturalis Principia Mathematica* (1687) that sets forth, in mathematical equations, the laws of motion
[21] A text on complex and imaginary number sequences in mathematics
[22] Laws of heat transfer as described in mathematical equations

He slept heavily but uneasily, and dreamed much, and when Mrs. Dempster woke him late in the morning he seemed ill at ease, and for a few minutes did not seem to realize exactly where he was. His first request rather surprised the servant.

"Mrs. Dempster, when I am out today I wish you would get the steps and dust or wash those pictures—specially that one the third from the fireplace—I want to see what they are."

Late in the afternoon Malcolmson worked at his books in the shaded walk, and the cheerfulness of the previous day came back to him as the day wore on, and he found that his reading was progressing well. He had worked out to a satisfactory conclusion all the problems which had as yet baffled him, and it was in a state of jubilation that he paid a visit to Mrs. Witham at "The Good Traveller."

He found a stranger in the cozy sitting-room with the landlady, who was introduced to him as Dr. Thornhill. She was not quite at ease, and this, combined with the doctor's plunging at once into a series of questions, made Malcolmson come to the conclusion that his presence was not an accident, so without preliminary he said: "Dr. Thornhill, I shall with pleasure answer you any question you may choose to ask me if you will answer me one question first."

The doctor seemed surprised, but he smiled and answered at once, "Done! What is it?"

"Did Mrs. Witham ask you to come here and see me and advise me?"

Dr. Thornhill for a moment was taken aback, and Mrs. Witham got fiery red and turned away, but the doctor was a frank and ready man, and he answered at once and openly: "She did, but she didn't intend you to know it. I suppose it was my clumsy haste that made you suspect. She told me that she did not like the idea of your being in that house all by yourself, and that she thought you took too much strong tea. In fact, she wants me to advise you, if possible, to give up the tea and the very late hours. I was a keen student in my time, so I suppose I may take the liberty of a college man, and without offence, advise you not quite as a stranger."

Malcolmson with a bright smile held out his hand. "Shake—as they say in America," he said. "I must thank you for your kindness, and Mrs. Witham too, and your kindness deserves a return on my part. I promise to take no more strong tea—no tea at all till you let me—and I shall go to bed tonight at one o'clock at latest. Will that do?"

"Capital," said the doctor. "Now tell us all that you noticed in the old house," and so Malcolmson then and there told in minute detail all that had happened in the last two nights. He was interrupted every now and then by some exclamation from Mrs. Witham, till finally when he told of the episode of the Bible the landlady's pent-up emotions found vent in a shriek, and it was not till a stiff glass of brandy and water had been administered that she grew composed again.

Dr. Thornhill listened with a face of growing gravity, and when the narrative was complete and Mrs. Witham had been restored he asked: "The rat always went up the rope of the alarm bell?"

"Always."

"I suppose you know," said the Doctor after a pause, "what that rope is?"

"No?"

"It is," said the Doctor slowly, "the very rope which the hangman used for all the victims of the Judge's judicial rancor!"

Here he was interrupted by another scream from Mrs. Witham, and steps had to be taken for her recovery. Malcolmson having looked at his watch, and found that it was close to his dinner-hour, had gone home before her complete recovery.

When Mrs. Witham was herself again she almost assailed the Doctor with angry questions as to what he meant by putting such horrible ideas into the poor young man's mind. "He has quite enough there already to upset him," she added.

Dr. Thornhill replied: "My dear madam, I had a distinct purpose in it! I wanted to draw his attention to the bell-rope, and to fix it there. It may be that he is in a highly overwrought state, and has been studying too much, although I am bound to say that he seems as sound and healthy a young man, mentally and bodily, as ever I saw—but then the rats—and that suggestion of the devil." The doctor shook his head and went on. "I would have offered to go and stay the first night with him but that I felt sure it would have been a cause of offence. He may get in the night some strange fright or hallucination, and if he does I want him to pull that rope. All alone as he is it will give us warning, and we may reach him in time to be of service. I shall be sitting up pretty late tonight and shall keep my ears open. Do not be alarmed if Benchurch gets a surprise before morning."

"Oh, Doctor, what do you mean? What do you mean?"

"I mean this, that possibly—nay, more probably—we shall hear the great alarm-bell from the Judge's House tonight," and the Doctor made about an effective an exit as could be thought of.

When Malcolmson arrived home he found that it was a little after his usual time, and Mrs. Dempster had gone away—the rules of Greenhow's Charity were not to be neglected. He was glad to see that the place was bright and tidy with a cheerful fire and a well-trimmed lamp.

The evening was colder than might have been expected in April, and a heavy wind was blowing with such rapidly-increasing strength that there was every promise of a storm during the night.

For a few minutes after his entrance the noise of the rats ceased, but so soon as they became accustomed to his presence they began again. He was glad to hear them, for he felt once more the feeling of companionship in their noise, and his mind ran back to the strange fact that they only ceased to manifest themselves when the other—the great rat with the baleful eyes—came upon the scene.

The reading-lamp only was lit and its green shade kept the ceiling and the upper part of the room in darkness so that the cheerful light from the hearth spreading over the floor and shining on the white cloth laid over the end of the table was warm and cheery. Malcolmson sat down to his dinner with a good appetite and a buoyant spirit. After his dinner and a cigarette he sat steadily down to work, determined not to let anything disturb him, for he remembered his promise to the doctor, and made up his mind to make the best of the time at his disposal.

For an hour or so he worked all right, and then his thoughts began to wander from his books. The actual circumstances around him, and the calls on his physical attention, and his nervous susceptibility were not to be denied.

By this time the wind had become a gale, and the gale a storm. The old house, solid though it was, seemed to shake to its foundation, and the storm roared and raged through its many chimneys and its queer old gables, producing strange, unearthly sounds in the empty rooms and corridors. Even the great alarm-bell on the roof must have felt the force of the wind, for the rope rose and fell slightly, as though the bell were moved a little from time to time, and the limber rope fell on the oak floor with a hard and hollow sound.

As Malcolmson listened to it he bethought himself of the doctor's words, "It is the rope which the hangman used for the victims of the Judge's judicial rancor," and he went over to the corner of the fireplace and took it in his hand to look at it.

There seemed a sort of deadly interest in it, and as he stood there he lost himself for a moment in speculation as to who these victims were, and the grim wish of the Judge to have such a ghastly relic ever under his eyes. As he stood there the swaying of the bell on the roof still lifted the rope now and again, but presently there came a new sensation—a sort of tremor in the rope, as though something was moving along it.

Looking up instinctively Malcolmson saw the great rat coming slowly down towards him, glaring at him steadily. He dropped the rope and started back with a muttered curse, and the rat turning ran up the slope again and disappeared, and at the same instant Malcolmson became conscious that the noise of the other rats, which had ceased for a while, began again.

All this set him thinking, and it occurred to him that he had not investigated the lair of the rat or looked at the pictures, as he had intended. He lit the other lamp without the shade, and, holding it up went and stood opposite the third picture from the fireplace on the right-hand side where he had seen the rat disappear on the previous night.

At the first glance he started back so suddenly that he almost dropped the lamp, and a deadly pallor overspread his face.

His knees shook, and heavy drops of sweat came on his forehead, and he trembled like an aspen. But he was young and plucky, and pulled himself together, and after the pause of a few seconds stepped forward again, raised the lamp, and examined the picture which had been dusted and washed, and now stood out clearly.

It was of a judge dressed in his robes of scarlet and ermine. His face was strong and merciless, evil, crafty and vindictive, with a sensual mouth, hooked nose of ruddy color, and shaped like the beak of a bird of prey. The rest of the face was of a cadaverous color. The eyes were of peculiar brilliance and with a terribly malignant expression.

As he looked at them, Malcolmson grew cold, for he saw there the very counterpart of the eyes of the great rat. The lamp almost fell from his hand, he saw the rat with its baleful eyes peering out through the hole in the corner of the picture, and noted the sudden cessation of the noise of the other rats. However, he pulled himself together, and went on with his examination of the picture.

The Judge was seated in a great high-backed carved oak chair, on the right-hand side of a great stone fireplace where, in the corner, a rope hung down from the ceiling, its end lying coiled on the floor. With a feeling of something like horror, Malcolmson recognized the scene of the room as it stood, and gazed around him in an awestruck manner as though he expected to find some strange presence behind him. Then he looked over to the corner of the fireplace—and with a loud cry he let the lamp fall from his hand.

There, in the judge's armchair, with the rope hanging behind, sat the rat with the Judge's baleful eyes, now intensified as with a fiendish leer. Save for the howling of the storm without there was silence.

The fallen lamp recalled Malcolmson to himself. Fortunately it was of metal, and so the oil was not spilt. However, the practical need of attending to it settled at once his nervous apprehensions. When he had turned it out, he wiped his brow and thought for a moment.

"This will not do," he said to himself. "If I go on like this I shall become a crazy fool. This must stop! I promised the doctor I would not take tea. Faith, he was pretty right! My nerves must have been getting into a queer state. Funny I did not notice it. I never felt better in my life. However, it is all right now, and I shall not be such a fool again."

Then he mixed himself a good stiff glass of brandy and water and resolutely sat down to his work.

It was nearly an hour when he looked up from his book, disturbed by the sudden stillness. Without, the wind howled and roared louder than ever, and the rain drove in sheets against the windows, beating like hail on the glass, but within there was no sound whatever save the echo of the wind as it roared in the great chimney, and now and then a hiss as a few raindrops found their way down the chimney in a lull of the storm.

The fire had fallen low and had ceased to flame, though it threw out a red glow. Malcolmson listened attentively, and presently heard a thin, squeaking noise, very faint. It came from the corner of the room where the rope hung down, and he thought it was the creaking of the rope on the floor as the swaying of the bell raised and lowered it. Looking up, however, he saw in the dim light the great rat clinging to the rope and gnawing it. The rope was already nearly gnawed through—he could see the lighter color where the strands were laid bare.

As he looked the job was completed, and the severed end of the rope fell clattering on the oaken floor, whilst for an instant the great rat remained like a knob or tassel at the end of the rope, which now began to sway to and fro. Malcolmson felt for a moment another pang of terror as he thought that now the possibility of calling the outer world to his assistance was cut off, but an intense anger took its place, and seizing the book he was reading he hurled it at the rat.

The blow was well-aimed, but before the missile could reach him the rat dropped off and struck the floor with a soft thud.

Malcolmson instantly rushed over towards him, but it darted away and disappeared in the darkness of the shadows of the room. Malcolmson felt that his work was over for the night, and determined then and there to vary the monotony of the proceedings by a hunt for the rat, and took off the green shade of the lamp so as to insure a wider spreading light. As he did so the gloom of the upper part of the room was relieved, and in the new flood of light, great by comparison with the previous darkness, the pictures on the wall stood out boldly.

From where he stood, Malcolmson saw right opposite to him the third picture on the wall from the right of the fireplace. He rubbed his eyes in surprise, and then a great fear began to come upon him.

In the center of the picture was a great irregular patch of brown canvas, as fresh as when it was stretched on the frame. The background was as before, with chair and chimney-corner and rope, but the figure of the Judge had disappeared.

Malcolmson, almost in a chill of horror, turned slowly round, and then he began to shake and tremble like a man in a palsy. His strength seemed to have left him, and he was incapable of action or movement, hardly even of thought.

He could only see and hear.

There, on the great high-backed carved oak chair sat the judge in his robes of scarlet and ermine, with his baleful eyes glaring vindictively, and a smile of triumph on the resolute cruel mouth, as he lifted with his hands a *black cap*.[23]

Malcolmson felt as if the blood was running from his heart, as one does in moments of prolonged suspense. There was a singing in his ears.

---

[23] Black square of fabric worn on the head of an English judge when pronouncing a death sentence

Without, he could hear the roar and howl of the tempest, and through it, swept on the storm, came the striking of midnight by the great chimes in the marketplace. He stood for a space of time that seemed to him endless still as a statue, and with wide-open, horrorstruck eyes, breathless. As the clock struck, so the smile of triumph on the Judge's face intensified, and at the last stroke of midnight he placed the black cap on his head.

Slowly and deliberately the Judge rose from his chair and picked up the piece of rope of the alarm bell which lay on the floor, drew it through his hands as if he enjoyed its touch and then deliberately began to knot one end of it, fashioning it into a noose.

This he tightened and tested with his foot, pulling hard at it till he was satisfied and then making a running noose of it, which he held in his hand. Then he began to move along the table on the opposite side of Malcolmson keeping his eyes on him until he had passed him, when with a quick movement he stood in front of the door. Malcolmson then began to feel that he was trapped, and tried to think of what he should do.

There was some fascination in the Judge's eyes, which he never took off him, and he had, perforce, to look. He saw the Judge approach—still keeping between him and the door—and raise the noose and throw it towards him as if to entangle him. With a great effort he made a quick movement to one side, and saw the rope fall beside him, and heard it strike the oaken floor.

Again the Judge raised the noose and tried to ensnare him, ever keeping his baleful eyes fixed on him, and each time by a mighty effort the student just managed to evade it.

So this went on for many times, the Judge seeming never discouraged nor discomposed at failure, but playing as a cat does with a mouse.

At last in despair, which had reached its climax, Malcolmson cast a quick glance round him. The lamp seemed to have blazed up, and there was a fairly good light in the room. At the many rat-holes and in the chinks and crannies of the wainscot he saw the rats' eyes, and this aspect, that was purely physical, gave him a gleam of comfort. He looked round and saw that the rope of the great alarm bell was laden with rats. Every inch of it was covered with them, and more and more were pouring through the small circular hole in the ceiling whence it emerged, so that with their weight the bell was beginning to sway.

Hark! it had swayed till the clapper had touched the bell. The sound was but a tiny one, but the bell was only beginning to sway, and it would increase.

At the sound the Judge, who had been keeping his eyes fixed on Malcolmson, looked up, and a scowl of diabolical anger overspread his face. His eyes fairly glowed like hot coals, and he stamped his foot with a sound that seemed to make the house shake.

A dreadful peal of thunder broke overhead as he raised the rope again, whilst the rats kept running up and down the rope as though working against time. This time, instead of throwing it, he drew close to his victim, and held open the noose as he approached.

As he came closer there seemed something paralyzing in his very presence, and Malcolmson stood rigid as a corpse. He felt the Judge's icy fingers touch his throat as he adjusted the rope.

The noose tightened—tightened.

Then the Judge, taking the rigid form of the student in his arms, carried him over and placed him standing in the oak chair, and stepping up beside him, put his hand up and caught the end of the swaying rope of the alarm-bell.

As he raised his hand the rats fled squeaking and disappeared through the hole in the ceiling. Taking the end of the noose which was round Malcolmson's neck he tied it to the hanging bell-rope, and then descending pulled away the chair.

* * * * *

When the alarm-bell of the Judge's House began to sound a crowd soon assembled. Lights and torches of various kinds appeared, and soon a silent crowd was hurrying to the spot. They knocked loudly at the door, but there was no reply. Then they burst in the door, and poured into the great dining-room, the doctor at the head.

There at the end of the rope of the great alarm-bell hung the body of the student, and on the face of the Judge in the picture was a malignant smile.

Robert Chambers
(1865-1933)

American Robert Chambers had little public renown until he published a collection of short stories at the age of thirty—*The King in Yellow* (1895). It contains a haunting church watchman that will not soon be forgotten. On the overall collection Lovecraft stated, "*The King in Yellow*, a series of vaguely connected shorts stories having as a background a monstrous and suppressed book whose perusal brings fright, madness and spectral tragedy, really achieves notable heights of cosmic fear . . .."[1]

The title of the book, which has an almost cheerful feel to it, reveals little of the horrific tales that await inside its cover. Chambers fashioned the title after a fictitious play of his own invention. Purportedly, it would cause any person who saw it acted out to go insane. The various supernatural stories of the collection reference parts of the play, giving it a nice touch of realism.

Throughout the collection the color yellow serves a ghastly purpose just as it does in fellow American Charlotte Perkins Gilman's "The Yellow Wallpaper" (1892), published three years earlier. In Gilman's horror story the wallpaper has a dire effect on the person staying in the room. In Chamber's collection of stories the color yellow is weaved throughout his supernatural stories as a warning sign of death and destruction that is surely to follow. Note also that the *The King in Yellow* was published the same year that

---

[1] *Supernatural Horror in Literature*, H. P. Lovecraft, 1927, pg. 29

follow American Ralph Adams Cram published his ominous collection *Black Spirits and White*.

"The Yellow Sign" is the best ghost short story Chambers wrote. H. P. Lovecraft called it a "most powerful tale."[2] Its symbols and archaic literary signs remind one of an M. R. James tale minus a protagonist who is an expert in medieval history.

Chambers would go on to pen a number of fantasy and horror novels in the years after *The King in Yellow*; they included *The Maker of Moons* (1896), *In Search of the Unknown* (1904), *The Slayer of Souls* (1920). In 1897 his play *The Witch of Ellangowan* was produced and had a short run. None would compare to the climatic ending of "The Yellow Sign."

---

[2] Ibid.

The Yellow Sign
1895

Let the red dawn surmise
What we shall do,
When this blue starlight dies
And all is through.[1]

I

THERE ARE SO many things which are impossible to explain!
Why should certain chords in music make me think of the
brown and golden tints of autumn foliage? Why should the Mass of
Sainte Cecile[2] send my thoughts wandering among caverns whose
walls blaze with ragged masses of virgin silver? What was it in the
roar and turmoil of Broadway[3] at six o'clock that flashed before my
eyes the picture of a still Breton forest[4] where sunlight filtered
through spring foliage and Sylvia bent, half curiously, half tenderly,
over a small green lizard, murmuring: "To think that this is also a
little ward of God!"

When I first saw the watchman his back was toward me. I
looked at him indifferently until he went into the church. I paid no
more attention to him than I had to any other man who lounged
through Washington Square that morning, and when I shut my
window and turned back into my studio I had forgotten him.

Late in the afternoon, the day being warm, I raised the window
again and leaned out to get a sniff of the air. A man was standing
in the courtyard of the church, and I noticed him again with as
little interest as I had that morning. I looked across the square to
where the fountain was playing and then, with my mind filled with
vague impressions of trees, asphalt drives, and the moving groups
of nursemaids and holidaymakers, I started to walk back to my
easel.

---

[1] First quatrain of "Let the Red Dawn Surmise," poem by Bliss Carman
(1861-1929) contained in *Pipes of Pan* series titled Songs of the Sea
Children, 1894, pg. 70
[2] St. Cecilia Mass is a dower mass composed by Frenchman Charles
Gounod (1818-1893) during 1855
[3] Famous street in New York, New York
[4] French forest

As I turned, my listless glance included the man below in the churchyard. His face was toward me now, and with a perfectly involuntary movement I bent to see it. At the same moment he raised his head and looked at me. Instantly I thought of a coffin-worm. Whatever it was about the man that repelled me I did not know, but the impression of a plump white grave-worm was so intense and nauseating that I must have shown it in my expression, for he turned his puffy face away with a movement which made me think of a disturbed grub in a chestnut.

I went back to my easel and motioned the model to resume her pose. After working awhile I was satisfied that I was spoiling what I had done as rapidly as possible, and I took up a palette knife and scraped the color out again. The flesh tones were sallow and unhealthy, and I did not understand how I could have painted such sickly color into a study which before that had glowed with healthy tones.

I looked at Tessie. She had not changed, and the clear flush of health dyed her neck and cheeks as I frowned.

"Is it something I've done?" she said.

"No—I've made a mess of this arm, and for the life of me I can't see how I came to paint such mud as that into the canvas," I replied.

"Don't I pose well?" she insisted.

"Of course, perfectly."

"Then it's not my fault?"

"No. It's my own."

"I'm very sorry," she said.

I told her she could rest while I applied rag and turpentine to the plague spot on my canvas, and she went off to smoke a cigarette and look over the illustrations in the *Courier Français*.[5]

I did not know whether it was something in the turpentine or a defect in the canvas, but the more I scrubbed the more that gangrene seemed to spread. I worked like a beaver to get it out, and yet the disease appeared to creep from limb to limb of the study before me. Alarmed I strove to arrest it, but now the color on the breast changed and the whole figure seemed to absorb the infection as a sponge soaks up water.

Vigorously I plied palette knife, turpentine, and scraper, thinking all the time what a séance I should hold with Duval who had sold me the canvas; but soon I noticed that it was not the canvas which was defective nor yet the colors of Edward.

It must be the turpentine, I thought angrily, *or else my eyes have become so blurred and confused by the afternoon light that I can't see straight.* I called Tessie, the model. She came and leaned over my chair blowing rings of smoke into the air.

"What have you been doing to it?" she exclaimed.

"Nothing," I growled, "it must be this turpentine!"

---

[5] *Le Courrier Français* was an illustrated Parisian weekly that appeared from 1884 to 1914

"What a horrible color it is now," she continued. "Do you think my flesh resembles green cheese?"

"No, I don't," I said angrily, "did you ever know me to paint like that before?"

"No, indeed!"

"Well, then!"

"It must be the turpentine, or something," she admitted.

She slipped on a Japanese robe[6] and walked to the window. I scraped and rubbed until I was tired and finally picked up my brushes and hurled them through the canvas with a forcible expression, the tone alone of which reached Tessie's ears.

Nevertheless she promptly began: "That's it! Swear and act silly and ruin your brushes! You have been three weeks on that study, and now look! What's the good of ripping the canvas? What creatures artists are!"

I felt about as much ashamed as I usually did after such an outbreak, and I turned the ruined canvas to the wall. Tessie helped me clean my brushes, and then danced away to dress. From the screen[7] she regaled me with bits of advice concerning whole or partial loss of temper, until, thinking, perhaps, I had been tormented sufficiently, she came out to implore me to button her waist where she could not reach it on the shoulder.

"Everything went wrong from the time you came back from the window and talked about that horrid-looking man you saw in the churchyard," she announced.

"Yes, he probably bewitched the picture," I said, yawning. I looked at my watch.

"It's after six, I know," said Tessie, adjusting her hat before the mirror.

"Yes," I replied, "I didn't mean to keep you so long." I leaned out the window but recoiled with disgust, for the young man with the pasty face stood below in the churchyard. Tessie saw my gesture of disapproval and leaned from the window.

"Is that the man you don't like?" she whispered.

I nodded.

"I can't see his face, but he does look fat and soft. Someway or other," she continued, looking at me, "he reminds me of a dream,—and awful dream I once had. Or," she mused looking down at her shapely shoes, "was it a dream after all?"

"How should I know?" I smiled.

Tessie smiled in reply.

"You were in it," she said, "so perhaps you might know something about it."

"Tessie! Tessie!" I protested, "don't you dare flatter by saying you dream about me!"

"But I did," she insisted; "shall I tell you about it?"

"Go ahead," I replied, lighting a cigarette.

---

[6] Likely a kimono, which is T-shaped and extends to the floor

[7] Dressing partition

Tessie leaned back on the open windowsill and began very seriously.

"One night last winter I was lying in bed thinking about nothing at all in particular. I had been posing for you and I was tired out, yet it seemed impossible for me to sleep. I heard the bells in the city ring ten, eleven, and midnight. I must have fallen asleep about midnight because I don't remember hearing the bells after that. It seemed to me that I had scarcely closed my eyes when I dreamed that something impelled me to go to the window. I rose, and raising the sash, leaned out. Twenty-fifth Street was deserted as far as I could see. I began to be afraid; everything outside seemed so—so black and uncomfortable. Then the sound of wheels in the distance came to my ears, and it seemed to me as though that was what I must wait for. Very slowly the wheels approached, and, finally, I could make out a vehicle moving along the street. It came nearer and nearer, and when it passed beneath my window I saw it was a hearse. Then, as I trembled with fear, the driver turned and looked straight at me. When I awoke I was standing by the open window shivering with cold, but the black-plumed hearse and the driver were gone. I dreamed this dream again in March last, and again awoke beside the open window. Last night the dream came again. You remember how it was raining; when I awoke, standing at the open window, my nightdress was soaked."

"But where did I come into the dream?" I asked.

"You—you were in the coffin; but you were not dead."

"In the coffin?"

"Yes."

"How did you know? Could you see me?"

"No; I only knew you were there."

"Had you been eating Welsh rare-bits,[8] or lobster salad?" I began laughing, but the girl interrupted me with a frightened cry.

"Hello! What's up?" I said, as she shrank into the embrasure by the window.

"The—the man below in the churchyard;—he drove the hearse."

"Nonsense," I said, but Tessie's eyes were wide with terror. I went to the window and looked out. The man was gone. "Come, Tessie," I urged, "don't be foolish. You have posed too long; you are nervous."

"Do you think I could forget that face?" she murmured. "Three times I saw that hearse pass below my window, and every time the driver turned and looked up at me. Oh, his face was so white and—and soft? It looked dead—it looked as if it had been dead a long time."

I induced the girl to sit down and swallow a glass of Marsala. Then I sat down beside her and tried to give her some advice.

---

[8] A vegetarian spread placed on sliced bread or toast and that derives its name as a joke on Welsh rabbit because the Welsh could not afford meat dishes

"Look here, Tessie," I said, "you go to the country for a week or two, and you'll have no more dreams about hearses. You pose all day, and when night comes your nerves are upset. You can't keep this up. Then again, instead of going to bed when your day's work is done, you run off to picnics at Sulzer's Park,[9] or go to the Eldorado[10] or Coney Island,[11] and when you come down here in the morning you are fagged out. There was no real hearse. That was a softshell crab dream."

She smiled faintly.

"What about the man in the churchyard?"

"Oh, he's an ordinary unhealthy, everyday creature."

"As true as my name is Tessie Reardon, I swear to you, Mr. Scott, that the face of the man below in the churchyard is the face of the man who drove the hearse!"

"What of it?" I said. "It's an honest trade."

"Then you think I did see a hearse?"

"Oh," I said diplomatically, "if you really did, it might not be unlikely that the man below drove it. There is nothing in that."

Tessie rose, unrolled her scented handkerchief, and taking a bit of gum from a knot in the hem, placed it in her mouth. Then drawing on her gloves she offered me her hand, with a frank, "Goodnight, Mr. Scott," and walked out.

II

The next morning, Thomas, the bellboy, brought me the *Herald*[12] and a bit of news. The church next door had been sold. I thanked Heaven for it, not that being a Catholic I had any repugnance for the congregation next door, but because my nerves were shattered by a blatant exhorter, whose every word echoed through the aisle of the church as if it had been my own rooms, and who insisted on his r's with a nasal persistence which revolted my every instinct. Then, too, there as a fiend in human shape, an organist, who reeled off some of the grand old hymns with an interpretation of his own, and I longed for the blood of a creature who could play the doxology[13] with an amendment of minor chords which one hears only in a quartet of very young undergraduates.

I believe the minister was a good man, but when he bellowed: "And the Lorrrrd said unto Moses, the Lorrrrd is a man of war; the Lorrrrd is his name. My wrath shall wax hot and I will kill you with

---

9 Sulzer's Harlem River Park was an amusement park in New York that bounded First and Second Avenues and 126th and 127th Streets and was destroyed by fire on February 18, 1923

10 First apartment building at 300 Central Park West in New York

11 Amusement park and residential area in the borough of Brooklyn in New York City

12 *The New York Herald* was a large daily newspaper founded in 1835 and printed until 1966

13 Songs delivered during Catechism of the Catholic Church

the sworrrrd!"[14] I wondered how many centuries of purgatory it would take to atone for such a sin.

"Who bought the property?" I asked Thomas.

"Nobody that I knows, sir. They do say the gent wot owns this 'ere 'Amilton flats was lookin' at it. 'E might be a bildin' more studios."

I walked to the window. The young man with the unhealthy face stood by the churchyard gate, and at the mere sight of him the same overwhelming repugnance took possession of me.

"By the way, Thomas," I said, "who is that fellow down there?"

Thomas sniffed. "That there worm, sir? 'E's night-watchman of the church, sir. 'E maikes me tired a-sittin' out all night on them steps and lookin' at you insultin' like. I'd a punched 'is 'ed, sir—beg pardon sir—"

"Go on, Thomas."

"One night a comin' 'ome with 'Arry, the other English boy, I sees 'im a sittin' there on them steps. We 'ad Molly and Jen with us, sir, the two girls on the tray service, an' 'e looks so insultin' at us that I up and sez: 'Wat you looking hat, you fat slug?'—beg pardon, sir, but that's 'ow I sez, sir. Then 'e don't say nothin' and I sez; 'Come out and I'll punch that puddin' 'ed.' Then I hopens the gate an' goes in, but 'e don't say nothin', only looks insultin' like. Then I 'its 'im one, but ugh! 'is 'ed was that cold and mushy it ud sicken you to touch 'im."

"What did he do then?" I asked, curiously.

"'Im? Nawthin'."

"And you, Thomas?"

The young fellow flushed in embarrassment and smiled uneasily.

"Mr. Scott, sir, I ain't no coward an' I can't make it out at all why I run. I was with the 5th Lawncers, sir, bugler at Tel-el-Kebir, an' was shot by the wells."

"You don't mean to say you ran away?"

"Yes, sir; I run."

"Why?"

"That's just what I want to know, sir. I grabbed Molly an' run, an' the rest of us just as frightened as I."

"But what were they frightened at?"

Thomas refused to answer for a while, but now my curiosity was aroused about the repulsive young man below and I pressed him. Three years' sojourn in America had not only modified Thomas' cockney dialect but had given him the American's fear of ridicule.

"You won't believe me, Mr. Scott, sir?"

"Yes, I will."

"You will lawf at me, sir?"

"Nonsense!"

---

[14] Exodus 15:3 and 22:24, King James version

He hesitated. "Well, sir, it's God's truth that when I 'it 'im 'e grabbed me wrists, sir, and when I twisted 'is soft, mushy fist one of 'is fingers come off in me 'and."

The utter loathing and horror of Thomas' face must have been reflected in my own for he added:

"It's orful, an' now when I see 'im I just go away. 'E maikes me hill."

When Thomas had gone I went to the window. The man stood beside the church-railing with both hands on the gate, but I hastily retreated to my easel again, sickened and horrified, for I saw that the middle finger of his right hand was missing.

At nine o'clock Tessie appeared and vanished behind the screen with a merry "Good-morning, Mr. Scott." While she had reappeared and taken her pose upon the model-stand I started a new canvas much to her delight. She remained silent as long as I was on the drawing, but as soon as the scrape of the charcoal ceased and I took up my fixative she began to chatter.

"Oh, I had such a lovely time last night. We went to Tony Pastor's."[15]

"Who are 'we'?" I demanded.

"Oh, Maggie, you know, Mr. Whyte's model, and Pinkie McCormick—we call her Pinkie because she's got that beautiful red hair you artists like so much—and Lizzie Burke."

I sent a shower of fixative over the canvas and said: "Well, go on."

"We saw Kelly and Baby Barnes the skirt-dancer and—and all the rest. I made a mash."[16]

"Then you have gone back on me, Tessie?"

She laughed and shook her head.

"He's Lizzie Burke's brother, Ed. He's a perfect gen'l'man."

I felt constrained to give her some parental advice concerning mashing, which she took with a bright smile.

"Oh, I can take care of a strange mash," she said, examining her chewing gum, "but Ed is different. Lizzie is my best friend."

Then she related how Ed had come back from the stocking mill in Lowell, Massachusetts, to find her and Lizzie grown up, and what an accomplished young man he was, and how he thought nothing of squandering half a dollar for ice-cream and oysters to celebrate his entry as clerk into the woolen department of Macy's.[17] Before she finished I began to paint, and she resumed the pose, smiling and chattering like a sparrow. By noon I had the study fairly well rubbed in and Tessie came to look at it.

"That's better," she said.

---

[15] Tony Pastor (1837-1908) was a vaudeville theatre owner in New York who leased the former Germania Theatre in 1881

[16] Term for introducing multiple people to one another

[17] Famous New York department store that now has many locations around the United States and is still in operation

I thought so too, and ate my lunch with a satisfied feeling that all was going well. Tessie spread her lunch on a drawing table opposite me and we drank our claret from the same bottle and lighted our cigarettes from the same match. I was very much attached to Tessie. I had watched her shoot up into a slender but exquisitely formed woman from a frail, awkward child.

She had posed for me during the last three years, and among all my models she was my favorite. It would have troubled me very much indeed had she become "tough" or "fly," as the phrase goes, but I had never noticed any deterioration of her manner, and felt at heart that she was all right. She and I never discussed morals at all, and I had no intention of doing so, partly because I had none myself, and partly because I knew she would do what she liked in spite of me.

Still I did hope she would steer clear of complications, because I wished her well, and then also I had a selfish desire to retain the best model I had. I knew that mashing, as she termed it, had no significance with girls like Tessie, and that such things in America did not resemble in the least the same things in Paris. Yet, having lived with my eyes open, I also knew that somebody would take Tessie away some day in one manner or another, and though I professed to myself that marriage was nonsense, I sincerely hoped that, in this case, there would be a priest at the end of the vista. I am a Catholic.

When I listen to high mass, when I sign myself, I feel that everything, including myself, is more cheerful, and when I confess, it does me good. A man who lives as much alone as I do, must confess to somebody. Then, again, Sylvia was Catholic, and it was reason enough for me.

But I was speaking of Tessie, which is very different. Tessie also was Catholic and much more devout than I, so, taking it all in all, I had little fear for my pretty model until she should fall in love. But then I knew that fate alone would decide her future for her, and I prayed inwardly that fate would keep her away from men like me and throw into her path nothing but Ed Burkes and Jimmy McCormicks, bless her sweet face!

Tessie sat blowing smoke up to the ceiling and tinkling the ice in her tumbler.

"Do you know, Kid, that I also had a dream last night?" I observed. I sometimes called her "the Kid."

"Not about that man," she laughed.

"Exactly. A dream similar to yours, only much worse."

It was foolish and thoughtless of me to say this, but you know how little tact the average painter has.

"I must have fallen asleep about 10 o'clock," I continued, "and after a while I dreamt that I awoke. So plainly did I hear the midnight bells, the wind in the tree-branches, and the whistle of steamers from the bay, that even now I can scarcely believe that I was not awake.

"I seemed to be lying in a box which had a glass cover. Dimly I saw the streetlamps as I passed, for I must tell you, Tessie, the box in which I reclined appeared to lie in a cushioned wagon which jolted me over a stony pavement. After a while I became impatient and tried to move but the box was too narrow. My hands were crossed on my breast so I could not raise them to help myself. I listened and then tried to call.

"My voice was gone. I could hear the trample of the horses attached to the wagon and even the breathing of the driver. Then another sound broke upon my ears like the raising of a window sash. I managed to turn my head a little, and found I could look, not only through the glass cover of my box, but also through the glass panes in the side of the covered vehicle. I saw houses, empty and silent, with neither light nor life about any of them excepting one. In that house a window was open on the first floor and a figure all in white stood looking down into the street. It was you."

Tessie had turned her face away from me and leaned on the table with her elbow.

"I could see your face," I resumed, "and it seemed to me to be very sorrowful. Then we passed on and turned into a narrow black lane. Presently the horses stopped. I waited and waited, closing my eyes with fear and impatience, but all was silent as the grave. After what seemed to me hours, I began to feel uncomfortable. A sense that somebody was close to me made me unclose my eyes. Then I saw the white face of the hearse-driver looking at me through the coffin-lid—"

A sob from Tessie interrupted me. She was trembling like a leaf. I saw I had made an ass of myself and attempted to repair the damage.

"Why, Tess," I said, "I only told you this to show you what influence your story might have on another person's dreams. You don't suppose I really lay in a coffin, do you? What are you trembling for? Don't you see that your dream and my unreasonable dislike for that inoffensive watchman of the church simply set my brain working as soon as I fell asleep?"

She laid her head between her arms and sobbed as if her heart would break. What a precious triple donkey I had made of myself! But I was about to break my record. I went over and put my arm about her.

"Tessie, dear, forgive me," I said; "I had no business to frighten you with such nonsense. You are too sensible a girl, too good a Catholic to believe in dreams."

Her hand tightened on mine and her head fell back upon my shoulder, but she still trembled and I petted her and comforted her.

"Come, Tess, open your eyes and smile."

Her eyes opened with a slow languid movement and met mine, but their expression was so queer that I hastened to reassure her again.

"It's all humbug, Tessie, you surely are not afraid that any harm will come to you because of that."

"No," she said, but her scarlet lips quivered.

"Then what's the matter? Are you afraid?"

"Yes. Not for myself."

"For me, then?" I demanded gaily.

"For you," she murmured in a voice almost inaudible, "I—I care—for you."

At first I started to laugh, but when I understood her, a shock passed through me and I sat like one turned to stone. This was the crowning bit of idiocy I had committed. During the moment which elapsed between her reply and my answer I thought of a thousand responses to that innocent confession. I could pass it by with a laugh, I could misunderstand her and reassure her as to my health, I could simply point out that it was impossible she could love me. But my reply was quicker than my thoughts and I might think and think now when it was too late, for I had kissed her on the mouth.

That evening I took my usual walk in Washington Park,[18] pondering over the occurrences of the day. I was thoroughly committed. There was no back out now, and I stared the future straight in the face. I was not good, not even scrupulous, but I had no idea of deceiving either myself or Tessie. The one passion of my life lay buried in the sunlit forests of Brittany. Was it buried forever? Hope cried "No!"

For three years I had been listening to the voice of Hope, and for three years I had waited for a footstep on my threshold. Had Sylvia forgotten? "No!" cried Hope.

I said that I was not good. That is true, but still I was not exactly a comic opera villain. I had led an easy-going reckless life, taking what invited me of pleasure, deploring and sometimes bitterly regretting consequences. In one thing alone, except my painting, I was serious, and that was something which lay hidden if not lost in the Breton forests.

It was too late now for me to regret what had occurred during the day. Whatever it had been, pity, a sudden tenderness for sorrow, of the more brutal instinct of gratified vanity, it was all the same now, and unless I wished to bruise an innocent heart my path lay marked before me. The fire and strength, the depth of passion of a love which I had never even suspected, with all my imagined experience in the world, left me no alternative but to respond or send her away. Whether because I am so cowardly about giving pain to others, or whether it was that I have little of the gloomy Puritan[19] in me, I do not know, but I shrank from disclaiming responsibility for that thoughtless kiss, and in fact had no time to do so before the gates of her heart opened and the flood poured forth.

---

[18] Washington Square Park encompasses nearly ten acres in the Greenwich Village neighborhood of New York and was started in 1871

[19] A sect of English protestants who abstained from nearly all physical pleasures under the guise of religion

Others who habitually do their duty and find a sullen satisfaction in making themselves and everybody else unhappy, might have withstood it. I did not. I dared not. After the storm had abated I did tell her that she might better have loved Ed Burke and worn a plain gold ring, but she would not hear of it, and I thought perhaps that as long as she had decided to love somebody she could not marry, it had better be me. I, at least, could treat her with an intelligent affection, and whenever she became tired of her infatuation she could go none the worse for it.

For I was decided on that point although I knew how hard it would be. I remembered the usual termination of Platonic liaisons and thought how disgusted I had been whenever I heard of one. I knew I was undertaking a great deal for so unscrupulous a man as I was, and I dreaded the future, but never for one moment did I doubt that she was safe with me. Had it been anybody but Tessie I should not have bothered my head about scruples. For it did not occur to me to sacrifice Tessie as I would have sacrificed a woman of the world. I looked the future squarely in the face and saw the several probable endings to the affair.

She would either tire of the whole thing, or become so unhappy that I should have either to marry her or go away. If I married her we would be unhappy. I with a wife unsuited to me, and she with a husband unsuitable for any woman. For my past life could scarcely entitle me to marry. If I went away she might either fall ill, recover, and marry some Eddie Burke, or she might recklessly or deliberately go and do something foolish.

On the other hand if she tired of me, then her whole life would be before her with beautiful vistas of Eddie Burkes and marriage rings and twins and Harlem flats[20] and Heaven knows what. As I strolled along through the trees by Washington Arch,[21] I decided that she should find a substantial friend in me anyway and the future could take care of itself. Then I went into the house and put on my evening dress for the little faintly perfumed note on my dresser said, "Have a cab at the stage door at eleven," and the note was signed "Edith Carmichael, Metropolitan Theater,[22] June 19th, 189—."

I took supper that night, or rather we took supper, Miss Carmichael and I, at Solari's and the dawn was just beginning to gild the cross on the Memorial Church[23] as I entered Washington Square after leaving Edith at the Brunswick. There was not a soul in the park as I passed among the trees and took the walk which

---

[20] Apartments in Harlem, New York were expensive and fashionable

[21] Washington Square Park's large stone arch built in 1892 to commemorate George Washington's (1732-1799) centennial inauguration as the first President of the United States

[22] New York theatre founded in 1883 and is still home to the Metropolitan Opera

[23] Judson Memorial Church, whose sanctuary was finished in 1893, is located in Greenwich Village has a metallic cross mounted on top of it

leads from the Garibaldi statue[24] to the Hamilton Apartment House,[25] but as I passed the churchyard I saw a figure sitting on the stone steps.

In spite of myself a chill crept over me at the sight of the white puffy face, and I hastened to pass. Then he said something which might have been addressed to me or might merely have been a mutter to himself, but a sudden furious anger flamed up within me that such a creature should address me.

For an instant I felt like wheeling about and smashing my stick over his head, but I walked on, and entering the Hamilton went to my apartment. For some time I tossed about the bed trying to get the sound of his voice out of my ears, but could not. It filled my head, that muttering sound, like thick oily smoke from a fat-rendering vat or an odor of noisome decay. And as I lay and tossed about, the voice in my ears seemed more distinct, and I began to understand the words he had muttered. They came to me slowly as if I had forgotten them, and at last I could make some sense out of the sounds. It was this:

"Have you found the Yellow Sign?"
"Have you found the Yellow Sign?"
"Have you found the Yellow Sign?"

I was furious. What did he mean by that? Then with a curse upon him and his I rolled over and went to sleep, but when I awoke later I looked pale and haggard, for I had dreamed the dream of the night before and it troubled me more than I cared to think.

I dressed and went down into my studio. Tessie sat by the window, but as I came in she rose and put both arms around my neck for an innocent kiss. She looked so sweet and dainty that I kissed her again and then sat down before the easel.

"Hello! Where's the study I began yesterday?" I asked.

Tessie looked conscious, but did not answer. I began to hunt among the piles of canvases, saying, "Hurry up, Tess, and get ready; we must take advantage of the morning light."

When at last I gave up the search among the other canvases and turned to look around the room for the missing study I noticed Tessie standing by the screen with her clothing still on.

"What's the matter," I asked, "don't you feel well?"

"Yes."

"Then hurry."

"Do you want me to pose as—as I have always posed?"

Then I understood. Here was a new complication. I had lost, of course, the best nude model I had ever seen. I looked at Tessie. Her face was scarlet. Alas! Alas! We had eaten of the tree of

---

[24] Statue in Washington Square Park representing General Giuseppe Garibaldi (1807-1882) and dedicated in 1888
[25] Early New York apartment building on Hamilton and Main that added a four story extension in 1905

knowledge,[26] and Eden and native innocence were dreams of the past—I mean—for her.

I suppose she noticed the disappointment on my face, for she said: "I will pose if you wish. The study is behind the screen here where I put it."

"No," I said, "we will begin something new"; and I went to my wardrobe and picked out a Moorish costume[27] which fairly blazed with tinsel. It was a genuine costume, and Tessie retired to the screen with it enchanted. When she came forth again I was astonished. Her long black hair was bound above her forehead with a circlet of turquoises, and the ends curled about her glittering girdle.

Her feet were encased in the embroidered pointed slippers and the skirt of her costume, curiously wrought with arabesques in silver, fell to her ankles. The deep metallic blue vest embroidered with silver and the short Mauresque jacket[28] spangled and sewn with turquoises became her wonderfully. She came up to me and held up her face smiling. I slipped my hand into my pocket and drawing out a gold chain with a cross attached, dropped it over her head.

"It's yours, Tessie."

"Mine?" she faltered.

"Yours. Now go and pose." Then with a radiant smile she ran behind the screen and presently reappeared with a little box on which was written my name.

"I had intended to give it to you when I went home tonight," she said, "but I can't wait now."

I opened the box. On the pink cotton inside lay a clasp of black onyx, on which was inlaid a curious symbol or letter in gold. It was neither Arabic nor Chinese, nor as I found afterwards did it belong to any human script.

"It's all I had to give you for a keepsake," she said, timidly.

I was annoyed, but I told her how much I should prize it, and promised to wear it always. She fastened it on my coat beneath the lapel.

"How foolish, Tess, to go and buy me such a beautiful thing as this," I said.

"I did not buy it," she laughed.

"Where did you get it?"

Then she told me how she had found it one day while coming from the Aquarium in the Battery,[29] how she had advertised it and watched the papers, but at last gave up all hopes of finding the owner.

---

[26] Reference to the Tree of Knowledge discussed in Genesis chapters 2-3 and where the serpent caused Eve to eat of its fruit and was sentenced to die by God

[27] Ornate, ankle length dress

[28] Short jacket that did not meet at the front

[29] The New York Aquarium opened in 1896 in the Battery Park of New York

"That was last winter," she said, "the very day I had the first horrid dream about the hearse."

I remembered my dream of the previous night but said nothing, and presently my charcoal was flying over a new canvas, and Tessie stood motionless on the model-stand.

III

The day following was a disastrous one for me. While moving a framed canvas from one easel to another my foot slipped on the polished floor and I fell heavily on both wrists. They were so badly sprained that it was useless to attempt to hold a brush, and I was obliged to wander about the studio, glaring at unfinished drawings and sketches until despair seized me and I sat down to smoke and twiddle my thumbs with rage. The rain blew against the windows and rattled on the roof of the church, driving me into a nervous fit with its interminable patter. Tessie sat sewing by the window, and every now and then raised her head and looked at me with such innocent compassion that I began to feel ashamed of my irritation and looked about for something to occupy me.

I had read all the papers and all the books in the library, but for the sake of something to do I went to the bookcases and shoved them open with my elbow. I knew every volume by its color and examined them all, passing slowly around the library and whistling to keep up my spirits. I was turning to go into the dining-room when my eye fell upon a book bound in yellow, standing in a corner of the top shelf of the last bookcase. I did not remember it and from the floor could not decipher the pale lettering on the back, so I went to the smoking-room and called Tessie. She came in from the studio and climbed to reach the book.

"What is it?" I asked.

"*The King in Yellow.*"

I was dumbfounded. Who had placed it there? How came it to my rooms? I had long ago decided that I should never open that book, and nothing on earth could have persuaded me to buy it. Fearful lest curiosity might tempt me to open it, I had never even looked at it in bookstores. If I ever had had any curiosity to read it, the awful tragedy of young Castaigne, whom I knew, prevented me from exploring its wicked pages. I had always refused to listen to any description of it, and indeed, nobody ever ventured to discuss the second part aloud, so I had absolutely no knowledge of what those leaves might reveal. I stared at the poisonous yellow binding as I would at a snake.

"Don't touch it, Tessie," I said, "come down."

Of course my admonition was enough to arouse her curiosity, and before I could prevent it she took the book and, laughing, danced away into the studio with it. I called to her but she slipped away with a tormenting smile at my helpless hands, and I followed her with some impatience.

"Tessie!" I cried, entering the library, "listen, I am serious. Put that book away. I do not wish you to open it!"

The library was empty. I went into both drawing-rooms, then into the bedrooms, laundry, kitchen, and finally returned to the library and began a systematic search. She had hidden herself so well that it was half an hour later when I discovered her crouching white and silent by the latticed window in the storeroom above.

At the first glance I saw she had been punished for her foolishness. *The King in Yellow* lay at her feet, but the book was open to the second part. I looked at Tessie and saw it was too late. She had opened *The King in Yellow*. Then I took her by the hand and led her into the studio. She seemed dazed, and when I told her to lie down on the sofa she obeyed me without a word.

After a while she closed her eyes and her breathing became regular and deep, but I could not determine whether or not she slept. For a long while I sat silently beside her, but she neither stirred nor spoke, and at last I rose and entering the unused storeroom took the yellow book in my least injured hand. It seemed heavy as lead, but I carried it into the studio again, and sitting down on the rug beside the sofa, opened it and read it through from beginning to end.

When, faint with the excess of my emotions, I dropped the volume and leaned wearily back against the sofa, Tessie opened her eyes and looked at me.

We had been speaking for some time in a dull and monotonous strain before I realized that we were discussing *The King in Yellow*. Oh the sin of writing such words,—words which are clear as crystal, limpid and musical as bubbling springs, words which sparkle and glow like the poisoned diamonds of the Medicis![30]

Oh the wickedness, the hopeless damnation of a soul who could fascinate and paralyze human creatures with such words, -- words understood by the ignorant and wise alike, words which are more precious than jewels, more soothing than Heavenly music, more awful than death itself.

We talked on, unmindful of the gathering shadows, and she was begging me to throw away the clasp of black onyx quaintly inlaid with what we now knew to be the Yellow Sign. I never shall know why I refused, though even at this hour, here in my bedroom as I write this confession, I should be glad to know what it was that prevented me from tearing the Yellow Sign from my breast and casting it into the fire. I am sure I wished to do so, but Tessie pleaded with me in vain.

Night fell and the hours dragged on, but still we murmured to each other of the King and the Pallid Mask, and midnight sounded

---

[30] The Italian Medici family is reported to have poisoned a number of its enemies in the sixteenth century, including Catherine de Medici (1519-1589) who used diamond powder mixed in food to poison

from the misty spires in the fog-wrapped city. We spoke of Hastur[31] and of Cassilda,[32] while outside the fog rolled against the blank windowpanes as the cloud waves roll and break on the shores of Hali.[33]

The house was very silent now and not a sound from the misty streets broke the silence. Tessie lay among the cushions, her face a gray blot in the gloom, but her hands were clasped in mine and I knew that she knew and read my thoughts as I read hers, for we had understood the mystery of the Hyades[34] and the Phantom of Truth was laid.

Then as we answered each other, swiftly, silently, thought on thought, the shadows stirred in the gloom about us, and far in the distant streets we heard a sound. Nearer and nearer it came, the dull crunching of wheels, nearer, nearer and yet nearer, and now, outside the door it ceased, and I dragged myself to the window and saw a black-plumed hearse.

The gate below opened and shut, and I crept shaking to my door and bolted it, but I knew no bolts, no locks, could keep that creature out who was coming for the Yellow Sign. And now I heard him moving very softly along the hall. Now he was at the door, and the bolts rotted at his touch.

Now he had entered. With eyes starting from my head I peered into the darkness, but when he came into the room I did not see him. It was only when I felt him envelop me in his cold soft grasp that I cried out and struggled with deadly fury, but my hands were useless and he tore the onyx clasp from my coat and struck me full in the face.

Then, as I fell, I heard Tessie's soft cry and her spirit fled to God, and even while falling I longed to follow her, for I knew that the King in Yellow had opened his tattered mantle and there was only Christ to cry to now.

I could tell more, but I cannot see what help it will be to the world. As for me I am past human help or hope. As I lie here, writing, careless even whether or not I die before I finish, I can see the doctor gathering up his powders and phials with a vague gesture to the good priest beside me, which I understand.

---

[31] Known in gothic mythology as The Horrible One or The Unspeakable One and appearing four years before "The Yellow Sign" in "Haïta the Sheperd," (1891), Abrose Bierce's short story, and years later in H. P. Lovecraft's "The Whisperer in Darkness (1931), "There is a whole secret cult of evil men (a man of your mystical erudition will understand me when I link them with Hastur and the Yellow Sign) devoted to the purpose of tracking them down and injuring them on behalf of the monstrous powers from other dimensions."

[32] The four quatrains of "Cassilda's Song" are found in Act 1. Scene 2 of *The King in Yellow*, which repeatedly mentions the fictional city of Carcosa that is the subject of Ambrose Bierce's "An Inhabitant of Carcosa" (1886)

[33] Fictional lake in the fictional city of Carcosa used in Ambrose Bierce's "An Inhabitant of Carcosa" (1886)

[34] A group of sister nymphs in Greek mythology who cried when Hyas was slain and morphed into a cluster of mysterious stars

They will be very curious to know the tragedy—they of the outside world who write books and print millions of newspapers, but I will write no more, and the father confessor will seal my last words with the seal of sanctity when his holy office is done. They of the outside world may send their creatures into wrecked homes and death-smitten firesides, and their newspapers will batten on blood and tears, but with me their spies must halt before the confessional. They know that Tessie is dead and that I am dying.

They know how the people in the house, aroused by an infernal scream, rushed into my room and found one living and two dead, but they do not know that the doctor said as he pointed to a horrible decomposed heap on the floor—the livid corpse of the watchman from the church: "I have no theory, no explanation. That man must have been dead for months!"

I think I am dying. I wish the priest would—

Edward Bulwer-Lytton
(1803-1873)

Edward Bulwer-Lytton is an oddity of English aristocracy due to his wide commercial success as a writer. This was not entirely by choice. In 1827, in defiance of his mother's wishes, he married Rosina Wheeler, an Irish woman from a working-class family. Out of spite, Bulwer-Lytton's mother withdrew his lavish stipend and he was forced to make his own way in the world. Fortunately for literary readers, he turned to writing.

The year after his wedding he wrote *Pelham*, a novel that brought wide commercial success and launched his British literary career that lasted until his death in 1873. Two years after the success of *Pelham*, Bulwer-Lytton published his first ghost short story, "Monos and Diamonos" (1830). It was also popular in England.

He became well-known in America, too. The same year Bulwer-Lytton published *Rienzi, the Last of the Roman Tribunes*, Edgar Allan Poe satirized him in his short story "Lion-izing" (1835) for his long novels, likening them to his long nose.[1] Satire aside, Poe thought highly of his writing:

> From the brief Tale—from the "Monos and Daimonos" [sic]
> of the author—to his most ponderous and labored novels—
> all is richly, and glowingly intellectual—all is energetic, or
> astute, or brilliant, or profound.[2]

---

[1] *Edgar Allan Poe's Annotated Short Stories*, Andrew Barger, 2008, pg. 259
[2] "Bulwer's Rienzi," Edgar Allan Poe, *Southern Literary Messenger*, Vol. II, 1836, pg. 197

Bulwer-Lytton had been honing his craft for over thirty years when he published "The Haunted and the Haunters" (1859), a ghost story praised by many famous authors though lacking in some originality as you will see below.

Montague Summers said he "immensely" admired it and when surmising how the author wrote such good supernatural stories relayed that "Bulwer-Lytton was a serious and discriminating student of the occult."[3]

"The Haunted and the Haunters" is based on a real life story.[4] In 1840 an obscure journal, published by the husband-wife team of William and Mary Howitt, printed a series of letters from Edward Drury to the owner of a "haunted house at Willington near Newcastle-on-Tyne" named Joseph Proctor.

Drury, on hearing of the eldritch place and being a staunch denier of all things supernatural, wrote to Proctor on June 17, 1840, expressing his resolve to stay there alone for the night with only his dog.[5]

Proctor agreed to the evening of July 3, 1840, though by the time the fateful night approached, Drury decided to take his friend, Thomas Hudson, instead of his dog. He also packed "a brace of pistols." This is the chilling account of what he experienced.

Sunderland, July 13, 1840.

DEAR SIR,—I hereby, according to promise in my last letter, forward you a true account of what I heard and saw at your house, in which I was led to pass the night from various rumours circulated by most respectable parties, particularly from an account by my esteemed friend, Mr. Davison, whose name I mentioned to you in a former letter. Having received your sanction to visit your mysterious dwelling, I went on the 3d of July, accompanied by a friend of mine, T. Hudson.

This was not according to promise, nor in accordance with my first intent, as I wrote you I would come alone; but I felt gratified at your kindness in not alluding to the liberty I had taken, as it ultimately proved for the best. I must here mention that, not expecting you at home, I had in my pocket a brace of pistols, determining in my mind to let one of them drop before the miller, as if by accident, for fear he should presume to play tricks upon me; but after my interview with you, I felt there was no occasion for weapons, and did not load them, after you had allowed us to inspect as minutely as we pleased every portion of the

---

[3] *The Supernatural Omnibus: Being a Collection of Stories of Apparitions, Witchcraft, Werewolves, Diabolism, Necromancy, Satanism, Divination, Sorcery, Goety, Voodo, Possession, Occult, Doom and Destiny,* Montague Summers, 1931, pg. 12

[4] Ibid.

[5] "Visits to Remarkable Places," William Howitt, *Howitt's Journal: Literature and Popular Progress,* Vol. I, 1847, pg. 290

house. I sat down on the third story landing, fully expecting to account for any noises that I might hear, in a philosophical manner.

This was about eleven o'clock, P.M. About ten minutes to twelve we both heard a noise, as if a number of people were pattering with their bare feet upon the floor; and yet, so singular was the noise that I could not minutely determine from whence it proceeded.

A few minutes afterwards we heard a noise, as if someone was knocking with his knuckles among our feet; this was followed by a hollow cough from the very room from which the apparition proceeded. The only noise after this was as if a person was rustling against the wall in coming up-stairs. At a quarter to one I told my friend that, feeling a little cold, I would like to go to bed, as we might hear the noise equally well there; he replied that he would not go to bed till daylight.

I took up a note which I had accidentally dropped, and began to read it, after which I took out my watch to ascertain the time, and found that it wanted ten minutes to one. In taking my eyes from the watch, they became rivetted upon a closet door, which I distinctly saw open, and saw also the figure of a female attired in grayish garments, with the head inclining downwards, and one hand pressed upon the chest, as if in pain, and the other— viz. the right hand-extended towards the floor, with the index finger pointing downwards.

It advanced with an apparently cautious step across the floor towards me; immediately as it approached my friend, who was slumbering, its right hand was extended towards him; I then rushed at it, giving, as Mr. Procter states, a most awful yell; but instead of grasping it, I fell upon my friend, and I recollected nothing distinctly for nearly three hours afterwards. I have since learnt that I was carried down stairs in an agony of fear and terror.

I hereby certify that the above account is strictly true and correct in every respect.

EDWARD DRURY,
North Shields.[6]

In conclusion the article noted, "[w]e have lately heard that Mr. Proctor has discovered an old book, which makes it appear that the very same 'hauntings' took place in an old house on the very same spot, at least two hundred years ago."[7]

Though perhaps not entirely original in its foundations, H. P. Lovecraft picked the ghost short story as "one of the best short

---

[6] "Visits to Remarkable Places," William Howitt, *Howitt's Journal: Literature and Popular Progress*, Vol. I, 1847, pg. 291

[7] Ibid. at 293

haunted house tales ever."[8] It's the perfect tale to close out this collection and it's also the oldest. Boo!

---

[8] *Supernatural Horror in Literature*, H. P. Lovecraft, 1927, pg. 29

The Haunted and the Haunters
1859

A FRIEND OF mine, who is a man of letters and a philosopher, said to me one day, as if between jest and earnest, "Fancy! since we last met I have discovered a haunted house in the midst of London."

"Really haunted,—and by what?—ghosts?"

"Well, I can't answer that question; all I know is this: six weeks ago my wife and I were in search of a furnished apartment. Passing a quiet street, we saw on the window of one of the houses a bill, 'Apartments, Furnished.' The situation suited us; we entered the house, liked the rooms, engaged them by the week,—and left them the third day. No power on earth could have reconciled my wife to stay longer; and I don't wonder at it."

"What did you see?"

"Excuse me; I have no desire to be ridiculed as a superstitious dreamer,—nor, on the other hand, could I ask you to accept on my affirmation what you would hold to be incredible without the evidence of your own senses. Let me only say this, it was not so much what we saw or heard (in which you might fairly suppose that we were the dupes of our own excited fancy, or the victims of imposture in others) that drove us away, as it was an undefinable terror which seized both of us whenever we passed by the door of a certain unfurnished room, in which we neither saw nor heard anything. And the strangest marvel of all was, that for once in my life I agreed with my wife, silly woman though she be,—and allowed, after the third night, that it was impossible to stay a fourth in that house. Accordingly, on the fourth morning I summoned the woman who kept the house and attended on us, and told her that the rooms did not quite suit us, and we would not stay out our week."

She said dryly, "I know why; you have stayed longer than any other lodger. Few ever stayed a second night; none before you a third. But I take it they have been very kind to you."

"They,—who?" I asked, affecting to smile.

"Why, they who haunt the house, whoever they are. I don't mind them. I remember them many years ago, when I lived in this house, not as a servant; but I know they will be the death of me someday. I don't care,—I'm old, and must die soon anyhow; and then I shall be with them, and in this house still.' The woman spoke with so dreary a calmness that really it was a sort of awe that prevented my conversing with her further. I paid for my week, and too happy were my wife and I to get off so cheaply."

"You excite my curiosity," said I; "nothing I should like better than to sleep in a haunted house. Pray give me the address of the one which you left so ignominiously."

My friend gave me the address; and when we parted, I walked straight towards the house thus indicated.

It is situated on the north side of Oxford Street, in a dull but respectable thoroughfare. I found the house shut up,—no bill at the window, and no response to my knock. As I was turning away, a beer-boy, collecting pewter pots at the neighboring areas,[1] said to me, "Do you want any one at that house, sir?"

"Yes, I heard it was to be let."

"Let!—why, the woman who kept it is dead,—has been dead these three weeks, and no one can be found to stay there, though Mr. J—— offered ever so much. He offered mother, who chars[2] for him, £1 a week just to open and shut the windows, and she would not."

"Would not!—and why?"

"The house is haunted; and the old woman who kept it was found dead in her bed, with her eyes wide open. They say the devil strangled her."

"Pooh! You speak of Mr. J——. Is he the owner of the house?"
"Yes."

"Where does he live?"

"In G—— Street, No. ——."

"What is he? In any business?"

"No, sir,—nothing particular; a single gentleman."

I gave the pot-boy the gratuity earned by his liberal information, and proceeded to Mr. J——, in G—— Street, which was close by the street that boasted the haunted house. I was lucky enough to find Mr. J—— at home,—an elderly man with intelligent countenance and prepossessing manners.

I communicated my name and my business frankly. I said I heard the house was considered to be haunted,—that I had a strong desire to examine a house with so equivocal a reputation; that I should be greatly obliged if he would allow me to hire it, though only for a night. I was willing to pay for that privilege whatever he might be inclined to ask.

"Sir," said Mr. J——, with great courtesy, "the house is at your service, for as short or as long a time as you please. Rent is out of the question,—the obligation will be on my side should you be able to discover the cause of the strange phenomena which at present deprive it of all value. I cannot let it, for I cannot even get a servant to keep it in order or answer the door.

---

[1] In England boys would sell beer in large pewter pots to residential neighborhoods and pick up the pots the next day similar to milk delivery services
[2] Cleans house

"Unluckily the house is haunted, if I may use that expression, not only by night, but by day; though at night the disturbances are of a more unpleasant and sometimes of a more alarming character. The poor old woman who died in it three weeks ago was a pauper whom I took out of a workhouse; for in her childhood she had been known to some of my family, and had once been in such good circumstances that she had rented that house of my uncle. She was a woman of superior education and strong mind, and was the only person I could ever induce to remain in the house. Indeed, since her death, which was sudden, and the coroner's inquest, which gave it a notoriety in the neighborhood, I have so despaired of finding any person to take charge of the house, much more a tenant, that I would willingly let it rent free for a year to anyone who would pay its rates and taxes."

"How long is it since the house acquired this sinister character?"

"That I can scarcely tell you, but very many years since. The old woman I spoke of, said it was haunted when she rented it between thirty and forty years ago. The fact is, that my life has been spent in the East Indies, and in the civil service of the Company. I returned to England last year, on inheriting the fortune of an uncle, among whose possessions was the house in question. I found it shut up and uninhabited. I was told that it was haunted, that no one would inhabit it. I smiled at what seemed to me so idle a story.

"I spent some money in repairing it, added to its old-fashioned furniture a few modern articles,—advertised it, and obtained a lodger for a year. He was a colonel on half-pay. He came in with his family, a son and a daughter, and four or five servants: they all left the house the next day; and, although each of them declared that he had seen something different from that which had scared the others, a something still was equally terrible to all. I really could not in conscience sue, nor even blame, the colonel for breach of agreement. Then I put in the old woman I have spoken of, and she was empowered to let the house in apartments. I never had one lodger who stayed more than three days.

"I do not tell you their stories,—to no two lodgers have there been exactly the same phenomena repeated. It is better that you should judge for yourself, than enter the house with an imagination influenced by previous narratives; only be prepared to see and to hear something or other, and take whatever precautions you yourself please."

"Have you never had a curiosity yourself to pass a night in that house?"

"Yes. I passed not a night, but three hours in broad daylight alone in that house. My curiosity is not satisfied, but it is quenched. I have no desire to renew the experiment. You cannot complain, you see, sir, that I am not sufficiently candid; and unless your interest be exceedingly eager and your nerves unusually strong, I honestly add, that I advise you *not* to pass a night in that house."

"My interest *is* exceedingly keen," said I; "and though only a coward will boast of his nerves in situations wholly unfamiliar to him, yet my nerves have been seasoned in such variety of danger that I have the right to rely on them,—even in a haunted house."

Mr. J—— said very little more; he took the keys of the house out of his bureau, gave them to me,—and, thanking him cordially for his frankness, and his urbane concession to my wish, I carried off my prize.

Impatient for the experiment, as soon as I reached home, I summoned my confidential servant,—a young man of gay spirits, fearless temper, and as free from superstitious prejudice as any one I could think of.

"F——," said I, "you remember in Germany how disappointed we were at not finding a ghost in that old castle, which was said to be haunted by a headless apparition? Well, I have heard of a house in London which, I have reason to hope, is decidedly haunted. I mean to sleep there tonight. From what I hear, there is no doubt that something will allow itself to be seen or to be heard,— something, perhaps, excessively horrible. Do you think if I take you with me, I may rely on your presence of mind, whatever may happen?"

"Oh, sir, pray trust me," answered F——, grinning with delight.

"Very well; then here are the keys of the house,—this is the address. Go now,—select for me any bedroom you please; and since the house has not been inhabited for weeks, make up a good fire, air the bed well,—see, of course, that there are candles as well as fuel. Take with you my revolver and my dagger,—so much for my weapons; arm yourself equally well; and if we are not a match for a dozen ghosts, we shall be but a sorry couple of Englishmen."

I was engaged for the rest of the day on business so urgent that I had not leisure to think much on the nocturnal adventure to which I had plighted my honor. I dined alone, and very late, and while dining, read, as is my habit. I selected one of the volumes of *Macaulay's Essays*.[3] I thought to myself that I would take the book with me; there was so much of healthfulness in the style, and practical life in the subjects, that it would serve as an antidote against the influences of superstitious fancy.

Accordingly, about half-past nine, I put the book into my pocket, and strolled leisurely towards the haunted house. I took with me a favorite dog: an exceedingly sharp, bold, and vigilant bullterrier,—a dog fond of prowling about strange, ghostly corners and passages at night in search of rats; a dog of dogs for a ghost.

---

[3] Thomas Macaulay (1800-1859) contributed a number of essays or critiques to the *Edinburgh Review* in 1843 and one was on Horatio Walpole (1717-1797) who penned the haunting early Gothic novel *The Castle of Ortanto* (1764)

It was a summer night but chilly, the sky somewhat gloomy and overcast. Still there was a moon, faint and sickly but still a moon, and if the clouds permitted, after midnight it would be brighter.

I reached the house, knocked, and my servant opened with a cheerful smile.

"All right, sir, and very comfortable."

"Oh!" said I, rather disappointed; "have you not seen nor heard anything remarkable?"

"Well, sir, I must own I have heard something queer."

"What?—what?"

"The sound of feet pattering behind me; and once or twice small noises like whispers close at my ear,—nothing more."

"You are not at all frightened?"

"I! not a bit of it, sir;" and the man's bold look reassured me on one point,—namely, that happen what might, he would not desert me.

We were in the hall, the street-door closed, and my attention was now drawn to my dog. He had at first run in eagerly enough, but had sneaked back to the door, and was scratching and whining to get out.

After patting him on the head, and encouraging him gently, the dog seemed to reconcile himself to the situation, and followed me and F—— through the house, but keeping close at my heels instead of hurrying inquisitively in advance, which was his usual and normal habit in all strange places.

We first visited the subterranean apartments,—the kitchen and other offices, and especially the cellars, in which last there were two or three bottles of wine still left in a bin, covered with cobwebs, and evidently, by their appearance, undisturbed for many years. It was clear that the ghosts were not winebibbers. For the rest we discovered nothing of interest. There was a gloomy little backyard, with very high walls.

The stones of this yard were very damp; and what with the damp, and what with the dust and smoke-grime on the pavement, our feet left a slight impression where we passed.

And now appeared the first strange phenomenon witnessed by myself in this strange abode. I saw, just before me, the print of a foot suddenly form itself, as it were. I stopped, caught hold of my servant, and pointed to it. In advance of that footprint as suddenly dropped another.

We both saw it. I advanced quickly to the place; the footprint kept advancing before me, a small footprint,—the foot of a child: the impression was too faint thoroughly to distinguish the shape, but it seemed to us both that it was the print of a naked foot. This phenomenon ceased when we arrived at the opposite wall, nor did it repeat itself on returning. We remounted the stairs, and entered the rooms on the ground-floor, a dining parlor, a small back-parlor, and a still smaller third room that had been probably appropriated to a footman,—all still as death. We then visited the drawing-rooms, which seemed fresh and new. In the front room I seated myself in an armchair. F—— placed on the table the candlestick with which he had lighted us.

I told him to shut the door. As he turned to do so a chair opposite to me moved from the wall quickly and noiselessly, and dropped itself about a yard from my own chair, immediately fronting it.

"Why, this is better than the turning-tables," said I, with a half-laugh; and as I laughed, my dog put back his head and howled.

F——, coming back, had not observed the movement of the chair. He employed himself now in stilling the dog. I continued to gaze on the chair, and fancied I saw on it a pale, blue, misty outline of a human figure, but an outline so indistinct that I could only distrust my own vision. The dog now was quiet.

"Put back that chair opposite to me," said I to F——; "put it back to the wall."

F—— obeyed. "Was that you, sir?" said he, turning abruptly.

"I!—what?"

"Why, something struck me. I felt it sharply on the shoulder,—just here."

"No," said I. "But we have jugglers present, and though we may not discover their tricks, we shall catch *them* before they frighten *us*."

We did not stay long in the drawing-rooms,—in fact, they felt so damp and so chilly that I was glad to get to the fire upstairs. We locked the doors of the drawing-rooms,—a precaution which, I should observe, we had taken with all the rooms we had searched below.

The bedroom my servant had selected for me was the best on the floor,—a large one, with two windows fronting the street. The four-posted bed, which took up no inconsiderable space, was opposite to the fire, which burned clear and bright; a door in the wall to the left, between the bed and the window, communicated with the room which my servant appropriated to himself. This last was a small room with a sofa-bed, and had no communication with the landing-place,—no other door but that which conducted to the bedroom I was to occupy.

On either side of my fireplace was a cupboard without locks, flush with the wall, and covered with the same dull-brown paper. We examined these cupboards,—only hooks to suspend female dresses, nothing else; we sounded the walls,—evidently solid, the outer walls of the building. Having finished the survey of these apartments, warmed myself a few moments, and lighted my cigar, I then, still accompanied by F——, went forth to complete my reconnoiter. In the landing-place there was another door; it was closed firmly.

"Sir," said my servant, in surprise, "I unlocked this door with all the others when I first came; it cannot have got locked from the inside, for—"

Before he had finished his sentence, the door, which neither of us then was touching, opened quietly of itself. We looked at each other a single instant. The same thought seized both,—some human agency might be detected here. I rushed in first, my servant followed.

A small, blank, dreary room without furniture; a few empty boxes and hampers in a corner; a small window; the shutters closed; not even a fireplace; no other door but that by which we had entered; no carpet on the floor, and the floor seemed very old, uneven, worm-eaten, mended here and there, as was shown by the whiter patches on the wood; but no living being, and no visible place in which a living being could have hidden. As we stood gazing round, the door by which we had entered closed as quietly as it had before opened; we were imprisoned.

For the first time I felt a creep of undefinable horror. Not so my servant. "Why, they don't think to trap us, sir; I could break that trumpery door[4] with a kick of my foot."

"Try first if it will open to your hand," said I, shaking off the vague apprehension that had seized me, "while I unclose the shutters and see what is without."

I unbarred the shutters,—the window looked on the little backyard I have before described; there was no ledge without,— nothing to break the sheer descent of the wall. No man getting out of that window would have found any footing till he had fallen on the stones below.

F——, meanwhile, was vainly attempting to open the door. He now turned round to me and asked my permission to use force. And I should here state, in justice to the servant, that, far from evincing any superstitious terrors, his nerve, composure, and even gayety amidst circumstances so extraordinary, compelled my admiration, and made me congratulate myself on having secured a companion in every way fitted to the occasion.

I willingly gave him the permission he required. But though he was a remarkably strong man, his force was as idle as his milder efforts; the door did not even shake to his stoutest kick. Breathless and panting, he desisted.

I then tried the door myself, equally in vain. As I ceased from the effort, again that creep of horror came over me; but this time it was more cold and stubborn. I felt as if some strange and ghastly exhalation were rising up from the chinks of that rugged floor, and filling the atmosphere with a venomous influence hostile to human life. The door now very slowly and quietly opened as of its own accord.

We precipitated ourselves into the landing-place. We both saw a large, pale light—as large as the human figure, but shapeless and unsubstantial—move before us, and ascend the stairs that led from the landing into the attics.

---

[4] Ornate wooden door but thin

I followed the light, and my servant followed me. It entered, to the right of the landing, a small garret, of which the door stood open. I entered in the same instant. The light then collapsed into a small globule, exceedingly brilliant and vivid, rested a moment on a bed in the corner, quivered, and vanished.

We approached the bed and examined it,—a half-tester, such as is commonly found in attics devoted to servants. On the drawers that stood near it we perceived an old faded silk kerchief, with the needle still left in a rent half repaired. The kerchief was covered with dust; probably it had belonged to the old woman who had last died in that house, and this might have been her sleeping-room.

I had sufficient curiosity to open the drawers: there were a few odds and ends of female dress, and two letters tied round with a narrow ribbon of faded yellow. I took the liberty to possess myself of the letters.

We found nothing else in the room worth noticing,—nor did the light reappear; but we distinctly heard, as we turned to go, a pattering footfall on the floor, just before us. We went through the other attics (in all four), the footfall still preceding us.

Nothing to be seen,—nothing but the footfall heard. I had the letters in my hand; just as I was descending the stairs I distinctly felt my wrist seized, and a faint, soft effort made to draw the letters from my clasp. I only held them the more tightly, and the effort ceased.

We regained the bedchamber appropriated to myself, and I then remarked that my dog had not followed us when we had left it. He was thrusting himself close to the fire, and trembling. I was impatient to examine the letters; and while I read them, my servant opened a little box in which he had deposited the weapons I had ordered him to bring, took them out, placed them on a table close at my bed-head, and then occupied himself in soothing the dog, who, however, seemed to heed him very little.

The letters were short,—they were dated; the dates exactly thirty-five years ago. They were evidently from a lover to his mistress, or a husband to some young wife. Not only the terms of expression, but a distinct reference to a former voyage, indicated the writer to have been a seafarer. The spelling and handwriting were those of a man imperfectly educated, but still the language itself was forcible. In the expressions of endearment there was a kind of rough, wild love; but here and there were dark unintelligible hints at some secret not of love,—some secret that seemed of crime.

We ought to love each other, was one of the sentences I remember, *for how everyone else would execrate us if all was known.*

Again: *Don't let anyone be in the same room with you at night,— you talk in your sleep.*

And again: *What's done can't be undone; and I tell you there's nothing against us unless the dead could come to life.*

Here there was underlined in a better handwriting (a female's), *They do!* At the end of the letter latest in date the same female hand had written these words: *Lost at sea the 4th of June, the same day as—*

I put down the letters, and began to muse over their contents.

Fearing, however, that the train of thought into which I fell might unsteady my nerves, I fully determined to keep my mind in a fit state to cope with whatever of marvelous the advancing night might bring forth. I roused myself; laid the letters on the table; stirred up the fire, which was still bright and cheering; and opened my volume of Macaulay.

I read quietly enough till about half-past eleven. I then threw myself dressed upon the bed, and told my servant he might retire to his own room, but must keep himself awake. I bade him leave open the door between the two rooms.

Thus alone, I kept two candles burning on the table by my bed-head. I placed my watch beside the weapons, and calmly resumed my Macaulay. Opposite to me the fire burned clear; and on the hearthrug, seemingly asleep, lay the dog.

In about twenty minutes I felt an exceedingly cold air pass by my cheek, like a sudden draught. I fancied the door to my right, communicating with the landing-place, must have got open; but no,—it was closed. I then turned my glance to my left, and saw the flame of the candles violently swayed as by a wind.

At the same moment the watch beside the revolver softly slid from the table,—softly, softly; no visible hand,—it was gone. I sprang up, seizing the revolver with the one hand, the dagger with the other; I was not willing that my weapons should share the fate of the watch. Thus armed, I looked round the floor,—no sign of the watch. Three slow, loud, distinct knocks were now heard at the bed-head; my servant called out, "Is that you, sir?"

"No; be on your guard."

The dog now roused himself and sat on his haunches, his ears moving quickly backwards and forwards. He kept his eyes fixed on me with a look so strange that he concentered all my attention on himself.

Slowly he rose up, all his hair bristling, and stood perfectly rigid, and with the same wild stare. I had no time, however, to examine the dog. Presently my servant emerged from his room; and if ever I saw horror in the human face, it was then. I should not have recognized him had we met in the street, so altered was every lineament.

He passed by me quickly, saying, in a whisper that seemed scarcely to come from his lips, "Run, run! it is after me!"

He gained the door to the landing, pulled it open, and rushed forth. I followed him into the landing involuntarily, calling him to stop; but, without heeding me, he bounded down the stairs, clinging to the balusters, and taking several steps at a time. I heard, where I stood, the street-door open,—heard it again clap to. I was left alone in the haunted house.

It was but for a moment that I remained undecided whether or not to follow my servant; pride and curiosity alike forbade so dastardly a flight. I reentered my room, closing the door after me, and proceeded cautiously into the interior chamber.

I encountered nothing to justify my servant's terror. I again carefully examined the walls, to see if there were any concealed door. I could find no trace of one,—not even a seam in the dull-brown paper with which the room was hung. How, then, had the THING, whatever it was, which had so scared him, obtained ingress except through my own chamber?

I returned to my room, shut and locked the door that opened upon the interior one, and stood on the hearth, expectant and prepared. I now perceived that the dog had slunk into an angle of the wall, and was pressing himself close against it, as if literally striving to force his way into it. I approached the animal and spoke to it; the poor brute was evidently beside itself with terror.

It showed all its teeth, the slaver dropping from its jaws, and would certainly have bitten me if I had touched it. It did not seem to recognize me. Whoever has seen at the Zoological Gardens[5] a rabbit, fascinated by a serpent, cowering in a corner, may form some idea of the anguish which the dog exhibited.

Finding all efforts to soothe the animal in vain, and fearing that his bite might be as venomous in that state as in the madness of hydrophobia,[6] I left him alone, placed my weapons on the table beside the fire, seated myself, and recommenced my Macaulay.

Perhaps, in order not to appear seeking credit for a courage, or rather a coolness, which the reader may conceive I exaggerate, I may be pardoned if I pause to indulge in one or two egotistical remarks.

As I hold presence of mind, or what is called courage, to be precisely proportioned to familiarity with the circumstances that lead to it, so I should say that I had been long sufficiently familiar with all experiments that appertain to the marvelous. I had witnessed many very extraordinary phenomena in various parts of the world,—phenomena that would be either totally disbelieved if I stated them, or ascribed to supernatural agencies. Now, my theory is that the supernatural is the impossible, and that what is called supernatural is only a something in the laws of Nature of which we have been hitherto ignorant.

Therefore, if a ghost rise before me, I have not the right to say, "So, then, the supernatural is possible;" but rather, "So, then, the apparition of a ghost, is, contrary to received opinion, within the laws of Nature,—that is, not supernatural."

Now, in all that I had hitherto witnessed, and indeed in all the wonders which the amateurs of mystery in our age record as facts, a material living agency is always required. On the Continent you will find still magicians who assert that they can raise spirits. Assume for the moment that they assert truly, still the living

---

[5] The London Zoological Gardens opened for public visits in 1857, two years before publication of "The Haunters and the Haunted"
[6] Rabies

material form of the magician is present; and he is the material agency by which, from some constitutional peculiarities, certain strange phenomena are represented to your natural senses.

Accept, again, as truthful, the tales of spirit-manifestation in America,—musical or other sounds; writings on paper, produced by no discernible hand; articles of furniture moved without apparent human agency; or the actual sight and touch of hands, to which no bodies seem to belong,—still there must be found the MEDIUM, or living being, with constitutional peculiarities capable of obtaining these signs.

In fine, in all such marvels, supposing even that there is no imposture, there must be a human being like ourselves by whom, or through whom, the effects presented to human beings are produced. It is so with the now familiar phenomena of mesmerism[7] or electro-biology;[8] the mind of the person operated on is affected through a material living agent.

Nor, supposing it true that a mesmerized patient can respond to the will or passes of a mesmerizer a hundred miles distant, is the response less occasioned by a material being; it may be through a material fluid—call it Electric, call it Odic,[9] call it what you will— which has the power of traversing space and passing obstacles, that the material effect is communicated from one to the other.

Hence, all that I had hitherto witnessed, or expected to witness, in this strange house, I believed to be occasioned through some agency or medium as mortal as myself; and this idea necessarily prevented the awe with which those who regard as supernatural things that are not within the ordinary operations of Nature, might have been impressed by the adventures of that memorable night.

As, then, it was my conjecture that all that was presented, or would be presented to my senses, must originate in some human being gifted by constitution with the power so to present them, and having some motive so to do, I felt an interest in my theory which, in its way, was rather philosophical than superstitious.

And I can sincerely say that I was in as tranquil a temper for observation as any practical experimentalist could be in awaiting the effects of some rare, though perhaps perilous, chemical combination. Of course, the more I kept my mind detached from fancy, the more the temper fitted for observation would be obtained; and I therefore riveted eye and thought on the strong daylight sense in the page of my Macaulay.

I now became aware that something interposed between the page and the light,—the page was over-shadowed. I looked up, and

---

[7] Mesmerism was an early form of hypnotism practiced in the nineteenth century and based on the pseudo-theories of German Franz Anton Mesmer (1734-1815)

[8] Branch of biological studies that focuses on electric current in plants and animals, such as the electric eel

[9] Theory of a life force that was a combination of electricity and magnetism purported by Baron Carl von Reichenbach (1788-1869) as a reason for why mesmerism supposedly worked on patients

I saw what I shall find it very difficult, perhaps impossible, to describe.

It was a Darkness shaping itself forth from the air in very undefined outline. I cannot say it was of a human form, and yet it had more resemblance to a human form, or rather shadow, than to anything else. As it stood, wholly apart and distinct from the air and the light around it, its dimensions seemed gigantic, the summit nearly touching the ceiling. While I gazed, a feeling of intense cold seized me. An iceberg before me could not more have chilled me; nor could the cold of an iceberg have been more purely physical. I feel convinced that it was not the cold caused by fear. As I continued to gaze, I thought—but this I cannot say with precision—that I distinguished two eyes looking down on me from the height. One moment I fancied that I distinguished them clearly, the next they seemed gone; but still two rays of a pale-blue light frequently shot through the darkness, as from the height on which I half believed, half doubted, that I had encountered the eyes.

I strove to speak,—my voice utterly failed me; I could only think to myself, *Is this fear? It is* not *fear!*

I strove to rise,—in vain; I felt as if weighed down by an irresistible force. Indeed, my impression was that of an immense and overwhelming Power opposed to my volition,—that sense of utter inadequacy to cope with a force beyond man's, which one may feel *physically* in a storm at sea, in a conflagration, or when confronting some terrible wild beast, or rather, perhaps, the shark of the ocean, I felt *morally.* Opposed to my will was another will, as far superior to its strength as storm, fire, and shark are superior in material force to the force of man.

And now, as this impression grew on me,—now came, at last, horror, horror to a degree that no words can convey. Still I retained pride, if not courage; and in my own mind I said, *This is horror, but it is not fear; unless I fear I cannot be harmed; my reason rejects this thing; it is an illusion,—I do not fear.*

With a violent effort I succeeded at last in stretching out my hand towards the weapon on the table; as I did so, on the arm and shoulder I received a strange shock, and my arm fell to my side powerless. And now, to add to my horror, the light began slowly to wane from the candles,—they were not, as it were, extinguished, but their flame seemed very gradually withdrawn; it was the same with the fire,—the light was extracted from the fuel; in a few minutes the room was in utter darkness.

The dread that came over me, to be thus in the dark with that dark Thing, whose power was so intensely felt, brought a reaction of nerve. In fact, terror had reached that climax, that either my senses must have deserted me, or I must have burst through the spell. I did burst through it. I found voice, though the voice was a shriek.

I remember that I broke forth with words like these, "I do not fear, my soul does not fear;" and at the same time I found strength to rise. Still in that profound gloom I rushed to one of the windows;

tore aside the curtain; flung open the shutters; my first thought was—LIGHT. And when I saw the moon high, clear, and calm, I felt a joy that almost compensated for the previous terror. There was the moon, there was also the light from the gas-lamps in the deserted slumberous street.

I turned to look back into the room; the moon penetrated its shadow very palely and partially,—but still there was light. The dark Thing, whatever it might be, was gone,—except that I could yet see a dim shadow, which seemed the shadow of that shade, against the opposite wall.

My eye now rested on the table, and from under the table (which was without cloth or cover,—an old mahogany round-table) there rose a hand, visible as far as the wrist. It was a hand, seemingly, as much of flesh and blood as my own, but the hand of an aged person, lean, wrinkled, small too,—a woman's hand.

That hand very softly closed on the two letters that lay on the table; hand and letters both vanished. There then came the same three loud, measured knocks I had heard at the bed-head before this extraordinary drama had commenced.

As those sounds slowly ceased, I felt the whole room vibrate sensibly; and at the far end there rose, as from the floor, sparks or globules like bubbles of light, many colored,—green, yellow, fire-red, azure.

Up and down, to and fro, hither, thither, as tiny Will-o'-the-Wisps,[10] the sparks moved, slow or swift, each at its own caprice. A chair (as in the drawing-room below) was now advanced from the wall without apparent agency, and placed at the opposite side of the table.

Suddenly, as forth from the chair, there grew a shape,—a woman's shape. It was distinct as a shape of life,—ghastly as a shape of death.

The face was that of youth, with a strange, mournful beauty; the throat and shoulders were bare, the rest of the form in a loose robe of cloudy white. It began sleeking its long, yellow hair, which fell over its shoulders; its eyes were not turned towards me, but to the door; it seemed listening, watching, waiting. The shadow of the shade in the background grew darker; and again I thought I beheld the eyes gleaming out from the summit of the shadow,—eyes fixed upon that shape.

As if from the door, though it did not open, there grew out another shape, equally distinct, equally ghastly,—a man's shape, a young man's. It was in the dress of the last century, or rather in a likeness of such dress (for both the male shape and the female, though defined, were evidently unsubstantial, impalpable,—simulacra, phantasms); and there was something incongruous, grotesque, yet fearful, in the contrast between the elaborate finery, the courtly precision of that old-fashioned garb, with its ruffles and

---

[10] Tiny lights that appear above marshlands

lace and buckles, and the corpse-like aspect and ghost-like stillness of the flitting wearer.

Just as the male shape approached the female, the dark Shadow started from the wall, all three for a moment wrapped in darkness. When the pale light returned, the two phantoms were as if in the grasp of the Shadow that towered between them; and there was a bloodstain on the breast of the female; and the phantom male was leaning on its phantom sword, and blood seemed trickling fast from the ruffles, from the lace; and the darkness of the intermediate Shadow swallowed them up,—they were gone.

And again the bubbles of light shot, and sailed, and undulated, growing thicker and thicker and more wildly confused in their movements.

The closet door to the right of the fireplace now opened, and from the aperture there came the form of an aged woman. In her hand she held letters,—the very letters over which I had seen *the* Hand close; and behind her I heard a footstep. She turned round as if to listen, and then she opened the letters and seemed to read; and over her shoulder I saw a livid face, the face as of a man long drowned,—bloated, bleached, seaweed tangled in its dripping hair; and at her feet lay a form as of a corpse; and beside the corpse there cowered a child, a miserable, squalid child, with famine in its cheeks and fear in its eyes.

And as I looked in the old woman's face, the wrinkles and lines vanished, and it became a face of youth,—hard-eyed, stony, but still youth; and the Shadow darted forth, and darkened over these phantoms as it had darkened over the last.

Nothing now was left but the Shadow, and on that my eyes were intently fixed, till again eyes grew out of the Shadow,— malignant, serpent eyes. And the bubbles of light again rose and fell, and in their disordered, irregular, turbulent maze, mingled with the wan moonlight. And now from these globules themselves, as from the shell of an egg, monstrous things burst out; the air grew filled with them: larvae so bloodless and so hideous that I can in no way describe them except to remind the reader of the swarming life which the solar microscope brings before his eyes in a drop of water,—things transparent, supple, agile, chasing each other, devouring each, other; forms like nought ever beheld by the naked eye.

As the shapes were without symmetry, so their movements were without order. In their very vagrancies there was no sport; they came round me and round, thicker and faster and swifter, swarming over my head, crawling over my right arm, which was outstretched in involuntary command against all evil beings. Sometimes I felt myself touched, but not by them; invisible hands touched me.

Once I felt the clutch as of cold, soft fingers at my throat. I was still equally conscious that if I gave way to fear I should be in bodily peril; and I concentered all my faculties in the single focus of resisting stubborn will. And I turned my sight from the Shadow;

above all, from those strange serpent eyes,—eyes that had now become distinctly visible. For there, though in nought else around me, I was aware that there was a WILL, and a will of intense, creative, working evil, which might crush down my own.

The pale atmosphere in the room began now to redden as if in the air of some near conflagration. The larvæ grew lurid as things that live in fire. Again the room vibrated; again were heard the three measured knocks; and again all things were swallowed up in the darkness of the dark Shadow, as if out of that darkness all had come, into that darkness all returned.

As the gloom receded, the Shadow was wholly gone. Slowly, as it had been withdrawn, the flame grew again into the candles on the table, again into the fuel in the grate. The whole room came once more calmly, healthfully into sight.

The two doors were still closed, the door communicating with the servant's room still locked. In the corner of the wall, into which he had so convulsively niched himself, lay the dog. I called to him,—no movement; I approached,—the animal was dead: his eyes protruded; his tongue out of his mouth; the froth gathered round his jaws.

I took him in my arms; I brought him to the fire. I felt acute grief for the loss of my poor favorite,—acute self-reproach; I accused myself of his death; I imagined he had died of fright. But what was my surprise on finding that his neck was actually broken. Had this been done in the dark? Must it not have been by a hand human as mine; must there not have been a human agency all the while in that room? Good cause to suspect it. I cannot tell. I cannot do more than state the fact fairly; the reader may draw his own inference.

Another surprising circumstance,—my watch was restored to the table from which it had been so mysteriously withdrawn; but it had stopped at the very moment it was so withdrawn, nor, despite all the skill of the watchmaker, has it ever gone since,—that is, it will go in a strange, erratic way for a few hours, and then come to a dead stop; it is worthless.

Nothing more chanced for the rest of the night. Nor, indeed, had I long to wait before the dawn broke. Nor till it was broad daylight did I quit the haunted house. Before I did so, I revisited the little blind room in which my servant and myself had been for a time imprisoned. I had a strong impression—for which I could not account—that from that room had originated the mechanism of the phenomena, if I may use the term, which had been experienced in my chamber.

And though I entered it now in the clear day, with the sun peering through the filmy window, I still felt, as I stood on its floors, the creep of the horror which I had first there experienced the night before, and which had been so aggravated by what had passed in my own chamber. I could not, indeed, bear to stay more than half a minute within those walls. I descended the stairs, and again I heard the footfall before me; and when I opened the street door, I thought I could distinguish a very low laugh. I gained my own home, expecting to find my runaway servant there; but he had not presented himself, nor did I hear more of him for three days, when I received a letter from him, dated from Liverpool to this effect:—

> *HONORED SIR,—I humbly entreat your pardon, though I can scarcely hope that you will think that I deserve it, unless— which Heaven forbid!—you saw what I did. I feel that it will be years before I can recover myself; and as to being fit for service, it is out of the question. I am therefore going to my brother-in-law at Melbourne. The ship sails tomorrow. Perhaps the long voyage may set me up. I do nothing now but start and tremble, and fancy IT is behind me. I humbly beg you, honored sir, to order my clothes, and whatever wages are due to me, to be sent to my mother's, at Walworth,—John knows her address.*

The letter ended with additional apologies, somewhat incoherent, and explanatory details as to effects that had been under the writer's charge. This flight may perhaps warrant a suspicion that the man wished to go to Australia, and had been somehow or other fraudulently mixed up with the events of the night.

I say nothing in refutation of that conjecture; rather, I suggest it as one that would seem to many persons the most probable solution of improbable occurrences. My belief in my own theory remained unshaken.

I returned in the evening to the house, to bring away in a hack cab[11] the things I had left there, with my poor dog's body. In this task I was not disturbed, nor did any incident worth note befall me, except that still, on ascending and descending the stairs, I heard the same footfall in advance. On leaving the house, I went to Mr. J——'s.

He was at home. I returned him the keys, told him that my curiosity was sufficiently gratified, and was about to relate quickly what had passed, when he stopped me, and said, though with much politeness, that he had no longer any interest in a mystery which none had ever solved.

I determined at least to tell him of the two letters I had read, as well as of the extraordinary manner in which they had disappeared; and I then inquired if he thought they had been addressed to the woman who had died in the house, and if there were anything in her early history which could possibly confirm the dark suspicions to which the letters gave rise.

Mr. J—— seemed startled, and, after musing a few moments, answered, "I am but little acquainted with the woman's earlier history, except as I before told you, that her family were known to mine. But you revive some vague reminiscences to her prejudice. I

---

[11] Horse-drawn carriage for hire

will make inquiries, and inform you of their result. Still, even if we could admit the popular superstition that a person who had been either the perpetrator or the victim of dark crimes in life could revisit, as a restless spirit, the scene in which those crimes had been committed, I should observe that the house was infested by strange sights and sounds before the old woman died—you smile—what would you say?"

"I would say this, that I am convinced, if we could get to the bottom of these mysteries, we should find a living human agency."

"What! you believe it is all an imposture? For what object?"

"Not an imposture in the ordinary sense of the word. If suddenly I were to sink into a deep sleep, from which you could not awake me, but in that sleep could answer questions with an accuracy which I could not pretend to when awake,—tell you what money you had in your pocket, nay, describe your very thoughts,—it is not necessarily an imposture, any more than it is necessarily supernatural. I should be, unconsciously to myself, under a mesmeric influence, conveyed to me from a distance by a human being who had acquired power over me by previous *rapport.*"

"But if a mesmerizer could so affect another living being, can you suppose that a mesmerizer could also affect inanimate objects: move chairs,—open and shut doors?"

"Or impress our senses with the belief in such effects,—we never having been *en rapport* with the person acting on us? No. What is commonly called mesmerism could not do this; but there may be a power akin to mesmerism, and superior to it,—the power that in the old days was called Magic.

"That such a power may extend to all inanimate objects of matter, I do not say; but if so, it would not be against Nature,—it would be only a rare power in Nature which might be given to constitutions with certain peculiarities, and cultivated by practice to an extraordinary degree. That such a power might extend over the dead,—that is, over certain thoughts and memories that the dead may still retain,—and compel, not that which ought properly to be called the SOUL, and which is far beyond human reach, but rather a phantom of what has been most earth-stained on earth, to make itself apparent to our senses, is a very ancient though obsolete theory upon which I will hazard no opinion. But I do not conceive the power would be supernatural.

"Let me illustrate what I mean from an experiment which Paracelsus[12] describes as not difficult, and which the author of the *Curiosities of Literature*[13] cites as credible: A flower perishes; you burn it. Whatever were the elements of that flower while it lived are gone, dispersed, you know not whither; you can never discover nor

---

[12] Philip von Hohenhein (1493-1541) was a Swiss philosopher, occultist and mystic who gathered his theories by observing the natural world
[13] Isaac D'Israeli (1766-1848) anonymously compiled a collection of rare stories that he titled *Curiosities of Literature*, first published in 1791 with five more installments in succeeding years

recollect them. But you can, by chemistry, out of the burned dust of that flower, raise a spectrum of the flower, just as it seemed in life. It may be the same with the human being.

"The soul has as much escaped you as the essence or elements of the flower. Still you may make a spectrum of it. And this phantom, though in the popular superstition it is held to be the soul of the departed, must not be confounded with the true soul; it is but the eidolon[14] of the dead form.

"Hence, like the best attested stories of ghosts or spirits, the thing that most strikes us is the absence of what we hold to be soul,—that is, of superior emancipated intelligence. These apparitions come for little or no object,—they seldom speak when they do come; if they speak, they utter no ideas above those of an ordinary person on earth. American spirit-seers have published volumes of communications, in prose and verse, which they assert to be given in the names of the most illustrious dead: Shakespeare,[15] Bacon,[16]—Heaven knows whom. Those communications, taking the best, are certainly not a whit of higher order than would be communications from living persons of fair talent and education; they are wondrously inferior to what Bacon, Shakespeare, and Plato[17] said and wrote when on earth.

"Nor, what is more noticeable, do they ever contain an idea that was not on the earth before. Wonderful, therefore, as such phenomena may be (granting them to be truthful), I see much that philosophy may question, nothing that it is incumbent on philosophy to deny,—namely, nothing supernatural. They are but ideas conveyed somehow or other (we have not yet discovered the means) from one mortal brain to another. Whether, in so doing, tables walk of their own accord, or fiendlike shapes appear in a magic circle, or bodiless hands rise and remove material objects, or a Thing of Darkness, such as presented itself to me, freeze our blood,—still am I persuaded that these are but agencies conveyed, as by electric wires, to my own brain from the brain of another. In some constitutions there is a natural chemistry, and those constitutions may produce chemic wonders,—in others a natural fluid, call it electricity, and these may produce electric wonders.

"But the wonders differ from Normal Science in this,—they are alike objectless, purposeless, puerile, frivolous. They lead on to no grand results; and therefore the world does not heed, and true sages have not cultivated them. But sure I am, that of all I saw or heard, a man, human as myself, was the remote originator; and I believe unconsciously to himself as to the exact effects produced, for this reason: no two persons, you say, have ever told you that they experienced exactly the same thing.

---

[14] A specter
[15] William Shakespeare (1564-1616), famous English playwright
[16] Sir Francis Bacon (1561-1626), English philosopher and author
[17] Plato (428 B.C.-348 B.C.) was a famous Greek philosopher

"Well, observe, no two persons ever experience exactly the same dream. If this were an ordinary imposture, the machinery would be arranged for results that would but little vary; if it were a supernatural agency permitted by the Almighty, it would surely be for some definite end. These phenomena belong to neither class; my persuasion is, that they originate in some brain now far distant; that that brain had no distinct volition in anything that occurred; that what does occur reflects but its devious, motley, ever-shifting, half-formed thoughts; in short, that it has been but the dreams of such a brain put into action and invested with a semi-substance.

"That this brain is of immense power, that it can set matter into movement, that it is malignant and destructive, I believe; some material force must have killed my dog; the same force might, for aught I know, have sufficed to kill myself, had I been as subjugated by terror as the dog,—had my intellect or my spirit given me no countervailing resistance in my will."

"It killed your dog,—that is fearful! Indeed it is strange that no animal can be induced to stay in that house; not even a cat. Bats and mice are never found in it."

"The instincts of the brute creation detect influences deadly to their existence. Man's reason has a sense less subtle, because it has a resisting power more supreme. But enough; do you comprehend my theory?"

"Yes, though imperfectly,—and I accept any crotchet (pardon the word), however odd, rather than embrace at once the notion of ghosts and hobgoblins we imbibed in our nurseries. Still, to my unfortunate house, the evil is the same. What on earth can I do with the house?"

"I will tell you what I would do. I am convinced from my own internal feelings that the small, unfurnished room at right angles to the door of the bedroom which I occupied, forms a starting-point or receptacle for the influences which haunt the house; and I strongly advise you to have the walls opened, the floor removed,—nay, the whole room pulled down. I observe that it is detached from the body of the house, built over the small backyard, and could be removed without injury to the rest of the building."

"And you think, if I did that—"

"You would cut off the telegraph wires. Try it. I am so persuaded that I am right, that I will pay half the expense if you will allow me to direct the operations."

"Nay, I am well able to afford the cost; for the rest allow me to write to you."

About ten days after I received a letter from Mr. J——, telling me that he had visited the house since I had seen him; that he had found the two letters I had described, replaced in the drawer from which I had taken them; that he had read them with misgivings like my own; that he had instituted a cautious inquiry about the woman to whom I rightly conjectured they had been written. It seemed that thirty-six years ago (a year before the date of the letters) she had married, against the wish of her relations, an

American of very suspicious character; in fact, he was generally believed to have been a pirate.

She herself was the daughter of very respectable tradespeople, and had served in the capacity of a nursery governess before her marriage. She had a brother, a widower, who was considered wealthy, and who had one child of about six years old. A month after the marriage the body of this brother was found in the Thames, near London Bridge; there seemed some marks of violence about his throat, but they were not deemed sufficient to warrant the inquest in any other verdict than that of "found drowned."

The American and his wife took charge of the little boy, the deceased brother having by his will left his sister the guardian of his only child,—and in event of the child's death the sister inherited. The child died about six months afterwards,—it was supposed to have been neglected and ill-treated. The neighbors deposed to have heard it shriek at night.

The surgeon who had examined it after death said that it was emaciated as if from want of nourishment, and the body was covered with livid bruises. It seemed that one winter night the child had sought to escape; crept out into the backyard; tried to scale the wall; fallen back exhausted; and been found at morning on the stones in a dying state.

But though there was some evidence of cruelty, there was none of murder; and the aunt and her husband had sought to palliate cruelty by alleging the exceeding stubbornness and perversity of the child, who was declared to be half-witted. Be that as it may, at the orphan's death the aunt inherited her brother's fortune. Before the first wedded year was out, the American quitted England abruptly, and never returned to it.

He obtained a cruising vessel, which was lost in the Atlantic two years afterwards. The widow was left in affluence, but reverses of various kinds had befallen her: a bank broke; an investment failed; she went into a small business and became insolvent; then she entered into service, sinking lower and lower, from housekeeper down to maid-of-all-work,—never long retaining a place, though nothing decided against her character was ever alleged. She was considered sober, honest, and peculiarly quiet in her ways; still nothing prospered with her.

And so she had dropped into the workhouse, from which Mr. J—— had taken her, to be placed in charge of the very house which she had rented as mistress in the first year of her wedded life.

Mr. J—— added that he had passed an hour alone in the unfurnished room which I had urged him to destroy, and that his impressions of dread while there were so great, though he had neither heard nor seen anything, that he was eager to have the walls bared and the floors removed as I had suggested. He had engaged persons for the work, and would commence any day I would name.

The day was accordingly fixed. I repaired to the haunted house,—we went into the blind, dreary room, took up the skirting, and then the floors. Under the rafters, covered with rubbish, was found a trap-door, quite large enough to admit a man. It was closely nailed down, with clamps and rivets of iron. On removing these we descended into a room below, the existence of which had never been suspected. In this room there had been a window and a flue, but they had been bricked over, evidently for many years. By the help of candles we examined this place; it still retained some moldering furniture,—three chairs, an oak settle, a table,—all of the fashion of about eighty years ago.

There was a chest of drawers against the wall, in which we found, half-rotted away, old-fashioned articles of a man's dress, such as might have been worn eighty or a hundred years ago by a gentleman of some rank; costly steel buckles and buttons, like those yet worn in court-dresses, a handsome court sword; in a waistcoat which had once been rich with gold-lace, but which was now blackened and foul with damp, we found five guineas, a few silver coins, and an ivory ticket, probably for some place of entertainment long since passed away. But our main discovery was in a kind of iron safe fixed to the wall, the lock of which it cost us much trouble to get picked.

In this safe were three shelves and two small drawers. Ranged on the shelves were several small bottles of crystal, hermetically stopped. They contained colorless, volatile essences, of the nature of which I shall only say that they were not poisons,—phosphor and ammonia entered into some of them. There were also some very curious glass tubes, and a small pointed rod of iron, with a large lump of rock-crystal, and another of amber,—also a loadstone of great power.

In one of the drawers we found a miniature portrait set in gold, and retaining the freshness of its colors most remarkably, considering the length of time it had probably been there. The portrait was that of a man who might be somewhat advanced in middle life, perhaps forty-seven or forty-eight. It was a remarkable face,—a most impressive face. If you could fancy some mighty serpent transformed into man, preserving in the human lineaments the old serpent type, you would have a better idea of that countenance than long descriptions can convey: the width and flatness of frontal; the tapering elegance of contour disguising the strength of the deadly jaw; the long, large, terrible eye, glittering and green as the emerald,—and withal a certain ruthless calm, as if from the consciousness of an immense power.

Mechanically I turned round the miniature to examine the back of it, and on the back was engraved a pentacle;[18] in the middle of the pentacle a ladder, and the third step of the ladder was formed by the date 1765. Examining still more minutely, I detected a spring; this, on being pressed, opened the back of the miniature as a lid.

---

[18] A five pointed talisman designed to symbolize an earthly element

Within-side the lid were engraved, MARIANNA TO THEE. BE FAITHFUL IN LIFE AND IN DEATH TO ——.

Here follows a name that I will not mention, but it was not unfamiliar to me. I had heard it spoken of by old men in my childhood as the name borne by a dazzling charlatan who had made a great sensation in London for a year or so, and had fled the country on the charge of a double murder within his own house,— that of his mistress and his rival. I said nothing of this to Mr. J——, to whom reluctantly I resigned the miniature.

We had found no difficulty in opening the first drawer within the iron safe; we found great difficulty in opening the second: it was not locked, but it resisted all efforts, till we inserted in the chinks the edge of a chisel.

When we had thus drawn it forth, we found a very singular apparatus in the nicest order. Upon a small, thin book, or rather tablet, was placed a saucer of crystal; this saucer was filled with a clear liquid,—on that liquid floated a kind of compass, with a needle shifting rapidly round; but instead of the usual points of a compass were seven strange characters, not very unlike those used by astrologers to denote the planets.[19] A peculiar but not strong nor displeasing odor came from this drawer, which was lined with a wood that we afterwards discovered to be hazel.[20]

Whatever the cause of this odor, it produced a material effect on the nerves. We all felt it, even the two workmen who were in the room,—a creeping, tingling sensation from the tips of the fingers to the roots of the hair. Impatient to examine the tablet, I removed the saucer. As I did so the needle of the compass went round and round with exceeding swiftness, and I felt a shock that ran through my whole frame, so that I dropped the saucer on the floor. The liquid was spilled; the saucer was broken; the compass rolled to the end of the room, and at that instant the walls shook to and fro, as if a giant had swayed and rocked them.

The two workmen were so frightened that they ran up the ladder by which we had descended from the trapdoor; but seeing that nothing more happened, they were easily induced to return.

Meanwhile I had opened the tablet: it was bound in plain red leather, with a silver clasp; it contained but one sheet of thick vellum, and on that sheet were inscribed, within a double pentacle, words in old monkish Latin, which are literally to be translated thus: "On all that it can reach within these walls, sentient or inanimate, living or dead, as moves the needle, so work my will! Accursed be the house, and restless be the dwellers therein."

---

[19] Reference to liquid gyromancy, which is divination through movement of a disk in liquid

[20] Hazel is a hard wood tree whose branches were used as divining rods to find gold in Greece, which perhaps is a reference to the pirate husband from America in the story, and were used in England as early as the eighteenth century, see *Aboretum et Fruticetum Brittannicum; or, The Trees and Shrubs of Britain*, J. C. Loudon, Vol. III, 1838, pg. 2021

We found no more. Mr. J—— burned the tablet and its anathema. He razed to the foundations the part of the building containing the secret room with the chamber over it. He had then the courage to inhabit the house himself for a month, and a quieter, better-conditioned house could not be found in all London.

Subsequently he let it to advantage, and his tenant has made no complaints.

Ghost Short Stories Considered

J.Y. Akerman
1853 The Miniature

Anonymous
1878 The Story of Clifford House
1872 The Haunted Enghenio
1868 Pichon & Sons, of the Croix Rousse
1865 The Ghost of Rosewarne

Louisa May Alcott
1867 The Abbot's Ghost

Alexa
1880 The Spectre Bridgegroom

Edwin Arnold
1895 A Dreadful Night

John Kendrick Bangs
1898 The Mystery of Barney O'Rourke
1891 The Water Ghost of Harrowby Hall

S. Baring-Gould
1897 Colonel Halifax's Ghost Story

Walter Besant
1876 The Case of Mr. Lucraft

Ambrose Bierce
1871 The Haunted Valley
1887 An Inhabitant of Carcosa
1890 The Middle Toe of the Right Foot
1890 An Occurrence At Owl Creek Bridge
1891 A Tough Tussle

Algernon Blackwood
1899 A Haunted Island

Mary E. Braddon
1860 The Cold Embrace
1871 At Chrighton Abbey
1879 The Shadow in the Corner
1894 Herself

Amelia Edwards
    1867 The Four-Fifteen Express
    1860 My Brother's Ghost Story
    1863 How the Third Floor Knew the Potteries
    1864 The Phantom Coach
    1867 The Story of Salome
    1881 Was It an Illusion?

Joseph Le Fanu
    1853 An Account of Some Strange Disturbances in Aungier Street
    1851 Ghost Stories of Chapelizod
    1861 Ultor de Lacy: A Legend of Cappercullen
    1862 An Authentic Narrative of a Haunted House
    1863 The Ghost of a Hand
    1867 Devereux's Dream
    1867 Doctor Feversham's Story
    1868 The Spirit's Whisper
    1868 Squire Toby's Will
    1870 Madam Crowl's Ghost
    1870 Stories of Lough Guir
    1870 The Vision of Tom Chuff
    1872 Dickon the Devil
    1872 Mr. Justice Harbottle
    1872 The Familiar
    1896 Catherine's Quest
    1896 A Debt of Honor. A Ghost Story.
    1896 Haunted
    1896 The Phantom Fourth

Elizabeth Gaskell
    1852 The Old Nurse's Story

Theophile Gautier
    1856 The Spirit

Charlotte Perkins Gilman
    1891 The Giant Wistaria

B. M. Croker
    1890 To Let

Thomas Hardy
    1891 The Superstitious Man's Story

Bret Harte
    1865 Selina Sedilia
    1871 The Haunted Man: A Christmas Story By Ch-r-s D-c-k-n-s

R. S. Hawker
    1867 The Botathen Ghost

Lafcadio Hearn
    1874 The Cedar Closet

Hildegarde Hawthorne
    1891 A Legend of Sonora

E and H Heron (Kate and Hesketh Prichard)
    1898 The Story of the Spaniards, Hammersmith

Tom Hood
    1869 The Shadow of a Shade

Washington Irving
    1855 Guests from Gibbet Island

Henry James
    1868 The Romance of Certain Old Clothes
    1892 Sir Edmund Orme
    1896 The Friends of the Friends

Montague Rhodes (M. R.) James
    1895 Lost Hearts
    1899 Number 13

Jerome K. Jerome
    1891 The Haunted Mill
    1892 The Man of Science
    1895 The Priest and His Cook

Rudyard Kipling
    1885 The Phantom 'Rickshaw
    1887 By Word of Mouth
    1887 Haunted Subalterns
    1888 My Own True Ghost Story
    1890 At the End of the Passage
    1891 The Recrudescence of Imray
    1893 The Lost Legion

Leopold Kompert
    1890 The Silent Woman

Andrew Lang
    1886 The House of Strange Stories

Fitz Hugh Ludlow
    1859 The Phial of Dread

George Macdonald
    1868 Uncle Cornelius His Story

Arthur Machen
    1894 Dr. Duthoit's Vision

Brander Matthews
    1889 The Rival Ghosts

Guy de Maupassant
    1883 The Specter
    1884 Was It a Dream?
    1889 The Terror

Thomas Street Millington
    1872 No Living Voice

Mary Louise Molesworth
    1887 The Story of the Rippling Train

Rosa Mulholland
    1891 The Haunted Organist of Hurly Burly

Dinah M. Mulock (Mrs Craik)
    1856 The Last House in C____ Street

Edith Nesbit
    1891 John Charrington's Wedding
    1893 Hurst of Hurstcote

Mrs. (Margaret) Oliphant
    1882 The Open Door

Vincent O'Sullivan
    1898 The Business of Madame Jahn

A. T. Quiller-Couch
    1895 The Roll-Call of the Reef

Bram Stoker
    1891 The Judge's House

Mark Twain
    1888 A Ghost Story

H. G. Wells
    1896 The Red Room
    The Plattner Story

Oscar Wilde
    1897 The Canterville Ghost

Ellen Wood
    1868 Reality or Delusion?

Connect with Andrew Online

Join Andrew's Email List:
media@AndrewBarger.com

Website:
AndrewBarger.com

Like His Facebook Page:
facebook.com/AuthorAndrewBarger

Blog:
AndrewBarger.blogspot.com

Goodreads:
goodreads.com/author/show/1362598.Andrew_Barger

Other Titles by Andrew Barger

<u>Phantasmal</u>
<u>Best Ghost Short Stories 1800-1849</u>

Ghost short stories became very popular in the first half of the nineteenth century and some thought too horrific were published anonymously like "A Night in a Haunted House" and "The Deaf and Dumb Girl," with the latter being anthologized for the first time since its original publication in 1839.

The other ghost short stories in this collection are by famous authors. "The Mask of the Red Death," is by Edgar Allan Poe; "A Chapter in the History of a Tyrone Family," by Joseph Sheridan Le Fanu; "The Spectral Ship," by Wilhelm Hauff; "The Old Maid in the Winding Sheet," by Nathaniel Hawthorne; "The Adventure of the German Student," and "The Legend of Sleepy Hollow," by Washington Irving; as well as "The Tapestried Chamber," by Sir Walter Scott. Andrew Barger has added his familiar scholarly touch to this collection by including annotations, story backgrounds, author photos and a foreword titled "All Ghosts Are Gray."

[A] unique perspective on this dawn of horror's early roots and their connections to our modern day. [A] choice pick with stories from many legendary authors such as Edgar Allan Poe and Washington Irving, very much recommended reading.
MIDWEST BOOK REVIEW

<u>Best Horror Short Stories 1850-1899</u>
<u>A 6a66le^{tm} Horror Anthology</u>

Historic horror. The finest Victorian and American horror from the last half of the nineteenth century have been combined in one undeniable collection. It includes horror stories from Bram Stoker, Arthur Conan Doyle, Joseph Le Fanu, Arthur Machen, W. C. Morrow, H. G. Wells, and others. "But it now struck me for the first time that there must be one great and ruling embodiment of fear, a King of Terrors to which all others must succumb." Fitz James O'Brien "What Was It?" (1859).

The Best Horror Short Stories 1800-1849 is a book for anyone who loves a classic horror story. Thanks to Edgar Allan Poe, Honoré de Balzac, Nathaniel Hawthorne and others, the first half of the nineteenth century is the cradle of all modern horror short stories. Andrew Barger read over 300 horror short stories and compiled the dozen best. A few have never been republished since they were first published in leading periodicals of the day such as *Blackwood's* and *Atkinson's Casket*. At the back of the book Andrew includes a list of all short stories he considered, background for each story in the book, author photos and annotations for difficult terminology.

'The Best Horror Short Stories 1800-1849' will likely become a best seller . . .What makes this collection (of truly terrifying tales!) so satisfying is the presence of a brief introduction before each story, sharing some comments about the writer and elements of the tale. Barger has once again whetted our appetites for fright, spent countless hours making these twelve stories accessible and available, and has provided in one book the best of the best of horror short stories. It is a winner.
AMZ TOP TEN REVIEWER

Through his introduction and footnotes, Barger aims for readers both scholarly and casual, ensuring that the authors get their due while making the work accessible overall to the mainstream.
BOOKGASM

A top to bottom pick for anyone who appreciates where the best of horror came from.
MIDWEST BOOK REVIEW

<u>BlooDeath</u>
<u>Best Vampire Short Stories 1800-1849</u>

Unearthed from long forgotten journals and magazines, Andrew Barger has found the very best vampire short stories from the first half of the 19th century, which are collected for the first time in this award-winning book on the origins of vampire lore. He combed forgotten journals and mysterious texts to collect the very best vintage vampire stories from this crucial period in vampire literature. In doing so, Andrew unearthed the second and third vampire stories originally published in the English language, neither printed since their first publication nearly 200 years ago.

Also included is the first vampire story originally written in English by John Polidori after a dare with Lord Byron and Mary Shelley. The groundbreaking book contains the first vampire short story by an American who happened to be a graduate of Columbia Law School. The book further contains the first vampire stories by an Englishman and German, including the only vampire stories by such renowned authors as Alexander Dumas, Théophile Gautier and Joseph Le Fanu. As readers have come to expect from Andrew, he has added his scholarly touch to this collection by including annotations, story backgrounds, author photos and a foreword titled "With Teeth."

<u>Shifters</u>
<u>Best Werewolf Short Stories 1800-1849</u>
Andrew has compiled the best tales from the period when werewolf short stories were first unleashed. The stories are "Hugues the Wer-Wolf: A Kentish Legend of the Middle Ages," "The Man-Wolf," "A Story of a Weir-Wolf," "The Wehr-Wolf: A Legend of the Limousin," and "The White Wolf of the Hartz Mountains." It is believed that two of these stories have never been republished in over 150 years since their original printing. Read *Shifters: The Best Werewolf Short Stories 1800-1849* by the light of a full moon.

A seminal work of impressive scholarship, "The Best Werewolf Short Stories 1800-1849: A Classic Werewolf Anthology" is highly recommended reading for fantasy fans, and a valued addition to academic library Literary Studies reference collections.
MIDWEST BOOK REVIEW

<u>Mesaerion</u>
<u>Best Science Fiction Short Stories 1800-1849</u>

Looking for sci-fi stories that defined a genre? How about what is possibly the first science fiction story by a female or the first steampunk short story? There is the first voyage to the moon and a meeting with a lunar alien—Zuloc! What about a darkness machine and the first robotic insect? There is also the first story that deals with cryogenic freezing and reanimation. Andrew has searched two-hundred-year-old magazines and journals to find the very best science fiction stories from the period when the genre came to life, some of which are published for the first time in nearly 200 years.

More than just a simple anthology, 'Mesaerion: The Best Science Fiction Stories 1800-1849' significantly benefits modern readers with the editor's story back ground commentaries, annotations, author photos, and in informative foreword.
MIDWEST BOOK REVIEW

<u>The Divine Dantes</u>
<u>Squirt Gun in Hades (Infernal Trilogy #1)</u>

An Indie Book Awards best second novel finalist, the first book in *The Divine Dantes* trilogy finds young rocker Edward T. Nad down on his luck after the other member of his two-person band (and girlfriend—Beatrice) leaves their small town for Europe. Once there, Beatrice has second thoughts about the breakup and asks their erstwhile manager cum travel agent, Virgil, to bring Edward to her without him knowing it. This sparks off the hilarious intercontinental journey of the staid, nerdy manager and the young rocker with an active and opinionated mind who struggles with the basics, like settling on a name for the band: "Grain of Sand and the Clams" versus "The Beelzebubbas." The novel contains the characters of "The Inferno" and tracks their movements through Hades in modern times. *Dante's Infernos: Squirt Guns in Hades* is the first in a trilogy of novels that parallel "The Inferno," "The Purgatorio," and "The Paradiso" of Dante's *The Divine Comedy* through modern times.

[A] lively and good-natured work . . ..
PUBLISHER'S WEEKLY REVIEWER

[R]eminds me a little of the fun I find in Carl Hiaasen or Christopher Moore, but he definitely has his own vibe . . ..
AMZ BREAKTHROUGH *NOVEL AWARD EXPERT REVIEWER*

<u>Coffee with Poe</u>
<u>A Novel of Edgar Allan Poe's Life</u>

Coffee with Poe brings Edgar Allan Poe to life within its pages as never before. The book is filled with actual letters from his many romances and literary contemporaries. Orphaned at the age of two, Poe is raised by John Allan—his abusive foster father—who refuses to adopt him until he becomes straight-laced and businesslike. Poe, however, fancies poetry and young women. The contentious relationship culminates in a violent altercation, which causes Poe to leave his wealthy foster father's home to make it as a writer. Poe tries desperately to get established as a writer but is ridiculed by the "Literati of New York." "The Raven" gains Poe renown in America yet he slips deeper into poverty, only making $15 off the poem's entire publication history. Desperate for a motherly figure in his life, Poe marries his first cousin who is only thirteen. Poe lives his last years in abject poverty while suffering through the deaths of his foster mother, grandmother, and young wife.

To give us a historical fiction look at Edgar Allan Poe is great. The start where we are at his mom's funeral gives a little insight into why he may write the way he does. It is very interesting the ideas the author has put into the story about Poe. I like the idea of detailing the life of Edgar Allan Poe into a historical fiction novel. . . . A great idea to give us some insight into why Poe may be the way he is.
AMZ BREAKTHROUGH NOVEL AWARD EXPERT REVIEWER

<u>Edgar Allan Poe</u>
<u>Annotated and Illustrated Entire Stories and Poems</u>
For the first time in one compilation are background information for Poe's stories and poems, annotations, foreign word translations, photographs of individuals Poe wrote about, and poetry to Poe from his many romantic interests. Here is a sampling of the tales and poems included: "Annabel Lee," "The Bells," "The Black Cat," "[The Bloodhounds]," "The Cask of Amontillado," "The Conqueror Worm," "A Descent into the Maelstrom," "The Fall of the House of Usher," "The Gold-Bug," "The Haunted Palace," "Lenore," "The Masque of the Red Death," "MS. Found in a Bottle," "Murders in the Rue Morgue," "The Oblong Box," "The Pit and the Pendulum," "The Premature Burial," "The Purloined Letter," "[The Rats of Park Theatre]," "The Raven," "Some Words with a Mummy," "The Swiss Bell-Ringers," "The System of Doctor Tarr and Professor Fether," "The Tell-Tale Heart," and "Thou Art the Man." The classic illustrations are by Gustave Dore and Harry Clarke, with a great introduction by Andrew Barger.

This is an ambitious work and one that immediately becomes the scholar's gold standard for research on this major writer of mystery and thrills.

Barger adds 'guidance' to his method of presenting these works by such devices as listing all of the poems under the subheadings of 'Women in Edgar Allan Poe's Life', 'Miscellaneous Poetry both Before and After Age 25', 'Autobiographical', and 'Men in Edgar Allen Poe's Life.' These may seem like minor adjustments to the collections, but in Barger's hands the divisions add meaning and context to the works.

This is simply a splendid book, handsomely written and produced, and a fine tribute to the literature of Poe - and to the scholarship of Andrew Barger! Highly Recommended.
AMZ TOP TEN REVIEWER

<u>Mailboxes – Mansions – Memphistophels</u>
<u>A Collection of Dark Tales</u>

A finalist in the International Book Awards anthology category, Andrew Barger's first short story collection unleashes a blend of character-driven dark tales, which are sure to be remembered. In "Azra'eil & Fudgie" a little girl visits a team of marines in Afghanistan and they quickly learn she is more than she seems. "The Mailbox War" is a deadly tale of a weekend hobby taken to extremes while "The Brownie of the Alabaster Mansion" sees a Scottish monster of antiquity brought back to life. "Memphistopheles" contains a tale of the devil, Memphis, barbeque and a wannabe poet. "The Serpent and the Sepulcher" is a prose poem that will be cherished by all who experience it. "The Gëbult Mansion" recounts a literary hoax played by Andrew on his unsuspecting social networking friends that involves a female vampire. Last, "Stain" is an unforgettable horror story about a stain that will not go away.

<u>Middle Unearthed</u>
<u>Best Fantasy Short Stories 1800-1849</u>

Long before *Game of Thrones*, *The Lord of the Rings* trilogy and the *Harry Potter* series, there were the ten best fantasy stories published in the early nineteenth century. In old magazines and forgotten journals, Andrew read over 100 forgotten fantasy stories to find the very best. They include great tales by Charles Dickens, Mary Shelley, Washington Irving and many others. Read it today.

www.ingramcontent.com/pod-product-compliance
Lightning Source LLC
Chambersburg PA
CBHW050528190726

48284CB00003B/977